TAKE
IT
OFF,
TAKE
IT
ALL
OFF !

BY DAVID RITZ

Novels

Glory
Search for Happiness
The Man Who Brought the Dodgers Back to Brooklyn
Dreams
Blue Notes Under a Green Felt Hat
Barbells and Saxophones
Family Blood
Passion Flowers
Take It Off, Take It All Off!

Biographies

Brother Ray (with Ray Charles)
Divided Soul: The Life of Marvin Gaye
Smokey: Inside My Life (with Smokey Robinson)
Rhythm and the Blues (with Jerry Wexler)

Lyrics

"Sexual Healing" (recorded by Marvin Gaye)
"Love Is the Light" (recorded by Smokey Robinson)
"Brothers in the Night" (theme song of film, *Uncommon Valor*)
"Release Your Love" (recorded by the Isley Brothers)
"Eye on You" (recorded by Howard Hewett)
"Get It While It's Hot" (recorded by Eddie Kendricks and
Dennis Edwards)
"Power" (recorded by Tramaine Hawkins)
"Velvet Nights" (recorded by Leon Ware)

TAKE IT OFF, TAKE IT ALL OFF !

DAVID RITZ

DONALD I. FINE, INC.
New York

Library of Congress Cataloging-in-Publication Data
Ritz, David.
Take it off, take it all off! / by David Ritz.
p.   cm.
ISBN 1-55611-366-8
1. Women detectives—New York (N.Y.)—Fiction.   2. Stripteasers—
New York (N.Y.)—Fiction.   I. Title.
PS3568.I828T34   1993
813'.54—dc20   92-54987
CIP

Manufactured in the United States of America

10 9 8 7 6 5 4 3 2 1

Designed by Irving Perkins Associates

For Richard Freed

TERESA

It made me sick to look.

This was a nice girl, this Teresa Johnson, a sweetheart. Polite like you wouldn't believe. A regular doll. Couldn't have been older than eighteen, nineteen tops. All the boys said she had a face like Betty Hutton and a body like Betty Grable. Cute and sexy at the same time. She called me Big Sis and I called her Tush because she had this sensational backside—the best of any of us strippers— plus a personality like sunshine and cornflakes. She had the kind of face that belonged on a cornflakes box. She looked like she was born in the cornfields or the wheatfields 'cause that's where she came from, somewhere in the middle of America where people are nice even though they don't know what's going on in places like New York City and downtown Newark, New Jersey.

Tush counted on me. She asked me to show her the ropes. I was supposed to be taking care of her. And then . . .

. . . there she was, on the bed of her tidy little one-room West Side apartment on Sunday morning, June 10, her arms, her legs spread out, flat on her back, dead . . . don't ask me to describe what I saw because me, well, I'm a lady and I wouldn't want other ladies to have to look at her, except it made me sick to see the sheets soaked in blood and it made me mad—madder than hell— and it had me hurting so hard because it was some twisted-in-the-head woman-hater who killed her. It had to be a woman-hater because I know men. Believe me. Some gals know nursing; some know typing; some girls can cook; but Rhonda Silverstar, she knows her men. My baby brother Leo's got a Ph.D. in math from Columbia—that's wonderful, Leo's a genius; just ask Mom and Pops, they'll tell you Leo's a genius—but if they gave out Ph.D.s in men, I'd have one with honors. Doesn't matter that I dropped out of high school and never went to college. I know psychology. I know how men think. Inside they're scared shitless. For instance, with the war in Europe over and some of us girls still working the factories, the guys are worried about getting their jobs back because we're doing a better job. If they let us, we'd do a better job at everything. Men are babies. A juicy lay and lots of mothering— that's what they live for. First they want you talking nasty like a hooker; then they want you talking sweet like mommy telling 'em they're the strongest bravest boys in the world with schlongs like golden rods bigger than the Empire State Building.

But Teresa, poor baby, she didn't know nothing about men. Because anyone who knew men wouldn't have opened the door for this man. The way he killed her . . . that's the worst part. It was a sex death. My boyfriend Sandy, the songwriter and song-plugger and hypochondriac, Sandy calls orgasms little deaths, but I don't know what the hell he means except he can't stop thinking about sex and dying. The only way he ain't scared of getting sick and dying is when he's screwing me, which is why he wants to be screwing me all the time. Now the man who killed Teresa was thinking about sex because the wounds—big gashing horrible wounds—were in the three places where men come for their pleasure, the spots most men can't wait to put their mouths, except for Bull Wallinsky, another boyfriend of mine who plays centerfield for the Newark Bears. Bull's dying to get called up to the Yankees except Bull's got lots of problems, especially when it comes to baseball and screwing, the way he gets the two mixed up.

Maybe I didn't understand that Teresa was mixed up. Maybe I didn't understand her at all. She kept on saying how she'd never met a Jew before—she didn't even know what a Jew was—and when I took her home to meet the family they all loved her because she was so sweet, even Leo who's two years younger than me and doesn't know how to talk to girls or even look them in the eye. Now I couldn't look at Teresa, spread out dead on the bed. I had to close my eyes. How could one human being do this to another?

I turned away and noticed all the stuffed kittens surrounding her on the bed—maybe a dozen, all colors and sizes. They looked so cute, so much more alive than Teresa. On the end table I spotted the yearbook from Teresa's high school. Valleyview High; Valleyview, Ohio. I turned a few pages and there she was, a blonde cheerleader with June Allyson bangs wearing one of those pleated skirts and shaking those pom-poms and I wondered—how the hell did a girl like that get to Plotsky's Burlesque in Newark, New Jersey? How'd she ever wind up as one of my backup broads on the chorus line? I sighed and thought . . . well, probably the same way I wound up at Plotsky's. We both decided life's more exciting when you're taking your clothes off.

I turned to Captain Mickey Donegan, a cop who's been coming over to Jersey to watch me take my clothes off for the past five years. Mick's a big guy with curly orange hair who's always got a half-smoked cigar in his mouth.

"Look, Mick," I said, "you gotta find this creep. You gotta nail this sicko, and you gotta make sure the son of a bitch fries."

"I thought you'd have some ideas, Rhonda," he told me. "That's why I called you soon as the fingerprint boys left. When was the last time you saw her?"

"Last night. We took the Tubes in from Newark after the late show."

"With dates?"

"What dates? We were dead tired. The late show was later than usual. It'd been a hell of a week. Fact is, Tush fell asleep on the Tubes. Fell asleep with her head on my shoulder. Poor baby. I hated to wake her up when we got to the city. I waited till she caught the subway uptown. Then I went home to Brooklyn."

"Maybe she had a late date," said Mickey. "There was no forced entry. What about the guys she associates with, the guys who hang around Plotsky's. Any perverts?"

"We got a good clientele, you know that. Execs. College boys. Police officers like you. We don't pander."

"I've seen some rough trade in there."

"She avoided them like the plague. I told her straight off—never mix business with pleasure. Just like I'm always telling you, Mick."

"What about her boyfriends?"

"On stage Tush didn't mind showing off, but off stage she was shy. I didn't see no boyfriends. This girl was a virgin."

"Come on, Rhonda. This ain't no time for fairy tales. A girl like this, a stripper? You're telling me this number was cherry?"

"I'm telling you, Mick, she didn't know nothing about men. Zip. Zero. I could tell by all the questions she asked me. I was her teacher, so to speak. I taught her how the subways run and how to pack a hatpin in her purse so if anyone goosed her during rush hour she could defend herself. But this was a girl, mind you, who spent her days poking around museums. She'd point at naked statues, asking me about men's private parts in a way that I knew she didn't know how the plumbing works. She liked old paintings. Once she even dragged me over to the Metropolitan Museum so I could see these paintings of Jesus bleeding all over the cross. She thought the paintings were beautiful. To me they were creepy. I told her I was Jewish. She didn't even know Jews don't go for Jesus."

"I didn't know you was Jewish, Rhonda . . ."

"Come on, Mick," I said, flicking my nose with my finger, "with this honker."

"My mom's got a bigger nose than yours."

"What kind of name you think Silverstar is?"

"Never thought about it."

"I changed it from Silverstern. Pops is still mad at me about that, but Pops was mad at me the day I was born. He considers me dead and buried. He says by working at Plotsky's I'm shaming my people and that I'm ashamed of myself, but that's bullshit because I kept the Silver part and I kept the star. Look," I said, pulling out my fourteen-karat gold chain from beneath my snug white blouse. Mickey's eyes went from my Star of David to my tits, but what else was new? Mickey was a tit man. I made my living off tit men. I ain't tall enough to appeal to leg men and my ass is a little too flat—it's a good ass but it ain't a sensational ass, not like Tush's—to grab the ass men. See, my tits are my jewels, my gifts from God. They jut straight out. They're firm enough so I wear a brassiere only if I feel like it. And I only feel like if I want to have something to take off to add to the excitement. By the time I was thirteen my boobs were already bigger than Mom's and Pops was having heart palpitations.

"I told Pops that Silverstar was just as Jewish as Silverstern," I told Mickey, "but Pops didn't hear me. I told him, I swore to him, I'd wear the six-pointed star he gave me for the rest of my life, I wouldn't ever be anything but Jewish no matter where I went or what I did, but Pops, he didn't listen. Truth is, he didn't even want a daughter, it's his son, his perfect son, that counts. Pops worships the ground his son walks on. You know something, Mick, if I ever told him the real truth about Leo, Pops would slit his throat."

"Whose throat—his own or his son's?"

"Both."

"Has anyone ever killed anyone in your family?"

"Come on, Mickey, I'm just talking. We're getting off the subject . . ."

"You were saying that Teresa had no boyfriends."

"She'd only been here six months. What is this? Second week of June? Well, she showed up a little after New Year's. You should have seen her with this white dress and puffed sleeves that looked like an apron. She looked like a storybook. I thought she was Little Miss Bo Peep looking for her sheep; I didn't think she'd know shit about stripping except those cheerleading moves aren't too far away from your basic bumps and grinds and with that tush and her attitude—she had a beautiful smile, friendly as anything—I figured I could whip her into shape in no time. And I did. But I told her, I said, 'Tush, stay close to Rhonda because working Plotsky's ain't no picnic in the park.' Specially last month with V-E Day and the city going nuts, I've never seen the city so wild. I told her that the soldiers would be running over to Plotsky's in droves and they'd be happy and celebrating and spending money but to be careful 'cause some of them had bad scares over there and some of them wouldn't be normal and it's hard to tell when a man's not normal until you get him in bed and then you see everything you need to know about him and sometimes you see too much."

"With me, Rhonda," said the captain, putting his arm around me in a way that was supposed to be comforting and something else at the same time, "you'd only get normal."

"This ain't right, Mick," I told him, removing his arm. "No one should have to die like this."

Just then the door opened and who should barge in but the Stickman with his big flash camera and all of sudden he's popping pictures and I'm saying, "Stickman, this ain't the time. For God's sake, have a heart." But you know Stickman, he's the tall skinny guy with the floppy green fedora who's there at every four-alarm fire and grizzly mob murder and the next morning I'm back in Brooklyn eating my breakfast and looking at the *Daily Mirror* with Stickman's picture of Tush on page one—PLOTSKY GIRL MURDERED!—with the stuffed kittens by her body which was covered up but her face was twisted with pain and looking ugly which wasn't fair—wasn't fair at all—'cause Teresa Johnson was beautiful, she was a decent gal, a damn decent gal, and I don't like it, I can't eat all day, which means something is really wrong with me, because my guts are a mess, and I'm mad, I'm furious, I want to know what happened, no one should have to die with so much god-awful fear and pain and maybe if I had spent a little more time with Tush, maybe if I had shown her around more, talked to her more about men, been a better Big Sis, maybe she'd be alive and I wouldn't be feeling like it was my fault, like I had to do something to set things right.

MILKMAN
KEEP THOSE
BOTTLES
QUIET

Sandy Singer ain't a great listener. He's either writing tunes or talking on the phone or running around to nightclubs to catch bandleaders to sell his songs. But he has bright eyes and a nice nervous way of making love—he always makes sure I come before him, which isn't always how Bull does it—and he has beautiful soft shoulders and makes beautiful music on his upright piano, but he drives me nuts the way he won't stop talking about getting sick and dying. Tonight, though, over at his apartment on Empire Boulevard in Flatbush just around the corner from me, I can't blame Sandy. Who can stop thinking about death with Tush staring at us in all the papers?

"Maybe it's the mob," said Sandy, who's bald as a bowling ball. Lots of gals don't like bald men. I do. Once upon a time Sandy must have had sandy-colored hair, but the shape of his head is pretty and what's inside is quality stuff and I think bald is beautiful. There's nothing between you and his brain except that tight naked flesh. Sandy might look a little older than his thirty years, he may be a little jittery, but he's definitely got a brain. And talent.

"What would the mob want with Tush?" I asked him. "Tush wouldn't know the mob from the NBC Symphony Orchestra."

"Maybe she got involved. She might have learned something. And they didn't like what she learned. The mob's all over the music business."

"You've told me."

"If they're all over the music business, they're all over burlesque."

"Plotsky's ain't mobbed up—I guarantee you. Herb Plotsky is
as legit as Eleanor Roosevelt."

"Plotsky . . . legit?"

"Plotsky ain't a bad egg. When he found out about Tush he
called me right away. He couldn't stop crying. Imagine, a sixty-
year-old man bawling like a baby."

"Think he was balling Tush?"

"Never in a million years. Plotsky never samples the merchandise. He said to me once when I was just starting out, 'If I ran a
candy store and ate all the candy, would I be a smart businessman
or a schmuck? Well, this is my candy store,' he said, 'and I'm no
schmuck.' "

"I've heard he's mob," said Sandy.

"By you, everyone including the Pope is mob."

"Show business is dangerous. Big money attracts big muscle. I
think Plotsky's a dangerous place for you. You oughta quit."

"You talk like my father."

"You've never bothered to introduce me."

"That's because I like you. He'd hate you because I like you. He
hates everyone I like. He pulled me out of high school because the
boys were too interested in me. He said girls don't need to know
what high school was teaching. He put me into a business school
and said, 'Learn something useful. Learn to type.' "

"Funny, I love to type. It's like playing the piano. And I always
feel like playing the piano. But now I'm not feeling great. I feel a
sore throat coming on."

"I've seen you type up your lyrics, Sandy. You're good. I took
typing long enough to type one letter that said, 'Dear Dad . . .
Now is the time for all good fathers to come to the aid of their
daughters and let them go back to their regular high schools.' See,
I wanted to get a regular degree and also take ballet lessons like
Minnie Binder up the street who was a fat slob and danced like a
hippo in a tutu."

"Did he let you go back?"

"Forget it."

"Your mother couldn't help?"

"Just about then Mom had a miscarriage—it was a girl, she wanted another girl and I wanted a little sister—and Pops said the miscarriage was my fault 'cause I gave everyone aggravation and why couldn't I be like Leo who stayed in his room and studied for hours on end, even though I knew he was back there beating his meat."

" 'I'm Dying for Your Love,' " said Sandy, going over to his piano. "What do you think of that for the title of a song?"

"How 'bout, 'I'm Living for Your Love'?"

"Dying is more dramatic," he explained, striking a couple of chords. The windows to his apartment were open and his neighbors didn't mind because he sang softly; he had this trick of turning whatever was on his mind into nice notes.

"I don't see how you can write right now," I said.

"My throat's killing me. They say a sore throat is the first sign of cancer."

"Write your song."

"I'm thinking about Tush," he said, tickling the ivories. "She had a beautiful voice."

"How do you know?"

"One night I heard her singing with the sax player in the Plotsky band."

"Abraham Jones? The colored guy?"

"The guy's brilliant. He talks foreign languages. Who's ever heard of a nigger talking French? He's one of these genius jazz musicians."

"If he's a genius, what are you doing calling him a nigger? I don't like that word. Abraham's classy. When I strip, he solos. I can't strip to anyone else's sax."

"Well, him and Tush were fooling around after rehearsal."

"How do you mean 'fooling around'?"

"Playing, singing. Tush could sing."

"She never said anything to me about singing."

"She said something to me. She told me she went up to Harlem with Abraham. She said they loved her up there."

"I don't believe it. She'd be too scared to go to Harlem."

"Abraham must have taken care of her. Maybe he had her singing something like this . . ."

And then Sandy started in, singing the song in a jazzy relaxed Bing Crosby-sounding voice, singing like the song was already written, even though he was making it up on the spot. I told you he was talented.

" 'I'm not what I seem,' he sang, 'and I'm living in a dream . . . dying . . . dying for your love."

"The melody's pretty," I said, "but I don't like the words."

"It's a hell of a lot better than 'Milkman Keep Those Bottles Quiet.' Do you realize that's a big hit? That's the kind of crap that's selling in 1945. My throat's killing me."

"I better talk to Abraham about Tush."

"Don't get involved. He could be mobbed up."

" 'Moonlight in Vermont' is a gorgeous song and it's popular. Why don't you write about moonlight instead of dying."

" 'Dying for your love.' It's a love song, baby. I'm dying for your love, especially the way you look tonight. Your beautiful brown eyes . . ."

"My eyes are too big. I got pop eyes and you know it."

"I love your eyes and I love your long silky black hair."

"My hair's kinky. To straighten it out takes me all day. And it never stays put. It never does right. I got hair like the coloreds have hair."

"And your breasts."

"There you go. You can talk about the eyes and the silky hair, but you're seeing boobs. You got boobs on the brain."

"You're wearing that lacy bra. I can see it under your blouse. You know what lace does to me."

"Sandy, please. How can you think about doing it when Tush is looking at us like that on page one of the *Mirror*? That bastard Stickman shouldn't have taken that picture."

"I'm not lying . . ." Sandy was singing, "just crying, baby, . . . no denying that I'm dying . . . just dying for your love."

"Forget it," I told him as he left the piano to paw me. I kissed him on the cheek and sent him back to the eighty-eights. "Work."

"I'm hurting, Rhonda."

"Gargle with seltzer and a little lemon."

"This awful thing with Tush . . . it's turned me into a nervous wreck."

"You know, Sandy," I said, feeling put out, "I came over here for a little comforting myself."

"And you'll get it, baby."

"Can't you see that's the last thing on my mind?"

"I see," he said. "I understand. But you gotta understand that for me there's only one way to lose the blues."

"Did you ever sell that song?"

"Woody Herman loved it. But he wanted to change it from 'I Wanna Lose My Blues' to 'Lose Your Blues.' "

"I like Woody's way. It's shorter."

"It changes the meaning, but if he'll do it, I'll take the money and run. If my throat gets any worse, I'm running to the emergency room. I can't swallow."

"Gargle. I'm going home."

"Maybe I should go with you. You're not safe."

"I'm sorry," I said before walking out the door, the melody of "I'm Dying for Your Life" rattling around in my brain, "but no one's safe, Sandy—not Tush, not me, not you. Life ain't safe."

A DOZEN
HOT BIALYS

Men.

Here a doll's been murdered and they're still thinking about getting laid. They're scared, I'm telling you, they're more scared than us. When we're scared we show it. We cry and scream our guts out. Least I do. But men, they gotta put on an act, they gotta be big shots, and only when they get naked do you even start to see what they're all about, except when they're banging you they're feeling terrific, acting like he-men conquerors. But some of them—a lot of them—need help about how to put it in and keep it in and you have to tell them—over and over again—how they're doing a good job. They can't hear that enough. They need comforting. I needed comforting. Sandy was in his own world. Why did I think he could take care of me when he needed me to take care of him?

I was hungry, and on a warm Sunday night there wasn't much open in Flatbush what with the Dodgers playing up in the Bronx at the Polo Grounds and the radios playing from everyone's open windows, Red Barber's Southern molasses voice describing the game, and I thought about maybe taking the subway over to Mom and Dad's apartment in Bensonhurst but it was nicer here by the park—on nights like this you can smell the grass and the flowers, Prospect Park is just like being in the country—and I wasn't sure Mom and Pops would make me feel any better. I thought of Bull Wallinsky, and how he'd run over from Hoboken in a second if the Bears were off tonight, but baseball was the last thing I needed to hear about—Bull's big bat, Bull's big slump, Bull's dick always needed a fix-me-up and the last thing I needed right now were men with dick problems even though I usually liked helping out. I got satisfaction that way but not tonight, not with my tummy hurting from thinking about Tush and skipping all these meals.

I turned on Bedford Avenue with the shadow of pitch-dark Ebbets Field at my back. A half moon hung low in the sky. There was a loud groan coming from a hundred apartments all over the neighborhood when Red Barber said Van Lingle Mungo struck out Dixie Walker in the top of the ninth and the Bums lost one-zip which serves 'em right 'cause Durocher should never have traded Mungo to the Giants and I rooted for the Yankees, maybe just to be different, maybe just to pull for a winner, maybe because I liked Bull or maybe just to piss off Pops 'cause all summer long he planted himself by the radio living and dying with the Dodgers. And it didn't matter to him that his son didn't know nothing about baseball and his daughter could name all the players; he still wouldn't talk to me about baseball. Tonight he'd be in a bad mood and he wouldn't want to see me anyway. Leave Pops alone.

Leave Brooklyn—that was my first thought when I left home when I was seventeen. That was nine years ago. And for a while I lived down in Florida with that circus, and then I was out in California with a hot coochy-coochy show—San Pedro, California, is really where I learned to strip—but when I came back to the city and tried living on Fourteenth Street around S. Klein on the Square—I've got some stories to tell you about the dressing rooms at S. Klein—it was too loud and Brooklyn is peaceful, Brooklyn is really gorgeous because it's green and you see lots of houses, it ain't all apartment buildings, and the people are down to earth and not everyone is like Pops, worried where the next nickel's coming from and ready to kill for a sale. I could live in Newark, where I wouldn't have to run back and forth on the Tubes, but I like going to sleep every night in Brooklyn. Brooklyn is home.

Brooklyn also has the best bread. Bread is my downfall 'cause if I have an extra few pounds to take off—with five less pounds, I'm perfect—I can't do it because I'm eating bialystockers, hot ones right out of the oven. I don't cut 'em open, I just smear butter over the top and it takes me four bites and one's gone and I'm ready for the next one, especially the chewy way they taste with the white powdery flour and diced-up onions sprinkled over the flat part in the middle. I save the middle part for last. Now Plotsky doesn't mind me with five extra pounds because he knows if I lose weight around my middle I lose bulk on top and that's no good for a stripper with tit and rotating tassle action like mine. Except if I wanted to do regular dancing up on Broadway, like a regular chorus girl, like a Rockette, I could use thinner hips, but let me tell you something: Those gals make about one-tenth as much as me 'cause at Plotsky's I'm a star; at Plotsky's they give me top billing, they got me on the marquee—Rhonda Silverstar and her Starlettes—and I'm changing my routine every month, I'm coming up with my own numbers and my own gimmicks, I'm going out there wearing a cape of real orchids and picking them off one by one, I'm pushing the limits and I'm driving the boys crazy, I'm giving them what they like. The boys love me. All during the war when no one had nylon stockings, I had enough nylons to open a store. The boys kept sending nylons back to my dressing room. So what if I have to schlep to Newark? LaGuardia, the bum, he ran live burlesque out of New York City years ago and it's a good thing he decided not to run for another term 'cause who wants the bluenose? The people want burlesque or they wouldn't pack the theaters. No matter what Pops thinks about strippers, I'm making more in a month than he makes in a year and if he won't take any of my money, Mom will, even if she's too scared to tell him. Everyone's scared.

"Give me a dozen, Jimmy," I tell the bialy man. "And make sure they're hot."

On my way back down Bedford Avenue, I take a few bites and I'm feeling a little bit better except Teresa Johnson is dead and what's Captain Mickey really going to do about it? For years I'd been hearing Mickey's on the take and what does he care about this kid Tush? He didn't believe me when I said she never had a man, but it's true; you'd be surprised how many strippers are cherry. Everyone thinks we're loose and wild but a lot of us are nice girls trying to get away from nutty families or just looking for a break. Like Tush.

I made up my mind to go see Mickey at the police station the next day. I wanted to see if he had come up with anything and maybe I'd talk to Abraham Jones once I got to Newark. Maybe Abraham knew something, or maybe Sandy got it wrong and Tush didn't have anything to do with the colored guy, which is how I figured it. Not that Abraham ain't nice. He's extra-nice. But I couldn't see Bo Peep riding the A train up to 125th Street. And what's more, I couldn't see anyone wanting to kill her. I'm telling you, it had to be some sicko, and if one girl got it yesterday maybe another gal will get it tomorrow because that's how sickos work.

When I got to my apartment building on Flatbush Avenue—my mind still thinking of Tush, two bialys already eaten—the last person in the world I expected to see was Bernie Silverstern, my father.

"I was worried," he said. Pops talks in a flat-pancake voice and has this habit of not looking at you when he's talking to you. He's only fifty, with a full head of wavy gray hair, but he looks sixty, with those sad watery eyes of his. He's taller than me—he's five eleven, I'm five nine—but he stoops over. He talks to the floor.

"Worried about what?" I asked.

"You. Who else should I be worried about?"

"You read about Tush?"

"What 'tush'?"

"Teresa. I called her Tush."

"That girl was Jewish?"

"No, I just called her Tush."

"She came once to the apartment. Very pleasant person."

"She had a good heart."

"You buy bialys?"

"You want one? They're hot."

"With a cup of coffee, I wouldn't mind."

I can't remember the last time I made anything for my father, even a cup of coffee. He'd never been to my apartment—not once. I couldn't help but be a little excited.

"Sorry about the Dodgers," I said when we got inside.

"Bums," he answered. "Last year they lost sixteen in a row. On the way over here tonight I heard how Walker struck out. I didn't even stay home to listen to the game." God, I thought, this was a big deal. Pops was so worried about me he gave up the game.

"I'm moving to a bigger apartment next month," I told him, apologizing for the sparse furnishings. I quickly closed the door to my bedroom where I kept my sewing machine. I sewed all my own breakaway dresses and special costumes which, I suppose, I didn't want Pops to see. Why remind him?

"I'm moving to Eastern Parkway," I told him. "A penthouse."

"A penthouse," Pops repeated. He had this habit of repeating whatever you said. "Fancy schmancy. What's wrong with this apartment? For one person it's very nice."

"Mom tell you how to get here?"

"She wrote down the address."

"I'll be right back with your coffee."

In the kitchen, I took a couple of deep breaths. It was strange having Pops in my place. And it was even stranger having him acting nice. Last time I was home for Sunday dinner he didn't take his head out of the paper, didn't say two words to me.

"You put in two sugars?" he asked me when I brought the coffee and bialy.

"You don't think I know to put in two sugars? Where's Mom?"

"Where's Mom? Mom is where Mom usually is. Playing mah-jongg."

"Is the coffee sweet enough?" I asked as he sipped.

"The coffee's fine."

"Well, I have to say that it's nice to know you care so much about me."

"What father doesn't care for his daughter?"

"Sometimes I can't tell."

"You should only know how much I care. How many nights I don't sleep . . ."

He was sitting on the couch and I was sitting on a folding chair facing him. His eyes wouldn't meet mine, but that's true of most men's eyes—except when they want to sleep with you.

"Well, you can sleep tonight," I told him, "because I'm fine."

"I'm not so sure."

"What do you mean?"

"I don't want to start in. I didn't come over to start in. But your mother's very worried about you."

"I thought you said you were the one who was worried."

"We want you to come home."

"What! I'm not a baby, I'm twenty-six years old."

"In my day children lived at home with their parents until they got married. Twenty six is not old."

"I told you, I'm moving into my own penthouse."

"I'm glad you have money, but a fancy penthouse is not what you need."

"Okay, Pops, *you* tell me what I need."

"A regular job."

"Here we go . . ."

"I'm saying something different this time. I'm not discussing Plotsky's. Your mother said, 'If you go to her, don't discuss Plotsky's,' so I'm not discussing Plotsky's. Plotsky's is your business. I don't know from Plotsky's. But I do know foundation garments."

"Well, that's the truth. If you don't know girdles, no one in the world does. You been selling them your whole life."

"I'm tired already. I'm tired from traveling from Poughkeepsie to Albany. From Rochester to Syracuse to Buffalo. No one in their right mind should have to work Buffalo. I want to give up the line and go back into business for myself again. The war in Europe is over and things are better. I found a location for a store on Fort Hamilton Parkway in Borough Park."

"Around your old store . . ."

"The old store was on Thirteenth Avenue."

"Do you know how many times I heard you say that never in a million years would you ever have a store again, not after what happened?"

"The Depression made a lot of people say a lot of things. My big brother Morris, he said he was gonna kill himself, and then he disappeared. His old crowd says he's out in California but after twelve years of silence—he doesn't write, he doesn't call—I say my poor brother's dead, may he rest in peace. Well, I'm no Morris. Mo was a spendthrift and a showboat. He had his silk suits and his fancy men's store on Broadway with the autographed pictures of Errol Flynn and Wallace Beery. He made fun of me for selling corsets in Brooklyn. I told him there was decent money in girdles but he'd laugh and turn up his nose and take his show ladies to Sardi's . . ."

"I loved Uncle Mo."

"You loved Uncle Mo? Uncle Mo was a bum. A regular bum. When his customers couldn't pay their fancy bills and he couldn't pay his fancy rent, what does he do? He runs."

"What did you do?"

"I lasted as long as I could. When I couldn't last any longer I did what Morris should have done but he'd never do it because he was too proud, this big brother of mine. Me, I got a job. I got a line. I went on the road. For thirteen, fourteen years I been on the road. I've had it. My eyes aren't as good as they used to be. I want to go into business for myself again. This time, though, your mother's going to help me. She's helping me find the money and she'll help me in the store. She has to. That's the only way to get the woman to stop spending money. With her it's a sickness. But she'll only help me, Rhonda, if you help. That's what she said. She wants us all to go into business together. She says we're a sure thing to make a bundle—and it'll be good for the family."

"What do you think I am, Pops, a saleslady?"

"Is there anything wrong with selling? We're all selling something."

"What about Leo? You going to get Leo in there to sell girdles?"

"Leo's a professor."

"Well, I'm a professional too."

"A professional what?"

"Dancer."

I saw my father silently count to ten. I knew what he wanted to say—and I couldn't help but dare him to say it.

"Say it," I said. "Say I'm a stripper. You're ashamed to say it."

"I told your mother I wouldn't say nothing. I promised I'd be good—no fights, no discussions about Plotsky's. I'm here because of your mother. The poor woman's worried to death about you, what with this murder, this horrible thing that happened to that girl that could have happened to you, God forbid, because these places, these God-awful places, they . . ."

"They *what*?"

"They make men crazy!" Pops finally exploded, his neck turning red,

"You mean it's Tush's fault that she was killed?"

"I don't know this Tush and I don't know from Plotsky's. I never been there. My brother Morris, he'd know better than me . . ."

I suddenly had a memory of Mo taking me backstage—I couldn't have been older than ten or eleven—on a Saturday afternoon at the Republic Theater on Forty-second Street where he introduced me to Rags Ragland and Georgia Sothern. Georgia Sothern was a big star then with gorgeous red hair. Uncle Mo would tell me stories about her, and he'd talk about Ann Corio and Margie Hart and Gypsy Rose Lee . . .

"He was poison, this brother of mine."

"He was swell. He'd take me around to the delis to meet the comics and the showgirls, where everyone was laughing and having a swell time. He'd introduce me as his pretty niece because he had no kids and he was a good guy, he always treated me good, no matter what you say . . ."

"Listen, Rhonda, why don't just come home with me?"

"Just like that?"

"Just like that."

"What makes you think I'm interested in business?"

"You did good in all your business classes."

"I hated those classes, I hated that business high school. You know that."

"So now it'll come in handy."

"Don't you understand, I'm making money hand over fist . . ."

"Your work is *schmutz*."

"What's dirty to you is art to me."

"Art?"

"Yes, goddamnit, art! That's how Ruby Keeler began, you know. She was a peeler. And so was Joan Crawford. They called her Lucille LeSueur back then and she was in a chorus line."

"I told your mother it'd be a waste of time. Why should I come to you? I knew you'd never do it. But she said you'd want to help."

"Help? You mean you want my money?"

"I have my own money, but I'm looking for a smart partner. Your mother said, 'Ask Rhonda. If she's in, I'm in.' "

"I'm out."

"I already figured."

"You said you were coming over because you were worried. But it wasn't that. It wasn't Tush. You weren't worried about her and you're not worried about me. You're worried about money. Money is all you're ever worried about."

"You're one to talk. Look what you're doing for money."

"It's not for the money. It's for . . ."

"What, Rhonda, what *is* it for? Tell me, please, so I can tell your cousins and your aunts and the neighbors, so at the next family affair, at the next wedding or bar mitzvah, I can explain when they ask me what a nice Jewish girl is doing parading around in her underwear in front of an audience of strange Gentile men."

"Tell them I'm not so nice."

"*That* they already know."

And with that he put down his coffee cup, polished off the bialy with one last bite, and headed for the door, never once letting his eyes meet mine.

I started to scream out after him—scream how he always favored Leo, how he really never cared about me, how lots of Jewish guys come to Plotsky's, not just Gentiles—but the sobs came before the words and there I was crying like a baby, crying for Tush, sobbing for myself, for the sound of the front door slamming and my father leaving and my father never understanding and me never wanting to see him again because he didn't even look me in the eye and he didn't know what a good dancer I was, he wouldn't let me take lessons, he thought I should be a secretary, well, I'm not a fuckin' secretary and there are secretaries in Mr. Plotsky's office who will type *my* letters and if I ever wrote him, if I ever spoke to Pops again—which I had no intention of doing, *ever*—I'd tell him to go to hell because all he does is make me feel like shit warmed over. That's all he's ever done.

"I hope your father didn't get you upset, darling."

That was Gert Silverstern, my mother, calling me three minutes after Pops left. I was still sobbing.

"Oh, Mom, why'd you send him over here?"

"Me? I was the one who told him not to go."

"He said it was your idea."

"I was coming myself, but he said, 'No, Gert, let me go. Let me see if my daugher is in trouble.' I knew he'd get you upset."

"He did."

"We've all been concerned. That girl. She had such lovely manners. What a thing to happen! You want me to stay with you, darling?"

"I'm not scared, Mom."

"You should be."

"Of what?"

"Men—that's what."

"In this whole crazy world, men are the one thing I understand."

"You should know that I appreciate all the things you do for me, Rhonda, I honestly do. You did a beautiful job hemming my green dress. Where'd you ever learn to sew like that?"

Not from you—I began to say, but didn't. Mom hated all household work, but who could blame her? Why should women be cooped up in the house? "Dorothea, the wardrobe lady at Plotsky's, she taught me three, four years ago," I explained. " 'If you want to make any money in this business,' she told me, 'learn to sew. They expect you to show up with your own clothes.' "

"Talking about clothes, I took that money you gave me for my birthday and I bought a silver fox stole, with his little face biting his tail and everything. The furrier gave me a price. It's stunning. Next time we have dinner, you'll see it."

"It's a little warm for fox, isn't it, Ma? Besides, what are you going to tell Pops?"

"What does he have to know? I'll wear it when I go hear this Yehudi Menuhin play his violin at Town Hall. So young, and such a nice-looking boy. A real talent. When he plays my eyes close and I think I'm living in a palace of gold, not this rotten apartment. Your father can't listen to music. He gets headaches. Me, I'm a lover of the finer things in life. Next weekend I'm meeting Bea— you remember my friend Bea, she's a teacher, she went to college— and we're going to the Cloisters up in Washington Heights to look at the tapestries. There's so much culture in every corner of this city that no one even appreciates. By the way, Rhonda, I found a rug for the living room. The living room needs something. It costs less than you'd think. It's a small Oriental rug, so your father will never notice. In beautiful taste. You get that from me, darling. Taste. It's inherited. Nobody can take it away from you. You can't buy it. You can't learn it. You're very lucky."

"Pops says you're going into business with him. He told me he wants to open another store."

"I said, 'Don't mention that to her, Bernie. She doesn't want to know from that.' "

"I don't."

"Now's not the time. With your friend and everything. Such a tragedy. I remember she told me about the museums she visited. She was trying to better herself, wasn't she? Do they have any ideas about who did it?"

"No."

"Horrible, just horrible. But in a couple of weeks you'll be feeling better and we'll talk about your father's store."

"You agree with him? You think I should put in money?"

"Your father has many faults, but he is your father and when it comes to running a store, he's no fool. The man knows corsets. Who can blame him for wanting to quit the road?"

"I don't care what he does. I'm not getting involved."

"You mean to work in the store? Of course not. If you're anything, you're a silent partner."

"He didn't put it that way. He said I should quit my job and we'd all work together."

"You and him, you'd kill each other. He's better off without you there."

"I don't care, Mom, I really don't. I'm not about to give him any money."

"Don't think of it as giving to him. You'll be giving to me. We're not talking about much. Maybe a couple of thousand dollars. Leo would give, but you know how little schoolteachers make. Your father, he's always giving to Leo."

"You think I have that kind of money?"

"When you were a little girl and I'd give you two nickels, you'd hide one of them under your pillow. With money you've always had a head on your shoulders."

"He's ashamed of what I do, but he's not ashamed to take the money I earn doing it."

"What you do for a living is your business. The less we talk about it, the better off we all are."

"Gee, that makes me feel great."

"I'm not saying good or bad, Rhonda. I'm just not saying. Who knows who you might meet at your job? Doctors go to those places. Lawyers. Dentists. Dentists make good money these days."

"Pops was too cheap to send me to a dentist when I was a kid," I reminded Mom. "When I first started looking for work, I had to fix my teeth—with my own money."

"So you know it's not easy living with your father. You get to leave. Leo gets to leave, but me, I'm here. I have to know what to say to Bernie and what not to say. On certain subjects he leaves me alone and I leave him alone. He doesn't know I've taken up golf, but I have. There's a public course in Dyker Beach. A man's giving me lessons. He's from Scotland. A regular pro. And did I tell you about the series, the Great Books of Western Civilization? I'm reading them all. One by one. Leo sent them. Your mother's turning into a regular philosopher. Every day I learn a new word. Today it's 'approbation.' Do you know what it means?"

"Something to do with jail?"

"Being praised. Approval. That's your father's problem. Bad credit. No bank will approve a loan. And I'm tired of going around to the aunts and uncles and begging like a pauper. Who needs the humiliation? I've asked everyone I know. Some will help out but most won't. To tell the truth, Rhonda—and this is just between mother and daughter—if he doesn't find the money, if he can't open the store, I can't see myself staying with him. Without a store he's a man without a future. Already I'm tired of his lousy moods. P.S. If something good doesn't happen soon, if he doesn't get off that lousy road and start making decent money, I'm leaving him, I swear to God."

"I can't believe I'm hearing this, Mom."

"Believe."

"Your marriage depends on whether I give him money to open a store—is that what you're saying?"

"I didn't put it that way. I'd never put it that way."

"Look, Mom, I lost a good friend. A sweet girl is dead, a young kid. I liked her. I liked her a lot. I worked with her five nights a week for the past six months, and the way she got it, Mom . . . anyway, I'm numb and now with you and Pops and this business about a store, I can't even think. Let me go to sleep."

"Of course, darling, whatever you want. You'll call me next week. You'll call when you feel better."

I felt worse. I felt like my parents were strangers, strangers who

I knew better than anyone in the world, but still strangers because I couldn't believe they were really my parents. I didn't think like them; I didn't act like them; I didn't believe what they believed and I didn't do what they wanted me to do. But I loved them. You have to love your parents, don't you? I know I wanted them to love me, and I thought they did, but Pops, he never paid much attention, and Mom, she was too busy trying to improve her lot in life, and it wasn't until I started making money—real money— that Mom started calling me and sure it felt good giving her stuff that the old man never could. They said I'd never amount to nothing and here I was about to make over $10,000 in a single year which was just unbelievable and just goes to prove I had to be good at what I did. Damn good. But to give money to Pops, Pops who never paid for a single dance lesson and wouldn't pay to fix my teeth, Pops who tried to turn me into some office secretary in Canarsie, Pops who gave me grief about Plotsky's and acted like I was committing some terrible sin . . . forget Pops.

I couldn't forget Tush. That was my problem—getting through Sunday night. I'd gone through most of the bialys. I was stuffed; I was fed up with my family. Sandy called, hoping I'd change my mind about making beautiful music with him, but I said, "Sandy, you gotta understand. I can't get this picture of Tush out of my head. I ain't in the mood." Bull called and said the Bears had lost and he'd gone 0 for four—two strikeouts, two little popouts—and could I, would I, 'cause they were playing tomorrow and I was the only thing that heated up his bat, but Bull hadn't even seen the papers and he didn't know about Tush and I didn't say nothing except I was tired and no, Bull, not tonight, you're a big sweet moose, but call me next week when I ain't so empty and exhausted.

I needed to sleep something awful. But I didn't need to dream. Not about Tush. I didn't need to see her again. And this time there were knives in her breasts and knives in her private parts and not just one guy was carving her up, but lots of guys, and their faces were hidden but I knew who they were, they were laughing, and one of them turned to me and yes, I recognized him—I swear I did!—but just when I was about to say his name I woke up and I thought I heard someone turning the knob to my bedroom door and my heart was beating like crazy and I jumped outta bed and reached for a weapon, but what kind of weapons do I have except for a couple of nail files and the bra I threw on the floor. Well, I'll poke out his eyes with the file and I'll strangle him to death with my bra, that's what I'll do. Except no one was there. It was five in the morning, still dark outside, my brains felt like scrambled eggs with me still wondering who in the hell would murder Tush, what kind of man would do that to a woman?

"PLOTSKY'S GOT A PROBLEM."

That's what Mr. Plotsky said to me.

"Because of Tush?" I asked him.

"They're putting on the heat. I can feel it already. Donegan was already by this morning."

"Does he know anything?"

"Do you?"

"Nobody knows nothing," I said. "Where's the heat coming from, Mr. Plotsky?"

"The mayor's office, the ethics committee, the people who hate burlesque."

Herb Plotsky was a veteran burlesque operator, a little man who wore his pants high over his waist. He had these bushy eyebrows and little wire glasses that made him look like the old guy in the storybook who carved Pinocchio out of a block of wood. His stomach was too big and his ears stuck out but his wife, Dolores, was a former showgirl, a regular knockout even though she had to be pushing sixty. Because Dolores was a couple of feet taller than Mr. Plotsky there were jokes about them in bed, but I figured she had the last laugh because they were living in a suite at the Essex House Hotel in Newark, not far from Plotsky's which is where I should be living to cut down on the wear and tear of running back and forth from Brooklyn but you already know how I feel about Brooklyn.

I was in Mr. Plotsky's backstage office on Market Street in

downtown Newark. It was Monday afternoon and even though there was no show that night I dropped by for one of our chats. Me and Mr. Plotsky always had these chats that made me feel better. His office was plastered with pictures of Phil Silvers, Abbott and Costello, Bert Lahr, Ed Wynn, Joe E. Brown and Eddie Cantor. Mr. Plotsky knew 'em all. He'd even know Uncle Mo. He bought suits and ties from Uncle Mo in the twenties and thirties and he always said Uncle Mo was a gentleman respected by everyone in the business.

"You should have seen the business back then," he said. "Back then burlesque was the biggest thing on Broadway. Everyone wanted to be in burlesque. Ziegfeld's girls knew the pay was better in burlesque. They wanted in. The money, the costumes, the lighting—we had it all. The chorus lines were fabulous . . ."

"We got a chorus line, Mr. Plotsky."

"You call it a chorus line, Rhonda, but it's only four girls behind you—well, three girls now—and they're not really dancers, they're just there to wiggle, they're only there to give the boys a little more to look at and if God forbid you get sick they can take your place. The chorus lines I'm talking about would have twenty gals. It was a regular musical show. It was class. For instance, when two of the Minksy brothers, H. K. and Morton—I knew them both, they were both good friends of mine—when they opened up their Oriental Theater near Fifty-first Street it was Christmas of 1936 and they even had a Park Avenue Row, a special seating section for the socialites who came in tuxes and evening gowns. You should have seen the stiltwalkers with sandwich boards out on the street selling the show and the classy Chinese girls they had dancing right in the lobby before you got into the theater. You see, Rhonda, the city was wild for burlesque. The National Winter Garden down on the Lower East Side was a jewel, that's what it was, and if you read your good newspapers like the New York *Times* you'd see that even the highbrow critics like Brooks Atkinson liked burlesque. Ever see the *New Yorker*? Well, A. J. Liebling, one of their biggest writers, he loved burlesque and the big-shot publisher Harold Ross, he'd come to the shows. Now the New York *Times* and the *New Yorker* won't show that picture of Teresa Johnson because they know all it does is give burlesque a bad name. They saw how LaGuardia killed off burlesque. Penal Code 1140A, Rhonda, that's what did us in. The hypocrites. The Minskys couldn't even use their own name anymore because the judge said the name was associated with filth, but what's filth to one man is paradise to another. We all had to run to Jersey. The Paradise was my first theater in Hoboken. Then there was the Apollo in Union City. These were shabby little theaters, but they were better than nothing. Burlesque ain't what it used to be. It used to be like grand opera, believe me. The sky was the limit. Now we're reduced to this."

"I don't think it's so bad, Mr. Plotsky."

"The Golden Age is gone. But you've heard all this before, Rhonda."

"I like listening to your stories, Mr. Plotsky." I wished my own father were here to listen.

" 'Use your own name,' I finally said to myself when I decided to open in Newark. The truth is I always wanted to see my name in lights. But who am I fooling, Rhonda? It's not the same. We have a small band. We have an old comic . . ."

"Danny's a very funny guy . . ."

"Danny's practically blind. I've seen how you lead him onstage. You stay out there with him and pretend like you're part of his act so you can lead him back to the wings. You're sweet to do it, Rhonda, but you're not fooling anyone. Without you, Danny's bumping into the footlights and he's falling into the pit. Danny has to go. He's old-time. Nowadays burlesque is down to girls like you."

"You make it sound terrible," I said.

"Not terrible, just different. More power to you, I say, because you carry the show. In the old days it was more than the peeler. It was a whole show. Now the whole show is you. You're terrific, Rhonda, I'm not saying you're not, but with this murder I'm afraid it'll happen here what happened in the city. They'll murder us. They'll say we're corrupting morals, causing violence . . ."

"But the violence was against *us*."

"You're telling me. You're talking logical, but the bluenoses, they don't know from logic. The politicians are looking for headlines. Logic doesn't enter. You're going to have to tone down the act, Rhonda. Give 'em the Boston version. Sew more beads on your G-strings. Stash the flesh-colored ones—at least for a while."

"But the boys go out of their minds with the flesh-colored G-string. They think I got nothing on. It's the best part of the act."

"And you do it with style, Rhonda, you really do, but we're being watched. I can't afford to be closed down."

"You'll be costing me, Mr. Plotsky. When I strip down to the flesh-colored G-strings the bills come flying on stage—fins, even sawbucks."

"I know, Rhonda. And you deserve that money. I wish I could tell you the sky's the limit, but we have to be practical."

"I'm working on a new routine."

"That's my girl, always working. What is it?"

"Pins, no zippers."

"Pins are good. Gypsy Rose uses pins. Zippers get caught. Less problems with pins."

"These are hat pins. Long pins, so the guys can see me taking them out. I take them out real slowly. I'm wearing nothing but little American flags, each one pinned to a see-through . . ."

"Rhonda, dear, please. I know you mean well . . ."

"It's patriotism. With the war in Europe over . . ."

"I understand. But not now, not when the ethics board is watching us like hawks. Your old routine is just fine, as long as you sew a few more beads on your G-string."

"I never thought I'd hear you talk this way, Mr. Plotsky. You liked me because I was daring. 'You have to be daring in this business,' you said. And now . . ."

"Now the world's changing and some maniac murdered one of my girls, and I'm telling you, this isn't the time to be draping American flags around yourself."

"You'll forgive me, boss, but maybe this is *just* the time. What with the publicity . . ."

"Publicity? I'm up to here with publicity! What do I want with more publicity? Please, Rhonda, you're a good stripper but I'm the businessman here so you'll just stick with stripping and forget the fancy stuff."

The meeting was over.

Mr. Plotsky had never been that short with me before. He hurt my feelings. I never thought Plotsky was anything like Pops, but now he was acting like Pops—cranky and worried about nothing but money. "A good stripper." Is that all I was to him? He used to say I was a good dancer, and he used to call me his star and now he's losing his temper with me. I know he's upset about Tush, but I am too. After all, she was my friend, my little sister. She was even my "catcher"—the one who stands in the wings and catches my clothes as I peel 'em off and fling 'em aside—skirt, blouse, stockings, gloves, the whole bit. Tush studied me. She said she wanted to strip too, but it's more than stripping I told her. It's wanting to please and wanting to excite and getting excited yourself—the boys can tell when you're faking and when you're not—and I'm no fake. Mr. Plotsky knows that. He knows I'm for real. Hell, I might as well tell you the truth: I get wet. Every time. With the thought of all the guys wanting me so bad, and how they're straining at the bit and how the house is crowded with hard-ons, all caused by me and aimed at me, their eyes aimed at me, their pricks aimed at me. "Can you think about that?" I asked Tush who blushed when I'd talk that way. Tush was fine as a backup but she never done a solo strip and maybe she could cut it and maybe she couldn't. She liked flattering me and I didn't mind being flattered because she said I did it right to the beat—and it's true, I strip on time, I strip in rhythm, I especially like to strip to jazz— and she liked jazz and come to think of it she once wanted to know if I'd go up to Harlem with her to hear some jazz but I was busy that night with Bull Wallinksy who'd been moved to the clean-up spot on the Newark Bears. The Bears are minor league but Bull is going to make the majors one day; I really believe in Bull.

Now Mr. Plotsky was telling me that Plotsky's wasn't the majors. Isn't that what he meant with all his talk about Minsky's and the glory days of the Oriental Theater on Broadway? "Just strip, Rhonda." That's all he wanted. "Just take it off, but leave on enough so we don't get in trouble."

The truth is that I wanted to take more off. I wanted to take it all off. You see, I made my way out of the chorus line into the spotlight by taking off more and more. You'd never know what I was going to do—I didn't even know—which is how I built my following. Being barebreasted was par for the course, but I'd go further. Sometimes I'd actually showed them bush. They were dreaming of sneaking a peek at the real deal, and there were times when I made those dreams come true. I'd slip my finger under my G-string and push it down on my thighs, if only for half a second. Maybe Mr. Plotsky saw this; maybe he was back in his office and didn't know a thing. Either way, he could hear the boys yelling for me and he sure as hell could count their money.

"This ain't no business for prudes"—that's what I'd tell Tush, and the way she'd stick out that ass of hers I knew she was no prude; she liked showing off her equipment, which is the first requirement of a peeler. You gotta like to give it up; or more to the point, you gotta make the boys *believe* you like giving it up. "Pussy is one thing," Danny the funny man used to tell me— Danny who's seen every stripper since the original Little Egypt— "but pussy with personality is a whole 'nother matter. You got pussy with personality."

Tush did too. She was just breaking out of her shell, just getting started. Before the late show we'd go over some routines together in my dressing room. She'd watch my moves. She'd understudy me. If I ever got sick, she was next in line to do my routine. Plotsky's got two other solo strippers, but he don't even bother to put their names on the marquees. One's a big Irish girl named Honey Pot who's pushing forty; the other is Nancy Nips who's gonna find her teeth down her throat if I see her using any of my moves again, especially this high hip grind I do from the floor, flat on my back, which is something I developed myself and was teaching to Tush when all of a sudden I see Miss Nips, who is one ugly bitch if you ask me, trying to grind the same way but, believe me, the boys ain't believing her, they know she really ain't thinking about grinding their meat which is what you have to do to get the boys up. Be sincere.

I thought my American flag idea was sincere as hell. It's how I felt about the boys who had fought for our freedom, it was my way to pay 'em back, give 'em a little pleasure. They went all the way for us, so why not go all the way for them? Well, if Mr. Plotsky was nervous there was nothing I could do. Sure, I'd sew a couple of more beads on my G-string but once I got on stage there were no guarantees. Besides, I wasn't thinking about that now. I was thinking about Tush and looking up a phone number for Abraham Jones the sax player and considering taking the Tubes back to the city and running up to Harlem to pay him a visit but first I'd drop in on Captain Mickey Donegan and see what was cooking.

THE SIZE
OF THEIR
SCHLONGS

This is what they're talking about at the precinct, I swear. Grown men, cops, sitting around discussing how they heard Joe Louis's schlong is the size of Long Island. I was standing out in the hallway and the door to Mickey's office was open. They didn't see me and I just wanted to listen 'cause this is when I learn even more about men. These are white guys, Irish guys, maybe Polish guys, maybe even Jewish guys, but one thing they got in common is that they're worried about their dicks. They ain't saying that, they're saying how the colored are this and the Italians are that but I ain't ever met a man—whether he's big, small or in between—who isn't always looking at it, pulling at it, wishing there was more of it. Now when I started going with guys—I was fourteen, maybe fifteen—I got educated right away. There was this guy named Arnold Levy, he was the first, and when he was soft he was real small but when I touched it—and I liked touching it, it felt friendly, like petting a friendly puppy or something—it got nice and long and stiff. Another guy they called Hebrew National 'cause he was supposed to be big as a salami—this was Sidney—but Sidney's schlong, even though it was a healthy slice of meat, never went anywhere when it got excited. It just sort of nodded upwards. I could tickle it, I could lick it, I could bite it (gently, of course), but nothing could make the thing stand straight up. In the locker room Sidney looks like the champ to the other guys, but in the bedroom give me Arnold every time. So size can fool you. It's all how they move in the groove. Are they digging deep or just scratching the surface? If they're interested in pleasing themselves first, forget it. They could have the leaning tower of fuckin' Pisa between their legs and it ain't gonna matter none. They gotta wanna make you happy. I ain't saying equipment ain't important. The tool must be in good working order. But attitude is everything. That's why Sandy the songwriter knocks me out. He can dance the dance of love while Bull . . . well, Bull's got good intentions; Bull just needs more batting practice.

I'd heard enough from the cops.

"So this is how guys go around solving crimes," I said, walking through the door.

The guys got out of their chairs—there were a half-dozen of them—and stood up like naughty little schoolboys who were just caught snitching candy.

"Rhonda!" said Captain Mickey Donegan, "what a nice surprise! Let me introduce you."

I could feel their eyes all over me. It felt good. I was glad I was wearing an orange jersey off-the-shoulders top and no bra so the circles of my nipples were aiming at everyone in the room. Bullseye. I was also glad I had tied up my hair high on my head 'cause my neck and back were tan from two weeks ago at Coney Island. I stood tall. If you keep your posture ramrod upright it makes a better impression and men notice you 'cause most tall women stoop, slumping their shoulders like they're apologizing for something. I ain't apologizing for shit. I keep my head high; I stand straight, like a queen.

After the introductions, the guys left the room, smiling and giving me one last once-over. When they were gone, I told Captain Donegan, "I came to see if you found out anything about my friend."

"We made some inquiries this morning," he said, "but there ain't a single clue. All the fingerprints were hers and nothing was out of place. I was by Plotsky's this morning . . ."

"They told me."

"Well, no one there knows nothing. They say the same thing you did. This girl was clean. Came to the city six months ago. Kept to herself."

I was going to say something about Abraham the sax player, but something told me not to. When white guys hear about colored guys even looking at white girls—especially when the white guys are the cops from this precinct—they start seeing dicks the size of dinosaurs. Besides, I liked Abraham, and I didn't want to get him in hot water, not before I knew the score myself.

"Who called her parents in Ohio?" I asked.

"Yours truly."

"Must have been hard."

"That's the understatement of the year. Her father thought she was in art school. He said he'd been sending her money for art school."

"You tell him about Plotsky's?"

"What do you take me for, Rhonda, a louse? I didn't say nothing. He'll be here tomorrow to claim the body. If you want to meet him, he'll be at the Savoy Plaza."

"Think I should, Mick?"

"Just don't say nothing about stripping. He thinks his daughter was a saint."

"She was a nice kid."

"The old man sounds nice too. He's a minister."

"You're kidding."

"Reverend Johnson."

"She never said nothing."

"He started praying, right over the phone."

"How many detectives you putting on the case, Mick?"

"You don't understand, Rhonda, I'm about to close this case out. We're jammed up. The chief's got us running down some outfit that's stealing cigarettes by the truckload and selling them out of state."

"Cigarettes? Who cares about a stack of hot smokes? This girl, this friend of mine, is dead."

"I did my best. I went to Newark."

"For an hour. You call that an investigation?"

"What do you want from us, Rhonda? I got nothing to go on."

"What about the coroner's report? Did he say she was raped first or what?"

"I'm telling you, no traces of semen, no pubic hairs, we don't got a clue."

"Funny. I figured . . ."

"You figured what?"

"Oh, I was just thinking how men usually don't pass up a woman, no matter what."

"Take it from me, Rhonda, there are all sorts of maniacs running around this city. It just so happened that one of them ran into Teresa Johnson."

"It ain't that simple, Mick. I know there's more to it than that. This isn't something you can just drop."

"The truth is that some people say girls in your line of work are asking for trouble."

"That ain't true. That's sick thinking, that's what it is."

"I'm trying to level with you, Rhonda. It boils down to this— the department doesn't regard a stripper as a high priority."

"Oh, yeah? Well, with all the time you spend at Plotsky's it seems like you give us strippers *very* fuckin' high priority."

"I give *you* high priority, Rhonda. If you want, we can work on this case together. Tonight."

Captain Mickey Donegan was a thick-skulled, red-haired meat-head. I didn't want to work with him. I didn't want to smell his nasty half-cigar. And I sure as hell didn't want to fuck him. I didn't even want to be in the same room with him, except that he was a loyal customer and brought in other customers and he did run a whole precinct. But it was obvious he didn't care nothing about finding the guy who rubbed out Tush. That made me mad. But what more could I say? A stripper—if she wants to stay popular— has to be a politician. He was insulting me and insulting my dead friend by calling us trash, just like my father thinks I'm trash, but this wasn't the time to call him a dumb-ass greasy-palmed flat-footed sonofabitch, which is what I wanted to say.

"If you learn anything, Mick," I said instead, "let me know 'cause I'm having trouble sleeping. She was good people, this Tush. She didn't deserve this."

"I can call you anytime?"

I thought about his question. "If it's about Tush, sure, you can call me anytime."

HARLEM
HIT
PARADE

To me Harlem is a happy place. When I think of Harlem I think of jazz and reefer and people who ain't putting on airs, people looking to laugh at life a little 'cause if we can't laugh we wind up nuts. Now I know I'm seeing Harlem through white eyes; I know the colored got their pain and heartaches like everyone else. They got to be worried about money like us. They got to be hurting by how they're treated bad and how they used to be slaves like the Jews were slaves except the colored were slaves right here in America and not just back in the Bible days. On the other hand, no one's putting them in concentration camps and killing 'em off in trainloads like the fuckin' Krauts were killing us off, except I truly believe in my heart most of the white people I know still think of the colored like slaves or monkeys and that makes me feel bad. Take the girlie magazines and the strip shows, which is something I know about. I modeled for those magazines when I was younger which is when I saw they had this policy: White girls can't show tit; only the colored girls can. White girls can never ever flash pussy; colored girls can. What does that mean? It means the guys who run the magazines think the colored gals are more like animals so it don't matter what they show. Ain't that some shit? I once got in a fight with one of those schmucks who owns a skin rag. I told him, "If you're gonna let this colored gal show snatch, you're gonna let me," and I flashed right then and there and the photographer snapped it up and the boss said do that again, waste more of my film and I'll put your ass on the street and I did it again and he tried to grab my arm but I smacked his face so hard he got scared.

P.S. When the magazine came out you could see my tits but they put a black strip over my bush while the colored girls were all-the-way nude.

I learn in Harlem. I learn from the shows and the colored strippers. When they're good, the colored strippers are the best. I pay real close attention how they bump to the beat, usually a little behind the beat to give it that extra edge that has the guys hanging on to their hard-ons. Compared to the colored, the white strippers are like soldiers—everything's too proper—while the colored girls are loose and full of surprises. If the world was fair, which it ain't, Plotsky's would have colored strippers right next to the white girls but they don't because Mr. Plotsky don't want a colored crowd. He won't even let me put a colored gal in the chorus line. He says Newark has too many coloreds already. One day, he says, the coloreds are going to take over and he calls them jungle bunnies and in that way he ain't no different from the guys who own the magazines.

I wasn't worried in Harlem. It was a sunny Monday afternoon and Lenox Avenue looked real peaceful with the kids playing in the water spraying from the fire hydrants just like they do down-town except here their skin was shiny black and their hair nappy but kids are kids and people are people and I don't understand why we gotta call each other names and go around hurting everyone's feelings. My feelings were hurt from the way Mickey Donegan talked to me and how he didn't care about Tush. Sure, he loves looking at strippers and putting his hand all over my ass back in my dressing room, but if some whacked-out lunatic carves me up like a fuckin' turkey don't count on this guy to do nothing except shrug his shoulders. Well, I was moving on. Long ago I taught myself it's better to do something than just feel sorry for myself, which is why I'd been trying to reach Abraham Jones. I wanted to get to the bottom of this thing. But no one answered the number

I got at Plotsky's off the sheet with all the band members' phones and addresses. So I decided to go uptown and talk to Abraham person to person. Person to person is better than the phone anyway.

He lived on 146th between St. Nicholas and Amsterdam in a brownstone that had seen better days but you wouldn't call it a slum. The mailbox said he lived in 5B and it wasn't bad climbing up five stories 'cause of the sound of his saxophone. The sound was sweet, like a faraway lover remembering some gal he loved real good. I followed the sound all the way to his door and just stood there for a while. I didn't want the sound to stop. It was a melody that could have been a song but wasn't a regular song, not like the kind that Sandy writes. Sandy's songs have a beginning, middle and end. This song was loose and wandered like a dirt path out in the country when the breeze is blowing and you're smelling the woods and maybe a bird, a bluebird is chirping over your head. Finally when he stopped I knocked on his door.

Abraham was surprised to see me. He was a nice-looking well-built man with thick glasses, a strong face and a soft voice. He spoke barely above a whisper, reminding me of the way he played the sax. He was gentle and well mannered with dark skin and good teeth. When he smiled, you felt like he meant it. There were books scattered around his place, some serious-looking books, a mess of magazines, some in foreign languages. I always knew Abraham was smart. He played burlesque for the bread, but Sandy said he was a true artist, one of those new be-boppers. He was sitting on a stool. A little upright piano stood in the corner. His horn rested in his lap and looked like magic the way it reflected the sun pouring through the window. He held his horn like a child. A golden child. He was wearing a white undershirt and I could see he had a nice chest—I don't like flabby men—and muscles up and down his arms.

"It's your friend, isn't it?" he asked. "You've come to ask me about Teresa."

"How'd you know?" I wanted to know.

"She was crazy about you. She kept talking about you like you were her sister. She must have told you about coming up here."

"She told Sandy."

"Sandy . . ." he said, trying to remember. "Oh yeah, Sandy Singer. The songwriter. Nice cat. Can he play piano?"

"He's mainly a writer."

"I write melodies, but I need to nail them down with some lyrics. Maybe I should get with Sandy."

"He'd like that. He thinks you're great."

"The thing with Teresa . . . grizzly . . . poor baby . . ."

"I can't believe it."

"You knew about her singing?"

"She mentioned it to Sandy."

"Did she and Sandy have something going on?"

The question startled me. Of course not. But why would Abraham even ask? "No," I told him. "They just knew each other."

"I see. Wonder who else she told about coming up here . . ."

"You worried about the cops?"

"White chick, black cat. Not exactly a hot number on the Harlem Hit Parade."

"I wouldn't say nothing to the cops, Abraham. Besides, they don't care about this case. A murdered stripper ain't a high priority."

"You want me to be straight with you, Rhonda?"

"Wouldn't want you to be anything else."

"Teresa had a beautiful voice. Natural voice. I'd be noodling on my horn after the gig and she'd sidle up beside me and start singing along, singing just what I was playing. I told her she could sing jazz and she really didn't know what jazz was and asked me whether I'd show her. I didn't know how to take that exactly. Being that she's white and fine I figured it best not to play with fire. But the flesh is weak and it didn't take too much to convince me. 'Please,' she kept asking me. 'Take me to hear a real jazz singer.' So I took her to hear the realest jazz singer there is—Billie Holiday. Teresa was spellbound. She sat through three straight sets of Lady Day, Teresa crying real tears for the feeling of Billie's songs. Lady noticed her and now Lady's got tears in *her* eyes. Afterwards, Billie comes over to the table and I introduce them. Teresa looks up at Lady like she's a goddess. Next thing I know Teresa wants to try to sing and she talks me into letting her rehearse with a little group I'm putting together in a chili house on Seventh Avenue between 139th and 140th where Bird used to jam. She makes me promise I won't tell no one because she's uneasy and unsure of herself but damned if that girl doesn't start sounding just a little like a white Billie Holiday."

"This doesn't sound like the Tush I knew. She liked paintings, going to museums . . ."

"That too. She was always talking about Dali's Christ."

"Dali?"

"Salvador. The weird painter. This chick was weird."

"I never saw that side of her."

"Well, she was learning to strip from you. You saw the stripper side."

"I guess so . . ."

"Want to know my take on Teresa?"

"If I didn't, I wouldn't be here."

"To me, she was the kind of chick who gets next to whatever's happening. If she's in a strip joint, she strips. If it's a jazz joint, she's down with jazz."

"I want to ask you a question, Abraham."

"You want to know if me and Teresa ever made it . . ."

"It ain't really my business, but . . ."

"She was different than you thought, and now you're trying to get to know her. Is that it?"

"That's it."

"Well, if we're going to be honest here, I intend to be *extra* honest. I'm not saying I didn't try. And I'm not saying I wasn't disappointed when I found out she wasn't interested. I was like you; I thought I understood her. I figured her for one of those white gals fascinated by the male Negroid anatomy. But, man, I figured wrong. Maybe if I hadn't taken her to hear Billie things might have turned out different. 'Cause Billie just scooped her up and carried her on out."

"Billie Holiday? You're telling me Tush and Billie Holiday . . ."

"I wasn't a bug in the rug in Lady's apartment. I'm not an eyewitness. All I can say is that Billie left with her that night. Two other times Billie came to fetch her after rehearsals. I didn't ask any questions."

"I don't . . . I just don't . . ."

"You don't want to believe it. And you don't have to, Rhonda. Teresa's gone."

"I wanna talk to Billie Holiday," I said.

"Now what good is that going to do you?"

"I'm not sure . . . I . . ."

"You don't think Billie did it, do you? Billie's already in enough hot water with the man. Undercover narcotic cops practically live on her doorstep. They're ready to bust her for looking the wrong way."

"I told you the cops are out of this."

There was a long pause. Abraham knew what I wanted to ask him. "You want to know where I was the night she was killed, don't you?"

I nodded.

"I went to jam. Went to the chili house and sat in with the cats. They'll tell you."

"I don't need to ask."

"Maybe you do need to ask. Looks like you want to keep asking questions. Well, that's your right, baby, but I say forget it. It was probably just some lunatic."

"That's what the cops said."

"Teresa might have met a weirdo. For a night or two, maybe she became a weirdo herself."

"I don't see that."

"We see what we want to see. Life is like the jazz music I play. We make it up as we go along."

"DO YOU UNDERSTAND THE NATURE OF HOMOSEXUALITY?"

Get this: One night, out of the blue, my brother Leo announces he's queer. Which is a little like Albert Einstein announcing he's Jewish. You had to be blind to miss it.

There I was, drained after this long Monday running from Plotsky's to Donegan's to Abraham's up in Harlem. I'd ridden the A train and the BMT and my tired ass was back in Brooklyn, my head aching with ideas that didn't go good together. Like Tush and Abraham. And Tush and Billie Holiday. And Tush and Sandy. To make matters even screwier, someone on the subway had left a *Life* magazine with a story about Salvador Dali with his crazed eyes and weird moustache sticking out and his paintings which aren't normal at all. Now I'm finding out maybe Tush wasn't normal. Maybe I'm not. Maybe none of us are.

"I knew you were never normal," I told Leo, who showed up after dinner. I had on my bathrobe and I'd put my hair up in rollers 'cause I was stripping tomorrow night and I did my own hair. It took a while to do my hair. I was going for a pageboy, which ain't a snap when your hair's kinky. I was in the middle of developing a little different look, and I wasn't in the mood for company. But Leo was my brother and it wasn't like I saw him every week. Months might pass before we talked and I guess I got a soft spot for my little brother, even though he's always been a pain in the ass and gotten all the attention because they say he's a mathematical genius. He's also got Pop's sad eyes but he's not as tall as me and Pops. He's more Mom's medium size and he'd look a lot better if he combed his hair and put on some pomade because his hair was sticking up and sticking out and made him look like the mad professor.

It didn't take long for Leo to say why he'd come to visit me.

"I'm moving to California."

"That sounds like fun."

"I'm moving there to be with my boyfriend."

I wasn't surprised. When Leo was a kid I'd catch him sneaking looks at Pops's crotch when Pops was wearing a robe, sitting and reading in his easy chair with his balls hanging out. I'd also never catch Leo sneaking looks at me—the way I'd catch Pops—which led me to suspect girls didn't interest Leo. Then there was his friend Howie Pasternak. Howie was always spending the night and I thought that was a little peculiar because girls had pajama parties but not guys. Besides, there was only one narrow bed in Leo's room and Mom thought they were camping out on the floor but when I looked in there they were cuddled up together. I could have busted him. I could have told my parents that their little prince was really a fairy but it was easier to get the fuck out of that house altogether than ruin my brother's life.

"You tell Mom and Pops about your boyfriend?" I asked Leo, knowing the answer was "no."

"That's why I'm here. I want to talk to you about that. I know you've known, Rhonda, but we've never discussed it."

"What's to discuss?"

"It's hard leading a secret life."

"I understand."

"Do you, do you really?"

"I think I do. You like men. I like men. We got that in common. Maybe that's all we got in common."

"It's easy for you . . ."

"Easy for *me*! Are you kidding? I was the nincompoop. I was the slut. I didn't even get to finish regular high school. Pops saw me as a filing clerk, a secretary at best."

"I had to hide everything I felt. I still do. At least you got to express your sexuality, Rhonda."

"What's that supposed to mean?"

"You got to be yourself."

"Because I busted out. I broke away . . ."

"That took balls."

"Look, Leo, you were the one who got to go to college. They paid for everything you ever wanted. They worship their little Leo . . ."

"That's why I can't tell them."

"Why do you have to go all the way to California to be with your boyfriend?"

"Because he hates New York. And I hate it too. I've got to get out of here."

"What about your teaching job?"

"I'll find another job out there."

"Is he Jewish?"

"That's a hell of a thing to ask."

"I'm curious."

"No, he's not Jewish. Why . . . do you think you'd have an easier time telling the folks if he were Jewish?"

"You want *me* to tell them?"

"I can't. You understand these sorts of things."

"Me?"

"You're experienced."

"This is great, just great. I'm the one who has to tell the folks that their precious Leo is moving to the other side of the country and then I got to say, 'By the way, your son likes dicks.' "

"Why do you put it like that? Do you really understand the nature of homosexuality?"

"I understand telling the fuckin' truth. And truthfully, that's how I look at it. Besides, what's wrong with liking dicks? I like dicks. They're funny-looking. They're fun to play with. The way they just hang there. The way they puff up. The way they work is interesting. Ain't we talking the same language?"

"I don't want to talk about it."

"Then don't. Don't talk to me and don't talk to Mom and Pops."

"Why are you getting mad?"

" 'Cause you're setting me up to do your goddamn dirty work. All that does is make me look dirtier to them. I'm carrying your dirty news. You're too clean, too pure to say it yourself. You know what they're going to say? 'It's not true . . . it's impossible.' Or else they'll say, 'You did it to him. You tried something with him, you touched him, and look what happened . . . you turned our precious Leo queer.' "

"It's important that they know."

"Why?"

"Because . . . well, to be truthful, I want to be like you. I want to live honestly, Rhonda. I want to be free. God, you don't know how much I admired you when Pops was grilling you about dating Arnold Levy and you said, just like it was nothing, 'Yes, we're dating and we're also sleeping together and I like it. It makes me feels great.' "

"You thought that was cute?"

"It was courageous . . ."

I was moved. I like being looked up to. "So why didn't you ever say anything to me?" I wanted to know.

"I was too scared."

"Well, maybe it's time not to be so scared. What can they do to you? You'll be gone anyway."

"Maybe it's better not to tell them at all. Just say I'm moving to California."

"I'm not saying a word, Leo. I ain't doing your talking for you. What with my friend dead . . ."

"What friend?"

"Tush. Teresa Johnson."

"The girl I met?"

"You were there that Sunday I brought her home. Mom and Pops didn't tell you? You didn't see it in the *Mirror*?"

"I don't read the *Mirror*. Mom and Pops didn't say a word. How'd she die?"

"Murdered. Sex murder."

"What do you mean 'sex murder'?"

"The points of pleasure—all mutilated."

"Jesus . . . someone who hated sex."

"That's what I think."

"What do the cops think?"

"They're snoozing on the job. They don't give a rat's ass. In their eyes, a stripper's a piece of garbage."

"I'm sorry, Sis, I really am."

He came and put his arm around me. This was the first time I could remember Leo touching me in years. He even kissed me on the cheek.

"I need a friend right now," he said. "And you're the only one who understands me, Rhonda. No one understands men like you. No one."

BATTER UP

"Please, baby, you gotta come to the game tonight."

"It's Tuesday," I told Bull. "I strip tonight. I don't have time to chitchat. I gotta make a living, you know."

"When I get traded to the Yankees, you won't have to work."

I could just see Bull sitting there, stroking his bat, his lucky bat, worrying about going hitless tonight. "I ain't seen you in a week," he told me.

"I've had problems." I didn't want to mention Tush 'cause I knew that would get him even more upset. Chances are Bull hadn't read about it because Bull doesn't read. He doesn't even like looking at newspaper pictures of car wrecks and murders. Bull's got a queasy stomach and a big heart. Some people say he looks a little like Joe Palooka from the funnies but they haven't seen him with his shirt off. He's got a chest like one of those gladiators in the movies and if the average red-blooded girl ever saw him with his pants off she'd want to rub her hands all up and down his calves and thighs 'cause he's steel. Bull doesn't have to be brainy because he's a baseball player; he's a good centerfielder who can run the bases. Slumps are his only problems. He's got slumping and humping mixed up in his head. See, sometimes he can't get it up. That can bring on his hitting slump or it can work the other way: if he's not batting he's not bumping. It's tricky. I got my own tricks, like putting on a private show for him or bathing him in a bubble bath like a little baby. But with Bull you never know when he'll get excited. It's frustrating. His slumps can go on forever. He'll go o for thirty, o for forty. Right now he hasn't hit in his last five games. He hasn't run my bases in over a month. I wouldn't be so understanding except that the lug is really a good guy and when he finally does connect it's a grand slam like you wouldn't believe. I get chills just thinking about it.

"I think I'm about to pull out of it tonight," he told me. "I want you to be there when it happens."

"It'll happen whether I'm there or not."

"Sure you can't take off?"

"Not a chance."

"Then I'll come by Plotsky's after the game."

"Alright," I said, remembering that Sandy would be busy playing a society party on Park Avenue, though he was still convinced his sore throat meant cancer.

I hung up. I had to finish dressing 'cause I was stopping off to see Teresa's father on my way to Newark. I'd called the hotel and told him I was his daughter's friend and wanted to come by to pay my respects. Would he mind? This deep radio announcer's voice said, "No, not at all," he had to go to the morgue to identify the body but he'd be back at three.

I wanted to look nice and proper which was no problem for me. If you'd seen me that afternoon riding up Fifth Avenue on the green and yellow double-decker bus you'd never take me for a stripper. I was wearing this dark blue dress that wasn't too tight in the bosom and I could have been Lynn Fontanne or Katharine Cornell, that's how classy I looked wearing a white hat and a pair of white gloves and navy blue high heel leather pumps that the Duchess of Windsor could have worn. I can look classy at the drop of a hat.

From the lobby of the Savoy Plaza I called up to Mr. Johnson's room. He said he'd be right down so I waited in a gold velvet chair, my legs properly crossed, and read the paper about how Truman was fucking around with the United Nations charter but if you ask me the nations ain't ever gonna be united because people are assholes and jealous of each other. I looked around the lobby and saw some other women—young women like me—with men who had to be loaded with dough. Was I jealous? I knew goddamn well that some of those gals were turning tricks. I could see that under their silky dresses they were selling pussy just like I was selling pussy except with me you can look but you can't touch. And if you don't think there's not a hell of a difference there, brother, you're dead wrong. Pops doesn't see the difference. He once told me that stripping was worse than tricking 'cause you're taking on a roomful of men when you strip. But the actual screwing—that's in their imagination. And mine. Maybe you won't believe this, but I'm telling the truth when I say I never put out for money. Not once. I'm not calling whores evil or anything like that. But whores have to shut down their minds when they're getting laid. If they don't, they go crazy. My mind can't be switched off, it's always going a mile a minute, which is why I know turning tricks would make me nuts.

No, I wasn't jealous of no Fifth Avenue hookers even though they had to have had some interesting adventures. I wasn't jealous of chorus girls or actresses . . . but, wait a minute . . . look who's passing through the lobby, passing right in front of me—if it ain't Miss Tallulah Bankhead herself, the Broadway star. Her hair's in a pageboy just like mine and her dress is the same blue as my dress. She walks with her back straight and her head high. Good posture. I believe in good posture.

"Did you hear?" I overhear one of those high-class hookers whisper to her gentleman friend who's sitting on a couch right in back of me.

"Hear what?"

"About Tallulah and Billie Holiday."

"Who's Billie Holiday?"

"A colored singer. Tallulah went to see her a couple of weeks ago at the Downbeat Club on Fifty-second Street and the two of them disappeared into Billie's dressing room. The door didn't open for two hours. Billie never did come out to sing that night."

"Miss Silverstar?"

I looked up. It was the radio announcer's voice.

"Mr. Johnson?"

"Reverend Johnson," he said.

"Reverend," I repeated, wondering if he'd also overheard what the hooker said about Billie Holiday. But why should he care? He'd never heard of Billie Holiday; he'd never heard of Plotsky's.

"May I offer you a cup of tea?"

I could have used a drink, but I had to say yes to tea. We went to the dining room which was stuffy with society types but pretty with fresh flowers in little crystal vases. Our table was by the window and I couldn't help but notice a cute soldier standing on the corner of Fifty-ninth Street looking lost. He had this little waist and these broad shoulders. My heart went out to him. Since the war in Europe was over I saw a lot of cute lonely-looking soldiers parading around the city. You couldn't call Teresa's father cute.

He was pudgy with a turkey neck and a little tomato nose. His hair was graying on the sides and he wore a black suit and black tie like an undertaker. His eyebrows were pencil thin and his skin pasty pink with all these broken red veins on his cheeks and chin. He looked like he never had to shave. The best thing about him was his smooth, deep voice. I guessed he was about fifty.

"It was kind of you to call, Miss Silverstar," he said. "Would you care for something to eat?"

I ordered a piece of chocolate layer cake. All I'd eaten all day was a grapefruit and toast. This was one of those days when I tried to skip lunch to knock off a pound or two, but here it was three o'clock and I was starving. I was caving in.

"I didn't know if you knew anyone in the city, Mr. Johnson," I told him between bites, "so I figured you'd be feeling rotten and I just wanted to tell you how much I loved Tush . . . Teresa . . . and what a swell gal she was."

"In what capacity did you know her, Miss Silverstar?"

I was ready for that question. "Art school. We met at the art school."

"I see. Are you a painter?"

"Trying to be. I wasn't as good as Teresa. She was terrific."

"She never sent us any of her sketches. And in her apartment I found no evidence of her work."

"She kept it all at school."

"Where is the school?"

"Uh . . . downtown . . ."

"Maybe if I went there . . ."

"It's closed for vacation." I hated lying. You start and you can't stop. I polished off the chocolate cake and thought about ordering another piece—the cake was moist, the frosting was creamy and I was still famished—but I couldn't act like a pig. I wasn't here to eat. "Did you talk to Captain Donegan?" I asked the reverend.

"Do you know him?"

"He asked me some questions 'cause he knew I was your daughter's pal."

"I see. Did you and Teresa attend church together?"

That threw me. "Well . . . not exactly . . ."

"Teresa spoke about attending church in New York City. Where do you attend church, Miss Silverstar?"

"Well, Jewish people don't go to church, we go to synagogue."

"I see, Miss Silverstar."

Now when he said "Silverstar" it was like he was saying "Jewishstar." His radio announcer's voice had gone cold. Ice cold. Suddenly he was out of questions. The silence between us made me nervous. I had to say something. "I just hope the police catch the guy. I hope they find him."

"We already know who it was, Miss Silverstar."

"What are you talking about? Who was it?"

"I'm talking about the devil, Miss Silverstar."

"The devil?"

"The human vehicle through whom Satan was working is irrelevant. The fact is that my daughter lost her life to evil. I had warned her that she was moving to a city marked by evil. In Valleyview, she was a good girl. She was a church girl. She was on the right path. I told her leaving was wrong, but she insisted she was strong enough to survive. She disobeyed my wishes. She was traveling the wrong path. My daughter was traveling with the wrong people."

"That ain't true, Mr. Johnson. She was going to these art museums all the time, looking at these pictures of Jesus. She even took me along. She loved that Jesus art."

"You don't go to a museum to find Jesus, Miss Silverstar. You go to a church, a *Christian* church. Now if you'll excuse me . . ."

He paid the bill and got up and left. He left me feeling like shit and he also left a shitty tip for the waitress. He left her a fuckin' nickel. Now is that Christian love, leaving someone a lousy nickel?

What was it with this guy? I know he had to be hurting for his daughter, but why does that mean he has to hurt me? I was just trying to be nice. When I said I was Jewish it was like saying I killed her. When I was a little girl this fat boy from the Catholic school down the block ran after me and called me a Christ killer. I didn't know what he was talking about. I don't have nothing against Jesus except he always looks creepy in all those bloody paintings. Far as I'm concerned, Jesus could have lived as long as he liked. But I guess Reverend Johnson thought like the kid from Catholic school, except I couldn't kick Reverend Johnson in the nuts like I kicked the fat boy. That's what I wanted to do—kick him in the nuts and then tell him to come see me take it all off tonight at Plotsky's, because, let me tell you, Reverend, the way I'm feeling right now I'm ready to let loose and give 'em their money's worth. Tonight I'm giving the boys an eyeful.

On the Tubes I was thinking how a painter does it with colors, a piano player with notes, a writer with words. Well, I do it with my body. That's how I express myself—with my body, but my body was hidden under this stupid navy blue dress that I bought last year for Aunt Minnie's funeral. Aunt Minnie and Mom were sisters who hadn't talked for twenty years, but still I had to buy a new dress for her funeral. So I was wearing a funeral dress and thinking how I'd like to tear it up—that's how steamed I was at the whole crew: Donegan, who's looking to get laid instead of looking for the murderer; Reverend Johnson, who hates Jews; Pops, who wants my money; Mom, who's taking up golf; and Leo, who's a goddamn mess.

The thing about stripping is that I just don't strip off my clothes,

I strip off my mind, strip off all the craziness inside my head. I completely lose myself when I strip, and I love it. I couldn't wait till the first show. Sitting on the train, hating this blue dress, I had an inspiration. I'd wear this blue dress on stage. I'd keep on the whole proper bit—the white hat and white gloves. I'd never done that before. I'd come on like a lady. I wouldn't come out in my zebra-striped robe or my feathery gown. I'd give the boys something to worry about; I'd look normal; I'd take them by surprise.

When I got to Newark it was pouring rain, a sticky summer thunderstorm exploding over the city. I took a cab to the theater and who should greet me at the stage door but Mr. Plotsky himself. He wanted to see me.

We went to his office and he shut the door. "It's getting serious," he said. "The city council of Newark is looking into every single girlie show in town. They've had complaints. I think it's got to do with the murder, but who knows. Anyway, I'm starting something new. I'm calling it 'Family Night.' Every Wednesday night. I'm going to have clowns and balloons, clean comics and maybe an animal act."

"And no girls?"

"Sure, I'm having girls. No one's coming to Plotsky's if Plotsky's doesn't have girls. But the girls have to tone down. Do you understand me, Rhonda? Not even G-strings on 'Family Night.' Bloomers."

"Bloomers? For God's sake, Mr. Plotsky, bloomers are old-timey."

"Bloomers are sexy. You'll wear bloomers on 'Family Night.'"

"I don't like it."

"You don't have to. You can get out if you don't like it."

"Just like that? Your leading girl?"

"If my leading girl is leading me to ruin, what good is she?"

"I'm still bringing them in. I saw the line outside, even in the rain."

"If they close me, Rhonda, I can't last. I need the cash flow."

"This ain't the thirties, Mr. Plotsky, it's the forties."

"It was 1942, only three years ago, when they ran us out of New York. They can do the same thing in Newark."

"I ain't scared."

"Why should you be scared? You just work here."

"I *star* here," I reminded him. "I don't work six days a week like the other girls—I work five. And I don't do afternoon shows. I only work nights. I've worked hard to be where I am, Mr. Plotsky, and I didn't do it by wearing bloomers on no fuckin' 'Family Night.' "

"You got a fresh mouth on you, Rhonda," Mr. Plotsky said, "but I don't got time to argue. You're on in a half-hour."

"What about Tush? Did Donegan find out anything about Tush? Has he called?"

"Forget Tush. She's dead. The cops ain't bringing her back, the cops don't care. She fooled around and she's dead. Get dressed."

And all this time I thought Plotsky was a nice guy. I thought he had a heart. Some heart. One day he's crying about Tush and the next day he's forgotten her. Everyone's forgotten her. They think she got what she deserved. Isn't that what he meant by saying she "fooled around"? Well, how the hell does he know that? What gives him the right to assume she egged on some guy? Is that what everyone thinks of strippers—that we egg on guys in private like we do in public? If he thinks I know how to egg on guys, let him watch me tonight. Let him see what I think of his fuckin' "Family Night."

I told Gus the bandleader that I was dropping my regular routine tonight. I wasn't using the backup girls and I didn't want no "Pretty Girl Is Like a Melody."

"Play 'Don't Fence Me In,' " I said. We had rehearsed the song about a week ago. "Play it slow and sexy with lots of back beat and grind and get Abraham to play his sax real high and hard. Don't play it like no Bing Crosby and the Andrews Sisters. Play it like you wanna start a riot."

I wanted to start a riot. I wanted to be bad. I wanted to strut and shock and show Plotsky and Pops and Mickey Donegan and the whole world that you can't take Rhonda Silverstar's ass for granted. Don't try to control me. If you think I can be tamed, think again.

I undressed and dressed again, replacing my regular bra and panties with the breakaway stuff. But I kept on the blue dress and the white hat and gloves. I told the lighting man I wanted all blue gels. When I hit the stage, I just smiled. The joint was packed. All my regular guys were there. They didn't know what to think. Silence. I didn't say nothing. Just watched the cigarette plumes from a hundred cigarettes curling up to the ceiling. Felt the blue lights on my skin. Heard the slow slithery backbeat of the band. Abraham's sax started climbing, like when I heard it yesterday on the staircase in Harlem, and it reached me just where I lived. The boys were waiting for me to do something, but I kept them waiting. I didn't have my usual smile; I was glaring, feeling my anger, all the anger of these past couple of days of my friend being killed and no one caring, feeling the frustration of not being able to do shit for her, feeling like I hated this "Family Night" bullshit and I'd be damned if I wasn't going to do exactly what the fuck I wanted to do. Right here. Right now. Don't fence me in, daddy. Don't even try.

I don't sing in my strip. I don't say witty shit like Gypsy Rose. I don't tell no lame jokes. I just *strip*. I know what I got; I know they want to see it, they want to *feel* it, so I feel it first. I touch myself. Over my clothes. Over that stupid navy blue dress I rub my hands all up and down my body. I reach for the stupid white hat, I grab it, and I fling it behind me. Take off your hat. Half-inch by half-inch, I slowly peel off my white gloves. Take off your gloves. I still ain't smiling 'cause I still ain't happy. I'm thinking about Reverend Johnson, that prick, and what he'd think about my opening the top buttons to this dress, one by one, except I'm getting tired of that old routine and I rip the top off—I mean, *rip*—so the dress is torn and my push-up see-through show bra is showing and my nipples are hard as rocks and I'm thinking how I hate this dress, how I hate funerals and I rip off the bottom and start ripping at the whole thing like a wild woman and the boys are going wild—they ain't ever seen me do nothing like this before—and I'm ripping off my slip and I'm tearing it with my bare fingers and Abraham's wailing on his sax and the boys are screaming, "Take it off, take it off . . . take it *all* off!" and they know I'm different tonight, everything's changing, and they're with me 'cause they ain't sure what I might do, they see me losing control, and I see a couple of those sweet-eyed sailors sitting in the first row and I aim my tits right at their eyes, and I wiggle and shimmy and snap off my bra and watch their eyes get bigger when they see my jugs sticking right out there, and I'm thinking how their dicks are steel-hard 'cause of how I'm crouching right in front of them, these lonely-looking sailor boys, and I'm back up straight, peeling off my little panties—"*all . . . all . . . all . . . take it all off!*"—it's more then a scream, it's a chant, and I can't hear nothing but the boys chanting, and now I'm on my back grinding so they can see my G-string—with no extra beads, Mr. Plotsky; Rhonda the rebel didn't sew on no extra beads—and I'm imagining how much these sailor boys want to be on top of me, and I'll let them take turns, I'll let 'em fuck me as long and hard as they want to, give 'em all the pussy they ever dreamed of when they were over their fighting that war, dreaming of fucking a hot dame like me, just fuck me, boys, fuck me harder and if you wanna see this pussy, if you wanna see some real bush, wanna see how wet a real woman gets, well, I'll rip off this G-string, I'll take it off, I'll take it *all* off, I'll snatch it off and you'll see it what you're dying for, oh man, Abraham's playing the shit out of that saxophone and the house is crazy, the chanting is louder and louder, the floor of the stage is covered with bills, they're throwing money at me and I'm holding back nothing, Mr. Plotsky, I'm still on my back and I'm wide open, yes I am, I'm showing snatch, I'm squeezing my nipples and swiveling my hips to give them all a good look and they're yelling and whistling and going crazy, they're tearing the roof off this joint, and I'm thinking of what it'd be like to take on these young sailor boys, to feel their love and taste their sweat, and my hands are rubbing my thighs and my things are sweating and my fingers are on my lips, my fingers are on my clit—I've never done this before, my heart's beating like mad, I'm pushing myself out, I'm breaking all the rules and doing what the boys want me to do, what I've always wanted to do out there—I'm bringing myself off, with one hand I'm sticking my fingers deep inside just like girls do when they're alone and lonely in their bedrooms, just like we do under the covers only the covers are pulled back and everyone's watching, and that's what's getting me hotter 'cause when I did it alone I imagined everyone watching but now they really are, it's really happening, and with the other hand I'm rubbing myself, fingering it, flicking it, pushing it, stroking it hard, my clit's burning, it's hot, it's red-hot, so hot all the screaming shuts off in my head, the music stops, and it's like I'm alone with a thousand eyes on my pussy and I'm squeezing my tits and I'm squeezing my clit and when I come I'm shot out of my body. Floating above it all, floating above the boys, flying over the theater, over the heads of everyone, I'm leaving my body and my mind, my pleasure mind is floating and free with no thoughts or nothing and I'm happy like I never been happy before because I did it, I did it, I took it to the limit and went past the limit and nothing and no one can stop me now.

My body was still shaking. Tears were still streaming down my cheeks when I stumbled off the stage. A stagehand was gathering up the money for me. Must have been three hundred bucks. But I didn't even make it to my dressing room. I was still in the wings when Mr. Plotsky, the blood-filled veins in his forehead about to pop, starting screaming at me.

"You're through!" he yelled. "You'll never perform in my theater again! You'll never perform in burlesque! You're filth! Do you hear me? Nothing but filth!"

I GOT
A JOB
TO DO

Bull was waiting for me in the dressing room. Thank God for Bull. He got there late and hadn't seen the show, didn't know what had happened. He was in a good mood 'cause he'd beat out a broken-bat dribbler down the third-base line for an infield hit. His slump was over and he wanted to celebrate. I told him I was glad for him, but my head was aching like someone had slammed me with a hammer and would he mind just driving me back to Brooklyn and not talking too much, which was easy for Bull. Bull's sweet. He was just what I needed—someone not to think, or ask me questions, but just be there. When we left Plotsky's through the stage door and the guys were still screaming at me—"You did it this time, Rhonda! You did it all, baby!"—Bull didn't pay them no mind and didn't care 'cause he had his hit on his mind. As we drove over the Pulaski Skyway, this dark bridge that looked like something out of a horror story, I could smell Newark Bay stinking below because the rains had stopped and the night was putrid damp and my head hurt so bad and the lights in the Holland Tunnel didn't help and lower Manhattan looked lonely and empty and over the Brooklyn Bridge, way out there on the water, I saw flashes of lightning and I thought about people who jump off the bridge to stop their heads from hurting.

"I can't sleep with you, Bull," I told him as his old Studebaker pulled up to my apartment house on Flatbush Avenue. "I just gotta be alone."

His whole pudgy face fell; he looked so disappointed. "Something I said?"

I kissed him on the cheek. "You're a doll. It's just that I feel rotten."

"I'll sleep on the couch," he offered.

"I'll call you tomorrow. Promise."

I didn't even let him see me to the door. The minute I fell asleep, I started dreaming like crazy:

I was stripping, but when I took off my blouse, my arms fell off; when I took off my bra, my breasts fell off; soon I had no legs and no head and everyone was pointing at me and laughing and I was feeling terror in my heart, like I had done something awful, like I was this puppet falling apart, like I was dying, or already dead, and I started scrambling around to gather up my body parts and put them back together, except they wouldn't fit, because I wasn't Rhonda, I was really Tush, I was trying to put together Tush's body, but her body had been slashed up with knives, knives still stuck all over her, and there was Mom and Pops screaming at me from high up in the balcony, they were yelling that I was a fool, and don't come running to them, 'cause they couldn't help, they couldn't take the knives out, and Plotsky was with them, he was telling them I was shit and they were nodding their heads and agreeing with everything and everyone was running from the theater except for me. I was left on stage with my limbs and Tush's bloody limbs all over the place—which limbs belonged to me? which belonged to Tush?—and I was running in circles and crying 'cause I couldn't figure it out, I didn't know how the pieces fit together.

When I woke up, the first thing I did was feel my body all over. Everything was in place. For a split second, I had believed my dream. For a split second, I thought what I'd done last night at Plotsky's had also been a dream. Then I remembered it wasn't. I'd actually done it. I didn't want to think about it, but I couldn't think about anything else. Sure, I had done it; and the boys loved it; and fuck Plotsky. Fuck him and his "Family Night." Let him find another peeler half as hot as me. I had nothing to be ashamed of. At the same time, I didn't want to get out of bed. I didn't want to answer the phone that kept ringing 'cause I knew it was either Sandy or Mom or brother Leo and I'd have to tell them why I wouldn't be working at Plotsky's and I didn't feel like talking. Besides, I didn't owe an explanation to anyone. So I stayed in bed—that morning, that afternoon, that night. I ate a little, I fixed myself some eggs, but I didn't answer the phone and the next day was Thursday and I stayed in bed some more and I was really feeling like shit and there wasn't anyone I wanted to see—no one in the whole world. I didn't feel like anyone understood me, and sure, I was feeling sorry for myself, but I was entitled. To hell with the world. I'd stay in my apartment for another day, for another week; I'd stay here for the rest of my life if I wanted to. For all I cared, the goddamn phone could ring off the wall.

By Friday night I was deep in the dumps. Couldn't ever remember feeling so low. I was even drinking wine to put me back to sleep. I don't even really like wine and I never drink alone, but strong red wine wiped out all the thoughts in my mind and, believe me, my mind had too many thoughts. I was tired of thinking about what was right and what was wrong when I knew damn well the only real wrong thing was how Tush got murdered.

The knock on my door was Sandy. He knocked with a special jazzy rhythm so I'd know it was him.

"I'm not sure you want to see me looking like this," I said.

"I don't care. I just wanna make sure you're alright."

I went to the bathroom and put my hair up in a towel, turban style, before slipping on a robe. No makeup, no nothing. I opened the door. "Sorry, Sandy, but I ain't been feeling that good."

Sandy walked in wearing a straw hat and a silky yellow sports shirt open at the neck. Compared to me—with my eyes all red and my heart half torn out—he looked real casual and carefree. He was even whistling.

"What the hell you so happy about?" I wanted to know.

"Came to cheer you up."

"What makes you think I need cheering up?"

"Abraham told me what happened."

"Oh, he did, did he?"

"Sort of."

"And . . . ?" I asked, my voice daring him—just daring him—to say something smart.

"And nothing." Sandy knew me. He knew how to tiptoe around my moods.

"So what's the point?" I wanted to know.

"Ain't no point, baby, except that Abraham and I got together and wrote a tune. Thought you'd like to hear it."

"Without a piano?"

"I can sing it."

"So sing."

The song was called "She Sure Can Swing." It was about some dame who not only swung when she danced, but also when she walked. There were all these sly references to her backside and I felt it was about Tush, and I hated it—I had to stop Sandy from singing before he was halfway through—I just hated the goddamn song.

"How could you write something like this?" I asked.

"What's wrong with this song?"

"It's about Tush, and Tush is dead, and here you two bums go writing some shit to make money off a dead girl. How could you, Sandy? How could Abraham? He had the hots for her—and now I see you did too—so you've turned it into a song."

"You're making up stuff that ain't there."

"Don't tell me. I know you. I know how you loved watching her swing her hips. You told me so yourself. And Abraham, he used to study her ass like it was a book—he played in the band right behind her, night after night—and now you guys come up with this. Well, I don't buy it, I don't like it, and I wish to hell you'd get the hell out of here and just leave me alone."

"I know you feel bad about what you did, but . . ."

"Don't ever—EVER!—tell me how I feel!" I exploded. "I'm the

only one who knows how I feel—and I feel fine, I feel perfect, I feel absolutely wonderful—and you and Abraham can go fly a fuckin' kite with your song as far as I'm concerned 'cause it ain't right, you're taking advantage, and I don't ever wanna hear that thing again as long as I live."

I slammed the door behind him. When he was down the stairs, I fell on the bed and started bawling like a baby. I don't even know why I was crying—maybe for Tush, maybe for myself, maybe 'cause guys like Sandy and Abraham, guys who I thought had hearts, turn out to be thoughtless and crude and I don't want nothing to do with them anymore, nothing in the world.

All these days and there I was, still crying. I probably needed to talk to someone. I couldn't talk to Mom, because Mom would only be worried that I wasn't making money. Couldn't talk to Pops because Pops had the sympathy of a lox. Leo had his own problems. But could I go crazy? I didn't even know what that meant. Never leave the apartment? Never stop crying? Cry myself to death? Do people ever cry themselves to death?

It wasn't until Sunday morning that I finally got out. Bull had come by, dying to try out his hard-on. He'd hit in three straight games and was feeling like Popeye. I had him bring me some take-out Chinese food and we had a nice meal, but I said, "Listen, Bull, I know you're doing good but I got this infection down there that I don't want to give you." A little lie was better than going into long explanations.

I talked to Leo. That was easy 'cause I just had to listen. Life is a breeze if you're willing to do nothing but listen to people. Let people talk about their problems and don't say nothing and suddenly, when the conversation's over, you're a genius for being so sweet and understanding even though you haven't opened your mouth. Now Leo wasn't really sure he wanted to move to California because he liked his job here and what if his feelings for his boyfriend went away when he got out West?

My feelings were that I was tired of thinking about problems—Leo's, mine and everyone else's. I just wanted to get out. If I didn't leave my apartment soon, I'd explode. I saw that the sun was shining and I was dying for a little relief, a little happiness, and the place that makes me feel happiest is the Lower East Side 'cause that's where we used to live before we moved to Brooklyn, and that's where my life began with the smells from the streets and the people I saw when I opened my little eyes and looked at the world for the first time. I wanted to feel like a little girl, not some woman weighted down with problems.

Sunday afternoon on Essex Street. It felt more like spring than summer, and the breezes along my skin were making me feel better. Better than the breezes were the flaky potato knishes at Yonal Schimmel's and the fresh challah bread at Gertel's and at Julius the Candy King I couldn't pass up a little treat since I'd been losing weight all week and, besides, now that I wasn't peeling I didn't have to worry about weight. I didn't have to worry about anything. Just enjoy the crowd, the kids with their parents and the old folks from the old country and the teenagers trying to look tough and the cute sailors looking over dames and the feeling that life was going on, life wasn't just staying cooped up in my apartment worrying about did I do the right thing or the wrong thing. Life was sitting down at Ratner's and enjoying a nice bowl of borscht with a big fat lump of sour cream plopped in the middle. Life was seeing that all these people were shopping and eating and carrying on, and so would I.

"I see your boyfriend Bull's on a streak."

I glanced up to lock eyes with Stickman the photographer. Stickman was standing there like a scarecrow. His Adam's apple looked bigger than my head and he had these bulging eyes.

"You follow the Newark Bears?" I asked.

"I like the team. I like taking the Tubes over to Jersey to watch the games. It's cheaper than the Stadium."

"What are you doing downtown?"

"Double murder over in Little Italy. I got there before any of the papers. This one's gonna sell for big money," he said, patting his camera.

"Husband and wife?"

"Husband and mistress. He kills her, then he gets his head blown off."

"He killed himself?"

"No, someone shot him. They don't know who, but already every detective in the city has been put on the case, even your buddy Donegan from uptown. They're sparing no expense. The dame was the daughter of a state senator. By the way, they ever find out anything about your partner?"

"Dropped the case."

"Figures."

"Why do you say that?"

"Stripper and all . . ."

"Goddamnit, you don't think a stripper is a human being like anyone else?"

"Easy, baby. I just take pictures. I ain't the cops. But I know the cops. When it comes to hookers and peelers . . ."

"Wait a minute, there's a helluva difference . . ."

"Sorry, didn't mean to step on your toes, Rhonda, but I always figured you got your eyes opened and your head on straight. I've never known you to put on airs."

What was the use of arguing with Stickman? He saw Tush as a whore; he saw me as a whore; the cops saw us as whores. Strippers, whores . . . it's all the same. Bad girls. They love bad girls 'cause we get 'em hot; but they really hate bad girls 'cause bad girls can't be controlled. So if someone cuts our throats or hacks us into little pieces, well, tough shit. If it's the daughter of a senator, they'll search every nook and cranny in the city until they solve the case. But if it's a girl who makes a legit living entertaining men, forget it. That way of thinking made me want to throw another fit—all I'd been doing recently was throwing fits—but why? Who was I fooling? Stickman was right about me; I try to keep my eyes open and see life the way it is. Stickman was a photo hack expressing the real-life attitude. I could accept it or I could go crazy. That's what I'd been doing back in my apartment all week—going crazy. No more.

"I ain't arguing with you, Stickman," I said. "No man out

there—no cop, no detective, no one at the club—absolutely no one gives a good goddamn about who killed Tush. If there's anyone who cares, it's got to be me. And you know something, I'm just crazy enough to go after the guy."

"Careful, Rhonda," he warned me. "I seen a bunch of sex crimes in my day and at the bottom of every one there's always some weirdo looney-tunes crazy son of a bitch who'd slice up his own mother if the mood struck him."

"I got a job to do," I told Stickman, "and I'm going to do it."

Enough feeling sorry for myself. I was ready to whip myself into action. I had plans to move into this penthouse on Eastern Parkway, and that meant I needed to find work. Nothing to it. I was a headliner. I was sure another burlesque theater would hire me in a second.

I was wrong.

Plotsky, that putz, had put out the bad word. And everywhere I went—the Empire in Newark, the Globe in Jersey City, the Palace in Hoboken—turned me away. They claimed they were worried about the censors. I told 'em I did a clean show. They understood, they said, but couldn't take a chance.

Well, hell, I'd find work anyway. I still had friends. When I was picking up my costumes at Plotsky's, for instance, Danny the comic, the guy's who's practically blind, came up to me with tears streaming down his face.

"My baby," he was bawling, "my little baby. How could the old man do such a thing? You're his star."

"It'll be alright, Danny. Everything happens for the best."

"But I'm next. I know he's going to ax me."

"Don't worry about nothing. You got your fans. You still leave 'em laughing."

"Look, Rhonda," he said, lowering his voice, "I wouldn't want Plotsky to know I'm telling you this, but I know this gent, see, this guy who gives private parties and well, if you don't think it's below you or nothing, I was telling him about you, and he's got money, this particular guy's loaded. He lives up on Park Avenue. What do you say?"

"He wants a stripper or he wants to get laid?"

"A stripper, a stripper. I tell him, I say, 'Look, this gal's strictly legit. Strictly on the up and up.' "

"Couldn't hurt to talk to him."

"The money's good, I guarantee you."

Here's the thing about Park Avenue: It ain't what it seems. Nothing is. It seems so calm and cultured with everyone listening to little piano recitals and sipping tea and pronouncing their words like they been to college. They got uniformed doormen all over the place and you'll see dames walking poodles dollied up with little red bows in their hair. My party was at Eighty-eighth Street and Park and while I was heading into the building I saw one of those frankfurter-shaped dogs taking a dump and the proper old gal holding the hound on a leash started yelling at the doorman to wipe up the mess. If it was me, I'd yell back and tell her to clean up the shit herself, but the doorman came running which meant I didn't have to announce myself, I just slipped inside and rode the elevator to the penthouse, reminding me of the penthouse that was still waiting for me over in Brooklyn. I hadn't moved yet 'cause I was worried about my unsteady income, but this party would help. At $250 for an hour's work, it would help a lot.

The guy's name was Skefington, Oliver Skefington, a limey who worked on Wall Street. God knows how he knew Danny, but he knew strippers. On the phone he mentioned a few ladies who'd entertained at his parties, and they were among the biggest names in the business. Maybe he was bullshitting or maybe he wasn't, but I wasn't taking any chances so I told him I wanted my money up front, before I took off my hat, and he said fine, no problem. I asked him about music. I strip to music. He said he had lots of records and a fancy record player and what kind of music did I prefer? Jazz, I told him. Good, he said, jazz was his favorite.

This was the kind of Englishman who said "I say" before he

said anything, and I thought he was kind of charming and I expected him to be an old geezer but when he answered the door Oliver Skefington didn't look any older than me. "I say," he said, "you're right on time, lovey."

"Oh, am I now?" I could put on a pretty good British accent myself.

"The boys are in the parlor and they're waiting for you—this is quite a special occasion—and I expect you'll want to prepare yourself and freshen up so let me escort you to the ladies' loo."

This was going to be alright. After three weeks off, I was ready to make some men happy, have myself a good time and pocket the quick cash that Skef just handed me. When I came out of the powder room, I was wearing a big feathery outfit. On the record player Billie Holiday was singing "That Old Devil Called Love." Strange that he would play Billie Holiday. It was a slow, sexy song and I liked the rhythm, I liked the attitude—"it's that sly old son of a gun again," Billie sang—"he keeps telling me I'm the lucky one again"—and it felt like she was talking to me, letting me know just when to drop a glove, when to peel off a nylon, how to prance around the room which looked like an enormous old library with bookcases up to the ceiling and the guys—I should really say "gentlemen" 'cause all twenty or so of them were wearing suits and ties and tuxes and their little moustaches were perfectly groomed—the guys sat real quiet and dignified and I wondered whether I was getting across 'cause there were no catcalls—no "take it off!" no "show me what you got, baby!"—this was Park Avenue, this crowd was real refined which was fine with me. I put on a classy show. But by the time I got down to my panties and pasties the gents were standing up, a couple were standing on their chairs to see better, so I knew I'd made my point.

"I say, ducky," said Skef, when I left the parlor to head back to the powder room, "I do expect you'll return for your famous encore."

"What famous encore?"

"I was made to understand that your specialty involves an extraordinary display of onanism."

"What's that supposed to mean?"

"You know, lovey, masturbation. That's what I paid you for."

I couldn't believe Danny sold me that way. Blind ol' Danny. Oh, well, that's men for you. "Look," I told the limey, "you paid me to strip and I stripped."

"But I understood . . ."

"Well, Skef, you understood *wrong*. I don't go around masturbing in front of strange men." Hearing myself, I heard the voice of my father. It was weird; I just wanted out.

"I'm afraid, Miss Silverstar, that you've greatly disappointed my guests. I led them to believe . . ."

"Oh, yeah?" I snapped back. "Well, they'll just have to be disappointed 'cause you got the wrong girl."

Red-faced and furious, I went to the bathroom, got dressed and was on my way out when Skef stopped me at the door.

"Look here, old girl," he said, "I wish you hadn't taken offense. I meant no harm. In fact, I'll be happy to double your earnings if only you'll accommodate us. Be a sport."

I glared. I was tempted to slap him across the face. I felt insulted, but I knew I'd brought this on myself. Skef had promised his friends the honeypot, and the honeypot wasn't there. "Sorry," I said, "but you got the best I could give. This isn't anything I fake."

"I appreciate that, but . . ."

I offered him a weak smile. That's all I had in me.

On the way back to Brooklyn, I blocked out the night, but I couldn't block out Billie Holiday. I kept hearing her voice, kept hearing her sing "That Old Devil Called Love." I knew I had been off tonight, and I knew Billie made me think of Tush, made me want to talk to Billie herself. I had to get back on the case, stop this dumb dancing and stripping once and for all and find out what really happened to my pal. It was time to talk to Billie.

"WHAT IS
THIS THING
CALLED
LOVE?"

"This funny thing called love," the song said, and when Billie Holiday sang it you knew she had the answer, but she just wouldn't tell. I was sitting there in the Decca recording studio on Fifty-seventh Street where she was singing into the microphone. Four fiddlers surrounded her, a bunch of horn men and a rhythm section. I was behind the glass with the guy pushing the buttons and another guy giving her gentle instructions. Billie didn't look like she needed any instructions. She sang "Don't Explain" and "Big Stuff" and "You Better Go" with the violins crying and Billie moaning real low like the words to the tunes were plucked from her heart. She was gorgeous. She was also sexy, but sexy like no one I'd ever seen—not out-there here-I-am sexy; she was soft in-there mysterious sexy, hidden but hot. I loved the hound's-tooth-check suit she was wearing—I wished I had one just like it—so streamlined and elegant, and her hair was shiny and gathered up in a bun on the back of her neck. She had this beautiful mouth and when the words came out, dripped out like honey, you couldn't stop looking at her and hoping she'd never stop singing. I could see what Tush saw— if Tush really saw what Abraham Jones said she saw. I've known women who like women, and I never thought twice about it. Like I was telling my brother Leo the other day, we're born the way we're born and you either go with it or you go crazy. At the same time, the way Billie was singing about love and life I also knew she was hooked into men, the way I'm hooked into men. She knew they were dogs, but she still loved them. That's me. When she sang "What Is This Thing Called Love?" there was this small smile on her face. She didn't move much when she sang, just tilted her head. Her accent sounded real Southern but also Harlem tough. "Why should it make a fool of me?" she sang about this thing called love. Her voice wasn't big, but it cut like a knife. Her posture was proud. She sang proud but sad. She carried herself like a queen, a queen who'd lost her king 'cause deep down something was so painful that I saw tears on the cheeks of the drummer, this big man who didn't seem like the kind of cat who ever cried.

"He's no saint," she sang, "heaven knows that's what he ain't." It was like she was making up these words as she went along, making 'em up about men I knew, men all us women know. "There've been other fools like me . . . born to be in love with a no-good man." Her singing was like talking. A few minutes later, I heard how her talking was like singing.

We were sitting around after the session—Abraham had arranged the meeting for me—and everyone had gone. She sat on a stool and chain-smoked cigarettes. Her brown eyes were cloudy and she spoke real soft. I had to lean in to hear. Sometimes it was like listening to a little girl and sometimes she sounded like an old woman. I started out by telling her how I stripped to her song the other night. I figured she'd like hearing that. She did. "I feel like I'm taking it off every time I sing," she said. "Stripping down to my soul."

Then I mentioned Teresa.

"Baby," she began—I loved that she called me "baby," like we were old friends—"Teresa had talent. That child could really sing. When she first came round I had my doubts. I figured her for another white chick looking for a window on the jungle. Those gals are all over Harlem."

"Bagel babies from Brooklyn."

The expression fractured Billie. Her face lit up with laughter.

"Never heard that before. Bagel babies. That's great. You a bagel baby, Rhonda?"

"I don't think so. Maybe once upon a time, but I've been around too long, Billie."

"Tell me about it. But you loved Teresa, didn't you?"

"Like a friend, yes."

"Y'all danced together over at the strip joint in Newark, is that it?"

"That's it." I looked for jealousy but didn't see any in Billie's eyes. All I saw was tired sadness.

"I can't understand it," she said to me. "Nice girl like that. Gentle soul. I found out about it down in Philly. I'd been playing there all week. Then I happened to see a New York paper. I wanted to call someone but there was no one to call. All I could do was sit and cry. How'd it happen? Why?"

"That's why I'm here, Billie. The cops don't care about finding out a damn thing . . ."

"Cops . . ." Billie shook her head, her eyes staring into space. "Lord save us from the police."

"But I care," I added. "I thought maybe you could help." I stopped short of saying more because I didn't want Billie to think I was prying. What happened between her and Tush was their business, not mine.

"I'll tell you the truth, honey," said the singer, lighting one Chesterfield with another before inhaling deeply. "Teresa was too trusting. I swear she was. The child was innocent. Least that's how I saw her. Like a baby. She'd tell me about these men coming 'round, and I'd question her, I'd ask her how she knew they were on the square. 'I can feel it, Billie,' she'd say. But a fine-looking gal like that—mercy, she can be hoodwinked. Jive artists run this city. There was one guy she told me about who even called himself Bull."

"Bull?" My heart started racing.

"I told her Bull stood for bullshit, but 'No, Billie,' she'd say, 'he's a famous ball player, he plays in the big stadiums, and he's on the level, he's really crazy for me. We go out all the time.' "

"Bull Wallinsky?"

"Something Polish like that. Sounds like a sausage, don't it?"

Now my head was reeling, my heart hammering. Bull? Bull and Tush? Impossible.

"What'd she say about Bull?"

"Only that he was leaning on her. Leaning on her real heavy. You know the cat?"

"I thought I did," I said, feeling faint, confused, feeling like I was hearing the last thing in the world I ever expected to hear.

I passed up the hot dogs, the popcorn and the big salty pretzels. I did all I could to sit through the game without running out on the field and screaming at Bull right then and there. I arrived late, so I couldn't talk to him beforehand. I had to sit out in Bears Stadium in Newark and watch the Bears get clobbered 8–0. It was painful. The big crowd was bored. Bull fanned twice but smacked one line-drive single. I almost cheered before I remembered what Billie had said. I tried to make believe she hadn't said it, but there was no fooling myself. It was a muggy night, my blouse stuck to the seat, my dress wrinkled, my head pounding. What was Bull doing making moves on Tush? How could he? Bull was the least likely guy in the world to hurt anyone. I knew him; I knew how he was in bed. He just wanted to please; he was always 'fraid of hurting me. Bull couldn't have killed Tush any more than Billie. At the same time, he'd fooled me; he'd been playing around with my friend behind my back. Maybe there was some misunderstanding. But what kind of misunderstanding? Billie had no reason to lie. How could she have even heard of Bull if Tush hadn't told her? Maybe Abraham fed her information about Bull to throw me off track. Maybe Abraham and Billie were in cahoots; maybe they both did Tush in. But that was nuts. Please, God, don't let me go nuts.

After the game I waited by the locker room as the guys started filing out. When Bull saw me he was all smiles. He smelled soapy and fresh from the shower. His big blue eyes made him look like an overgrown kid. He started hugging me and I pushed him away.

"See my hit?" he asked, like a kid asking his mama.

"I saw it. But we gotta talk."

We went to a diner near the ballpark. He ordered a couple of slices of hot apple pie a la mode. I drank coffee. A couple of female fans asked him for his autograph. That made me mad and jealous. I was all mixed up.

"You got mixed up with Tush, didn't you?"

"Who's Tush?"

"Quit playing dumb, Bull. The gal who stripped with me. Teresa."

"The blond one?"

"Yeah, the blond one."

"You introduced me once. I thought she was pretty."

"I bet you did. And you asked her out."

"Not me."

"Bull, I know you did. I got proof."

"Rhonda, I never said a word to the dame."

"Never called her? Never went out with her?"

"Never." His eyes were like two big swimming pools. The water looked clear. But something was screwy here, real screwy.

"This is serious, Bull," I said to him. "This girl's dead and . . ."

"Dead?"

"Dead as in not breathing."

"You're kidding."

"You didn't know?"

I kept looking at those eyes, and they kept looking back at me, sky blue and sugar sweet.

"How would I know?" asked Bull.

"It was in all the papers."

"I don't read the papers."

I knew that was true, but how could Billie have made up something like this? "Look," I said to him. "You carry a little black book, don't you, with everyone's phone number?"

"Sure . . . I got your number, the coach's number, Mom and Dad back in Buffalo . . ."

"Well, let me see it."

He didn't hestitate. He dug into his pocket and handed it over. I looked through it quickly. Looked under "T" for Teresa. Nothing there. Looked under "J" for Johnson. Nothing there. Then I looked through every page and every number—there were only about fifteen—and it wasn't there.

"What were you doing on the night of June ninth?"

"I don't remember. What night was that?"

"A Saturday night."

"I don't keep track. Here, look at our schedule."

He pulled a wrinkled piece of paper from his pocket, a schedule showing that the Bears had played that Saturday and the following Sunday in Pittsburgh.

"Have you made all the road trips this year?"

"Yeah."

He hadn't even been in town.

"Look, Rhonda," he said. "Why would I be dating her while I'm dating you? That'd be like if you was dating someone else."

I tried to hear whether Bull was being sarcastic, but he didn't even know what sarcastic meant. Bull seemed so fucking sincere. Meanwhile, I was sincerely confused. My stomach was cramping and my period was starting. I needed to get out of there.

"Let me take you home, Rhonda. I wanna go back to Brooklyn with you. It's been a long time."

"It's gonna have to be a little longer, Bull."

"But . . ."

"You're gonna have to leave me alone!" I exploded. *"Everyone's gonna have to just leave me the hell alone!"*

I was lost. I couldn't figure it out. When I was a kid, Mom bought me a jigsaw puzzle that was supposed to be a bowl of fruit. I tried putting the pieces together for a couple of hours. When they just wouldn't fit I threw the thing on the floor and started crying. Mom said I had a terrible temper and no patience. She was right. Right now I wanted to start crying and throw the puzzle on the floor. My stomach was still cramped up, my period was giving me fits, and what's worse, the phone was ringing off the wall. By the ring I knew it was Mom.

"I thought you had moved," she said.

"Postponed."

"Due to weather?"

"Due to my not working." There . . . I told her.

"When did this happen?"

"I quit," I lied.

"I can't believe my ears."

"Believe it. I haven't played Plotsky's in weeks."

"And you don't say anything to your mother?"

"I've been on vacation, Mom."

"What about the penthouse on Eastern Parkway?"

"Postponed."

"What will you do for money?"

"I've got savings."

"Of that I'm sure. But what about me and your father, what about his store?"

"God bless his store. God bless you and Pops. God bless and good luck."

"You won't help us. Is that what you're saying?"

"I'm saying I'm going a little crazy."

"You just said you were on vacation. Who goes crazy on vacation?"

"I'm not sure where I'm going. I may go out of town."

"Then I want to use your apartment while you're gone."

"What for?"

"I'm leaving your father. The least you could do is give me a bed to sleep in."

GOD
BLESS
AMERICA

It'd been so long since I'd seen the countryside. I was on a train looking out the window and thinking how in the world there could be so many different flowers out there in the fields, yellow and green and orange and purple flowers growing wild, blowing back and forth with the breeze like nothing in this world was wrong. The summertime sun was shining down and I didn't even know what state we were racing through. I didn't care. I was happy to get out of the city, out of Newark and Brooklyn and away from everything and everyone that was confusing me. I was still trying to find out the truth about Tush—I swore I'd never give up—but now I was taking a different approach. I was going to her hometown in Ohio to find out who she really was. I needed clues to put me on the right track. So far all tracks led to nowhere.

As the train was click-clicking over the tracks below, the rhythm of the ride had me thinking like crazy, thinking how I'd been trying to put together pieces that wouldn't fit. Yesterday, for example, I'd gone back to see Abraham who said he'd never even heard of Bull. "You never saw him at Plotsky's after the show?" I asked him, thinking he was the one who mentioned Bull to Billie. "No, Rhonda," he answered. "You know how many guys are always hanging around backstage. I don't know one cat from another."

I even swallowed my pride and called Nancy Nips, that conniving bitch, who'd grabbed star billing at Plotsky's after I was canned. I should have expected her answer. "Tush was after your man and everyone else's," she said. "Better ask me what men I *didn't* see her with." To prove she was lying, I called the other girls I worked with. I was shocked when they went along with Nancy. "You didn't see it, Rhonda," they said, "because you didn't want to see it. You saw Teresa as a little sister, but she was really a little slut. The kid was a sneak." *But what about Bull?* I wanted to know. *Had anyone actually seen her with Bull?* No one could remember—no one actually named Bull—and whatever the other girls said, well, maybe they were just jealous.

On the other hand, I had doubts. Too many people were saying too many strange things about Tush not to shake me up. As the train left the countryside behind and pulled into a gloomy city of brick factories and old churches, I thought about the first time I met Tush, the day she came to audition at Plotsky's. First she had to pass old man Plotsky's eagle eye, but naturally that was no problem for Tush. He brought her to me and I remember thinking how fresh-faced she looked. She was always smiling like she meant it, like she just had to smile. She had this laughing way of talking and I believed her when she said she didn't know too much but was willing to learn. She even had dimples in her cheeks and right away I didn't feel like she'd ever backbite me, like most of the girls did, or try to wiggle her way into my spotlight. I trusted the girl. And now . . .

Now the conductor was telling us we were in Roving, Pennsylvania. People were milling around the platform. I thought I knew people. And damnit, I thought this particular person called Teresa Johnson was a sweetheart. "You knew her, Sandy," I had asked my sometime boyfriend songwriter. "What do you think?" "I don't think we really know anybody," said Sandy. "Not really." Well, maybe he was right, 'cause Bull thought he knew me but he didn't; he didn't know I could never be a one-guy gal. In the same way, I thought I knew Bull, and then Billie tells me how he's chasing Tush. But Bull couldn't have killed Tush; Bull was in Pittsburgh and Billie was in Philly and yesterday Sandy wanted me and him to run off to the Catskills and get away from it all, but no, thanks,

Sandy, I gotta be alone. For the first time in a long time I wasn't even thinking about sex. Maybe it was seeing Tush that Sunday morning, maybe it was my "special encore" that night at Plotsky's. Who knows? Sex was always my way; the hotter the sex the better. But right now I wasn't hot for nothing or no one—not Sandy, not Bull, not even the guys who screamed for me to strip. I knew it when I was over on Park Avenue and that limey tried to egg me on. The heat was running low, maybe even running out. Everything was changing in my life. I felt a little scared, but not scared enough to stay locked up in my apartment. At least I was out there sniffing around.

The train pulled out of the station. I picked up a *Life* magazine and started reading about how big-time radio stars like Fred Allen and Fibber McGee and Molly were worried. They were scared that television, which is like having a little movie theater in your house, might do them in. They were worried about changes. What about the changes happening to me? For the longest time I saw stripping as my calling. I was good at it. Now I wasn't stripping anymore; I was going somewhere where I wasn't invited, seeing people who had no interest in seeing me, wanting to ask them questions I'm sure they didn't want to answer. Fred Allen was worried he'd be a flop on television. Maybe I was worried I'd be a flop in anything besides stripping—especially this detective work. But what the hell, I was on my way, and the train kept chugging along, the ride making me drowsy until I closed my eyes and dreamed myself back on the Lower East Side, where I was a baby again, only I could talk like a woman and I had a full figure and men kept touching me, tickling me, and I told them not to; I said, "Look, I'm just a baby," and my father came along and he picked me up and suddenly I was a doll, not a human person, and he pulled out my arms and ripped off my head—I was watching this; I was the doll but I was also Rhonda the grown-up woman—and when the conductor woke me up shouting "Valleyview! Valleyview!" I was startled and remembered that other dream where all the parts of my body were scattered over the stage.

Picking up my suitcase and walking off the train into a town I'd never seen before, I felt strange. Back in Brooklyn, just about now, my mother was moving into my apartment. I'm sure that had something to do with why I'd wanted to get out of town. I didn't want to know what was happening between her and Pops. I didn't know where to go, I was just wandering through the little train station, when I heard a brass band playing outside. I saw all these flags and banners and balloons. People were everywhere. The band was playing "God Bless America" and I felt good, I felt happy because I'd forgotten I'd been traveling on the Fourth of July and it looked like all of Valleyview, Ohio, was celebrating.

I felt like I was in one of those movies where Mickey Rooney and Judy Garland are running around this little town where the picket fences are painted white and no one has any problems except they want to stage a musical and get to Broadway. Well, Main Street sure wasn't Broadway. It was scrubbed clean and in the windows of the stores—the druggist, the grocer, the dress shop, the haberdasher—were photographs of servicemen from Valleyview who'd fought in the war. Those guys were being honored by a parade and they were walking proud in their neatly pressed uniforms—sailors, soldiers, airmen. Alongside the parade I noticed several women dressed in dark blue or black with tears in their eyes. Some of them were younger than me, some my mother's age, and I knew they had husbands and sons who hadn't come home. My heart went out to them, and I wanted to say, "I understand how you feel," but the truth is that you really don't understand until it happens to you.

Everyone else, though, was having a grand time and as I walked down Main Street, suitcase in hand, I saw in their faces that people here were friendly, not crabby like in New York. The parade led to a town square, a green park in the middle and stores on three sides and on the far end an old courthouse that took up a whole block. In front of the courthouse a platform had been set up where dignitaries were about to speak. I squeezed through the crowd so I could get a close-up view. From far away I'd been almost sure that was Reverend Johnson, Tush's dad, sitting up there; now I saw I was right. He had that turkey neck and small tomato nose. I remembered how he felt about Jews and I sure as hell didn't want to talk to him today—I wasn't sure I ever wanted to talk to him again—and I wondered whether the woman next to him, a birdlike lady with blue gray hair, plain gray dress, tiny feet and light blue eyes, was his wife and Tush's mom. She was pretty. By the way she neatly held her hands in her lap and stared up at the reverend, I figured her as one of those women who worship their husbands. He was starting the ceremonies with a prayer, talking about "Lord Jesus" and "this great Christian country" and "our only true savior." I wondered whether he was laying it on so thick because he'd spotted Jewish me in the crowd.

"You don't look like you like what he's saying."

The voice came from next to me. I turned and saw a man wearing a patch over his left eye. His good eye was a powerful shade of green, almost neon green. I'm telling you, this guy was handsome. All the other men were wearing straw hats, but not him. Maybe thirty, maybe a little older, he was taller than me with a nice-shaped head of dark wavy hair. He had a straight nose and a small soft mouth and I thought I smelled booze on his breath. His suit looked a little too baggy for him and his tie was loose around his neck.

"I was just listening," I said to him.

"Just arrived?" he asked, as I caught his eyes sliding up my suitcase and landing on my breasts. I felt a jolt.

"A short visit," I answered.

"My name's Calvin Bryant. The Rosslyn House at the end of the square is the cleanest hotel in town." He nodded toward a three-story red-brick building.

"Rhonda Silverstar," I said. "Nice to meet you." I was suspicious of this guy but it was a little town and I couldn't afford not to act friendly to everyone.

"You're from New York," he assumed.

My accent was like wearing a sign plastered across my forehead.

I noticed how he had an especially high forehead. Sitting around the dinner table, Mom used to say that guys with high foreheads were smart. Pops's forehead was low; Leo's was extrahigh.

"I'm from Brooklyn," I told Mr. High Forehead.

"Well, I hope you had a nice trip," he said. His voice was smooth and soothing. So was his smile. His smile just slid across his face. I liked looking at his face. He had good cheekbones and a strong chin. To me he looked a little like a movie actor, maybe Robert Montgomery. The black patch made him mysterious. The one green eye was so strong, like it was doing the work of two. I felt that eye all over me, and even though I was dressed real normal—in a plain yellow dress that wasn't really form-fitting—I knew he knew what was underneath.

"You'll be okay at the Rosslyn House," he said. "Tell Tillie Rosslyn that Cal Bryant sent you. Don't be put off by her looks, she's a mountain and talks like a foghorn, but except for being nosey, is harmless enough. And, by the way," he added, before moving on through the crowd, "I'm with you—I think Reverend Johnson's a first-class prick."

Tillie Rosslyn, like Cal Bryant said, was a talkative old battle-axe with a low hoarse voice who had something to say about everyone. I bet she weighed in at three hundred pounds and she wore blond store-bought hair in a pageboy style that on a woman her size looked sort of ridiculous. I liked her, though. I'd known women like Tillie Rosslyn—she reminded me of a seamstress who used to work at Plotsky's—except she had a heavy Southern accent like Tallulah Bankhead and the same low almost mannish voice. She came from Kentucky, where she said her husband owned a Ford dealership until he died years ago. "I've been running this hotel—everything deluxe—ever since, and you'd be surprised by all the people who stopped here on their way to Cleveland or Cincinnati. Why, honeychile, I've given rooms to Miss Hedy Lamarr and Miss Elsa Lanchester who was in *Lassie Come Home* and no one in this whole town knew who she was except for me. I love collie dogs. Mr. Rosslyn had two collies and they kept me company after he died, they certainly did, until right recently. I had to put them to sleep. Both died within a week of each other. Now isn't that something? Why do I have the feeling you're in the movies, honey?"

"I'm not. Just on vacation. On my way out West."

"You seem like the show business type."

"Well, I used to dance."

"You seem too young to 'used to' do anything."

"Thanks."

"You're snazzy enough to be in pictures. You headed for California?"

I hesitated. "Yes . . . I think I'll wind up there . . ."

"How long will you be with us?"

"A week."

"A week's a long time in Valleyview. Cal Bryant an old friend of yours?"

"Well . . . more like a new friend."

"You been over to the *Courier*?"

"The *Courier*?"

"He's the editor over there. He's also a writer. He once had a short story published in a book. Can't remember which book. But it was a good story, I can tell you that much. Racy for the folks around here but I liked it. I like Cal. You fill out your registration?"

I handed her the form.

"Brooklyn. How come in every war movie there's a soldier from Brooklyn? Frank Sinatra's from Brooklyn."

"Hoboken."

"Isn't that Brooklyn?"

"Jersey."

"I'm going to give you a nice room, honeychile, that overlooks the town square. The bureau in that room dates back to the War Between the States. It belonged to my grandmother. Business is a little off right now but it'll pick up next week when the tractor salesmen hit town. Valleyview has this big plant, Osgood Tractors, and they call in their salesmen for meetings every six months or so. The boys all stay here. I run the local post office from right here in the lobby and there's the restaurant next door—I run that, too—and if you come in before seven I'll make sure Mac gives you the best cut of beef. Beef around here is the best. Cal Bryant eats here three, maybe four times a week, being a bachelor and all."

Why was Tillie pushing Cal on me? I got the idea she was the frustrated type . . . Jesus, what man would want her? . . . who got her kicks thinking about other people's sex lives. But sex still wasn't on my mind—at least not entirely—as I went upstairs to look over the room. I was thinking about Tush growing up in Valleyview. Like the room, everything in Valleyview seemed airy and clean. Outside my window I saw how a group of school kids had volunteered to pick up the litter from the parade. Don't even think about that happening in New York. The girls and boys looked so wholesome, working like the devil to get the job done. No hanky-panky, no ass-grabbing. I started thinking about how when I was barely a teenager, I met this Italian girl who told me about blowjobs. She said it was the quickest way to get to be the most popular girl in the class. She was right. Looking over these Ohio kids, I wondered what I'd be like today if I'd grown up around here. Would I have ever run off to the circus? Or turned into a stripper? Well, Tush grew up here and turned into a stripper. I wanted to talk to her teachers, meet her boyfriends, put myself in her place, try and imagine what it was like. She grew up so different from me, and yet she wound up the same as me. Or did she?

What was I supposed to do? With Calvin Bryant sitting across Tillie's restaurant from me, how could I not invite him over? Besides, I'd spent my second day in Valleyview just walking around, going in and out of the stores, getting a feel for the place but not quite sure about how to make my next move. The editor of the local paper had to be helpful.

He was wearing that same baggy suit and I was in a blue and white dress that clung pretty tight to me. During the day, I looked like a schoolteacher, but at night, well, I can't say I wasn't giving off some signals about being lonely. He came to my table to say hello.

"How's the apple pie around here?" I asked him.

He sat down and said, "Scrumptious. Tillie bakes it herself."

I ordered apple pie for two.

Cal cleared his throat. "It's absolutely none of my business, but I'm going to be bold enough to guess that you're a dancer."

"What makes you say that?"

"Well, I suppose . . ." He hesitated to gather his thoughts before saying, "I suppose it's the way you move."

"You haven't seen me move anything but my mouth," I said. This guy was a little shy and a little pushy at the same time, a combination I liked maybe a little too much.

"I'm talking about subtle moves," he explained. "Like your hands, the way you hold a fork."

Gee, for being stuck out in the sticks, Cal Bryant had some pretty good lines. Well, I was in the sticks too—far from home—and I could say anything I wanted; I could be whoever I wanted. "You guessed right," I told him, getting a little excited. "I am a dancer."

"What kind?"

"Musicals. Broadway musicals."

"I'm impressed."

"You should be. Ever hear of *Oklahoma!*?"

"Of course."

"Well, I was an understudy. Got to perform six or seven times."

"Must be exciting."

"Very."

"And Tillie says you're off to California. You're going to dance in pictures, I suppose."

"Going to try."

"Wonderful. But it's no accident you decided to stop in Valleyview."

"Why do you say that?"

"Just guessing."

At night, his one eye looked calmer than the other day. Neon green turned to sea green. I was starting to trust him.

"You've probably already noticed," he said, "that this town's dry. It's a short ride to the next county—just a few miles—where I think you'd find this old bar very picturesque. Personally, I'm quite fond of the place. If you'd like to come along, I'd appreciate your companionship."

The invitation was so sweet I had to accept. On the way out, Tillie Rosslyn, standing at the cash register and counting receipts, looked up, winked and nodded her head, as if she'd known all along that this was going to happen. Wanted it to happen.

Cal drove an old Chevy left over from the thirties. It didn't smell great.

"Belonged to my daddy," he told me.

"Your parents live around here?"

"Mother died when I was young. And my father . . . well, he's . . . he's in a hospital."

The way he said that told me not to probe further. Instead of talking I rolled down the window and took a whiff of cool night air. Delicious. I looked over and saw Cal fish a flask out of his suit pocket and take a nip.

"Can't wait till we get to the bar?" I asked him.

"Feel free to join me," he answered, offering me the flask.

"No, thanks."

The bar looked like something from a hundred years ago, all this old dark wood and stained glass, the sort of joint where Robin Hood would take his merry men. It was in this tiny village on the edge of the woods and the doors were open so you could smell the wildflowers and the sweet perfume of nature. No garbage, no sewers, no subways roaring underground, nothing even faintly resembling New York City.

Cal ordered a double scotch but I didn't feel like drinking.

"How come?" he wanted to know.

"I don't know . . . just the way it smells so clean around here . . . doesn't seem like it goes with drinking."

He tilted his head, his good eye looking at me like he was a little hurt. "Sure you don't want to join me?"

I gave in and ordered sherry. I didn't even like sherry, but it sounded like the right thing to order in a bar in a little village in Ohio.

"So tell me about living in New York," said Cal.

"You never been?"

"Oh, I've been. But only as a visitor."

"Didn't like it?"

"Didn't understand it."

"What's to understand?"

"The hurry. What's the hurry?"

"Oh, that. We're a little nervous—that's all. When you're nervous you rush."

"Are you nervous now?"

"Hell, no. This is the most relaxed I've been since God knows when."

"I'm glad." He finished off his drink and ordered another. This guy could pack 'em away.

"Smoke?" he offered. I accepted one of his Pall Malls. As he lit us on the same match, the glow from the flame showed wrinkles around his eyes and mouth. For a young guy he had a lot of wrinkles, but they seemed to add to his character. He looked like he did a lot of worrying.

"You like working on a newspaper?" I asked.

"There's not much to it. This is a slow news town."

"Tillie told me you were an author, said you wrote a short story that . . ."

"Tillie talks too much."

"Sorry, I—"

"No need to apologize. It was just a silly story that Tillie happened to find in a book in the library. I never even told anyone."

"You were ashamed?"

"Wasn't that. It's just that it has nothing to do with my real life. Just something I once did."

"What's it about?"

"A mystery. A sort of miniature murder mystery. I make myself into a private detective looking to solve a crime."

Interesting. "And," I asked, "do you solve it?"

"No. I guess the story is more philosophical than realistic."

"What does that mean?"

"Probably that it's not very good."

"The people who published it must have liked it."

"Look," he said, "now that we've exhausted my literary career, how about another round?"

"Hey, I don't want you driving into a tree."

"Don't worry about that. I know the road from here to Valleyview like the back of my hand."

"I got a little murder mystery of my own."

"Tell me about it."

I was tempted—real tempted—but, well . . . I wasn't altogether convinced to spill my guts to this guy. Cal was working on his third double scotch, but his eye was clear; it had softened and looked a little dreamy. For a long time I just sat there in silence.

"So what's the mystery?" he wanted to know.

"I had a friend in New York, a girl who danced with me." More silence as I studied my drink.

"Go on," he urged.

"She was killed."

"I presume this isn't a made-up story, this is real life."

"Real as you can get."

"What did the cops say?"

"The cops never found the killer. Never really looked for him."

"Why?"

"Well, she wasn't important to the cops. They don't think dancers are important. Maybe she wasn't very important to anyone."

"Except you."

"She was my friend."

"You knew her well?"

"I thought I did. But then I found out I didn't. She wasn't who I thought she was."

"And now you want to find out just who she was."

"Right."

"So you've come to Valleyview to ask about Teresa Johnson."

"How'd you know I was talking about Teresa?" I was surprised and not surprised. After all, I'd been telling him without telling him.

"After the initial story broke, I was stunned by the lack of follow-up. Actually, I was all set to go to New York myself and look into it when my publisher advised me strongly against it. Fact is, he flat-out forbid it. You see, my publisher is an elder at Reverend Johnson's church, and one of the old man's best friends."

"But why wouldn't Reverend Johnson want you to look into it?"

"He wanted to forget about it—at least that's what I was told. Didn't want any more publicity."

"That doesn't make sense."

"You have to understand small-town mentality. But tell me about this dancing business. I thought Teresa was in art school."

"She loved art, but she could also dance. And sing."

"I wonder if her father knew."

"I don't think so. I met him when he came to New York, and I don't think he knew nothing."

"Fascinating," said Cal, ordering still another scotch.

"Did you know Teresa?"

"No, not really. She was a pretty girl, I remember that, but just another cheerleader around here."

As he steadily drained his fresh drink, I was wondering whether I had told him too much, wondering what his next move would be, and wondering how I'd respond. As things turned out, I didn't have to wonder too much longer.

"You know," he said to me, for the first time that evening touching my hand, "I really think a lot of you for caring about your friend, for coming all the way here to . . ."

Before he completed his thought, his eye, which I thought had been looking at me lovingly, slowly closed while his head tilted down. He didn't fall out; he didn't fall down; he just sort of sat there, slightly slumped over, dead to the world. Nothing could wake him. The bartender helped me drag him to the car and gave me directions. I drove back to Valleyview, got off at the Rosslyn House and left Calvin Bryant in the car, sleeping like a baby.

I wasn't furious, but I couldn't call myself happy. A man I thought was attracted to me had passed out on our first date. A man I damn well knew I was attracted to was nothing more than a small-town drunk. Maybe that was mean, but what else was I supposed to think? Tillie wasn't surprised when I told her what happened. "He's sweet," she said, "and the boy's smart as a whip. Probably could be a big-time writer if he could ever get out of here. But I think he's scared." "Scared of what?" I wanted to know. "Scared of what all the boys are scared of—scared of being a man, honeychile." Now Tillie was telling the truth, and I saw right away that here in the heartland men were the same as in Sin City. I'd just found myself another baby.

Better forget about Cal Bryant and go off by myself. Better get out there and do what I came here to do—learn about Teresa, talk to her teachers and friends. Better dress real simple and modest and walk over to the high school and start asking questions.

Summer school was on and the building was half-deserted, just a couple of classes in session. I walked down the hallway and stopped in front of a trophy case. There was a picture of the 1944 cheerleading squad—six gals—in pleated skirts and wool sweaters, each with a big *V* across it. Teresa had the prettiest face and the best figure. She was smiling like she didn't have a care in the world.

"She was a fine girl," Principal Jonathan Birchdale told me a couple of minutes later. "Reverend Johnson had every right to be proud of her. And I'm certainly proud to be a deacon in Reverend Johnson's church." I'd introduced myself as her friend from New York, who happened to be passing through and wanted to pay my respects to those who knew her best. "I was so shocked when it happened," I told him, "I didn't know what to do or who to talk to."

"I can understand that," said the principal, a plump pumpkin of a man in his fifties with hardly any hair, baggy frog eyes and a pipe between his teeth which forced him to talk out of the side of his mouth. He wore a shirt and a polka-dot bow tie—no jacket—with his big gut straining against the buttons. "You can imagine the shock around here. The memorial service was one of the most emotional events I can ever remember attending. Of course the reverend spoke, as well as myself and Miss Fletcher."

"Who's she?"

"Miss Fletcher is our speech teacher and drama coach. She adored Teresa, simply adored the girl. And Bobby Marks—everyone likes Bobby—he was her boyfriend."

"Are they around?"

"Miss Fletcher is in Room 109, just down the hall. Her class should be out in a few minutes," he said, taking out his pocket watch and checking the time. "Bobby works for his father over at the Texaco station on Elm and LaSalle."

I wondered if there was something wrong with Miss Fletcher's skin. The minute I saw her leaving the classroom, I noticed that practically every inch of her body was covered by clothing. She wore a turtle-neck collar right up to her chin and her long granny skirt practically touched the floor. Poor thing had a chest like an ironing board. She was way out of fashion and, for July, way overdressed. The outfit looked strange on her, especially 'cause she couldn't have been older than thirty-five. I told her just what I'd told the principal about wanting to pay my respects. But unlike the principal, Fletch seemed like she had half a brain. She suspected something. She started asking me questions as we went to the teachers' lounge where she lit up a Camel and didn't even bother to offer me one. This was one nervous lady.

"How did you say you knew her?" she wanted to know.

"We were friends."

"You're not with the police, are you?"

"No."

"Was she happy in New York?"

"I thought so. Was she happy in high school?"

"She was very talented. She starred in the senior production of *Show Boat*. Beautiful voice—when she'd listen to me and stick to the melody. She could dance too."

"I know."

"How do you know?" Damn, this woman was nosey.

"We'd go ballroom dancing."

"Then you knew about her private life."

"Very little. She was very private."

"Not here. Here she was the belle of the ball. Boys tripped over themselves trying to get to her. If you ask me, she made herself too available. I'm sure that's what happened in New York, aren't you?"

"I don't know. I heard she had one particular boyfriend here."

"Who'd you hear that from?"

"Your principal."

Fletch took a deep drag on her cigarette. She laughed. "This was one girl who could never have one particular boyfriend—no matter how gorgeous he might be."

He was plenty gorgeous. Bobby Marks was in the back of the Texaco station stacking up used tires. His shirt was off and his sweaty chest was rippled with muscles, his handsome face smudged with dirt. For a second I wished I wasn't dressed so plain and modest so he could see that I had plenty to offer myself. But that wasn't the reason I was there. I wasn't supposed to get all hot and bothered by this schoolboy with his blond hair and big blue bedroom eyes. I could sure see what Tush saw; I could see that his waist was real thin and his back real strong and when he lifted the tires his arms bulged all over the place and with the sun beating down I was feeling flushed and just wanted to look, not disturb his work, not say a word, except he glanced up and was surprised to see me and walked over, grabbing a towel and drying himself off. I wanted to ask him if I could help dry him off, but I was a good girl; I didn't say nothing. Sometimes it's not easy being good.

He had a little lisp that made everything he said sound even more genuine.

"You're her friend Rhonda?"

"How'd you know?"

"She wrote me about you. She said you were a dancer."

Tush was dead, I was alive, but here we were with the same lies. That actually made things easier.

"I'm on my way to California and I just wanted to see her hometown."

"You have time for a Coke? Can I buy you a Coke?"

I had time for a lot more than a Coke, I thought to myself as he washed up and put on a clean white T-shirt that fit him so snug his muscles looked like they were about to rip the thin fabric. We walked down to a little drugstore with a soda fountain. Someone had left a *Time* magazine on the counter with President Truman on the cover. The radio was playing "I'm a Big Girl Now" by Sammy Kaye and his Swing and Sway orchestra. I ordered a scoop of chocolate ice cream. Bobby drank a root beer.

"You're probably wondering why I wasn't in the Army?" he asked.

Actually I wasn't wondering that at all. I was wondering how Teresa could ever leave a guy who looked like this.

"My ticker," he said. "They discovered it when I was playing football. My heartbeat's not right."

Neither was mine . . . what with him sitting next to me, his leg brushing against mine.

"Anyway," he went on, "I'm stuck here. I feel bad about it, I wanted to serve my country."

"Did you ever want to come to New York to visit Teresa?"

"How well did you know her, Rhonda?"

"I'm not sure."

"See, I wasn't sure either. I thought I knew her. We started going steady in the tenth grade. And all through the eleventh grade too. But our senior year . . ."

He stopped, closed his eyes, took a deep breath.

"What happened?" I wanted to know.

"The football team."

"You told me you played football and then had to stop."

"Not me, Teresa."

"I don't get it."

"Turned out she was dating a couple of the other football players the same time she was dating me. And since we were going steady, well . . . that wasn't right."

"Well . . ." What could I say?

"I don't think she cared about hurting me. It was just her nature. But I told her when she got to New York, she'd better stop that business. In New York someone could hurt her. I wrote her all the time. But all I'd get back was a little postcard now and then. That's when she mentioned you. She said you were her best friend. Like her older sister."

I didn't like the way he emphasized *older*. It was hot in the drugstore, and I started undoing the top two buttons of my blouse, but stopped myself.

"Let me know if I can help you while you're in Valleyview, Rhonda," he offered.

I told him if he ever had any suspicions, even after I left town, to contact Captain Mickey Donegan in New York. I tried to look him in the eye, but it was tough because his baby blues were so blue I felt myself melting. I wanted to tell him exactly how he could help me, but I didn't. I couldn't. It just didn't seem right.

Back in the hotel, my head was aching. I was still seeing Bobby Marks's sweaty chest. At the same time I was thinking of how Tush had hurt him. She fucked his teammates behind his back. That didn't jibe with the girl I had known. But it sure did jibe with what the other strippers had said. "You see," Bobby had told me, "she seemed one way but was really another. She was sweet as sugar, but the sugar just stayed on the top." "She was interested in experience," the Fletcher woman had added. "She wanted to experience everything, and that's dangerous."

Is it? Didn't I feel the same way? Isn't that why I ran away and joined the circus? Why I started stripping? And wasn't that the reason I took stripping as far as I could? It was the same reason, I thought, that I got interested in Bull and the reason I got interested in Sandy. I liked being with a ballplayer, but I also liked being with a songwriter. One was swinging the bat, the other swinging the piano. Two different experiences. I liked them both. I bet Bobby was a hell of an experience—a young athlete like that. Or maybe he wasn't all that experienced, maybe he needed a little instruction. He sure looked like he needed some comfort. I know I did. It'd been too long since I'd been with a man . . . ever since this business with Tush began. I was no nun. And I also was no private detective. So what was I doing out here in the middle of Nowhere, America, looking for clues to a crime that happened back in New York City?

I was in the middle of dinner in Tillie's dining room, cutting into a lean slice of sirloin, when the waiter brought over a huge bouquet of flowers with a little note. The note said, "Sure, I'm a cad, but even cads deserve a second chance. Cal."

I was a little disappointed because I was half hoping the flowers had come from Bobby Marks. But that was stupid; Bobby Marks wasn't on the make; Cal Bryant was. And, I suppose, so was I. Birds of a feather.

I expected he'd show up during dessert, and he did. He looked real clean shaven and didn't smell of booze but splashy cologne; he smelled like he'd just stepped out of the shower. A bottle of champagne was cradled in his arm.

"This is a two-part apology," he said. "You got the flowers. Here's the imported champagne. Am I forgiven?"

I had to smile 'cause he was smiling. His eye-patch made him look like a pirate. I really liked this guy's eye-patch. Besides, what business did I have daydreaming about a schoolboy? Get real,

Rhonda. Calvin Bryant was real. He was real interested in me. He didn't ask pushy questions like the Fletcher teacher. He wasn't pushy at all, he was smooth. That's why I liked him. But I didn't like the way he started in on the champagne 'cause I figured he'd wind up like he did last night.

"Last night I had a bit of the flu," he said. "It wasn't the booze."

I've known a lot of lushes, and they all got excuses. I wasn't buying his bullshit.

"Alright," he promised. "No bubbly for me tonight. That make you feel better?"

"Much."

"Now tell me about your day."

"Why should I?"

"Well, because it must have been exhilarating—and I bet a little confusing."

"Why would you say that?"

"You look a little confused."

His green eye was looking right through me. I drank a little champagne. The tiny bubbles tickled my nose and started dancing around my brain. He was right. Why should I fight it? I *was* a little confused. I was still seeing Bobby's muscles.

"I saw her boyfriend, Bobby Marks."

"Former football star."

"You heard of him?"

"Heard of everyone in this town."

"And?"

"He was the town hero. Quiet kid. Not too bright."

"He said she cheated on him."

"Oh?"

"With his teammates." Why was I telling this guy everything? Why did I trust him?

"Hmmm," said Cal. "That makes him a suspect, doesn't it?"

"I didn't think of that."

"I'm surprised."

"The kid's sweet as sugar. He's a hayseed. I don't see him murdering anyone."

"You should have seen him on the football field."

"I don't believe he'd stab Tush to death."

"Who?"

"Tush. I called Teresa Tush."

Cal smiled. I guess he knew about tushes.

"Who else did you talk to?"

"Miss Fletcher."

"The former nun."

"I should've known."

"What'd she say?"

"Nothing much. Just that Teresa was looking for experiences."

"Did she say Teresa was promiscuous?"

"She hinted."

"And what was her attitude?"

"Hard to tell. Maybe a little disappointed in Tush."

"Wonder why. Wonder if Fletcher had a crush on Teresa?" Cal looked to see whether he was shocking me. He wasn't. Naturally this angle had come up before, but I didn't feel like telling Cal about Billie Holiday. I wasn't going to tell this guy *everything*.

"You suspect Fletcher?" he asked me.

"I guess I should have asked her where she was the night of the murder. I guess I should have asked Bobby Marks too."

"Might be easier if I asked them. If you go back, they'll suspect something. I can do it so they won't know I'm asking."

"Why are you interested in helping me?"

"Isn't it obvious? I like you. I like you very much. Besides, covering city council meetings and Fourth of July parades is boring. At least you're onto an interesting story."

After he made his case, he smiled. His smile wasn't sleazy, conniving or forced. I thought his smile was sincere. His words sounded sincere. Besides, he was right. I should suspect even Bobby, I should suspect everyone, except I was feeling a little lonely and far from home here in Tillie's dining room. I saw Cal moving his hand to touch mine—just to touch it—and I let him, I let his hand rest there, feeling the warmth of his skin, when all of a sudden the mood was broken and his hand pulled away when we heard—

"I didn't know you knew Miss Silverstar, Mr. Bryant"—and looked up and saw the loose turkey neck of Reverend Johnson and his hard eyes burning down on us.

I don't know why, but I felt guilty, like my father had caught me giving some guy a blowjob when all Cal had done was touch my hand. I almost said, "I'm sorry, reverend," and then I remembered that this was the clown who didn't have any use for Jews so I didn't even smile.

"Care to join us, reverend?" offered Cal.

"No, thank you. I simply came by to say that Principal Birchdale mentioned that you had paid him a visit today. I'm interested in learning the exact nature of your visit to Valleyview, Miss Silverstar."

I was flustered, but I managed to say something about just wanting to see Teresa's hometown and meeting her friends. When he answered, he didn't even look at me, but directed his words to Cal.

"I trust, Mr. Bryant, that you do not find this a matter suitable for your newspaper. I seriously doubt if your publisher would be the slightest bit interested in reviewing the facts of Teresa's demise."

"I'm sure he wouldn't," said Cal. "Miss Silverstar and I are merely friends."

"Fast friends I should say," said the minister.

What business is it of yours, buster? I wanted to ask, but Cal surprised me by speaking up. "Miss Silverstar was hoping that she'd be able to meet your lovely wife, reverend."

I was? The minister was caught off guard. He didn't know how to respond. "I'll mention that to Mrs. Johnson," he finally said. "How long do you plan to be here, Miss Silverstar?"

"A day or two," I answered.

"Then I shall phone you," he said, nodding before turning and leaving the dining room. He walked like he had a broomstick up his ass.

"Why'd you do that?" I asked Cal when the minister was gone.

"I figured you'd want to see Teresa's house, her bedroom, meet her mom, get the whole picture. Was I wrong?"

"I suppose you're right." Of course he was right; and of course I was getting mad at him for butting in like this. On the other hand, Cal had a way of stepping around my anger. Besides, how mad could I get at someone trying to help me?

"This trust business is interesting," he said, sipping on coffee while pouring me a little more champagne.

"What do you mean?" I wanted to know.

"You're a dancer—a showgirl—is that right?"

"I'm an artist," I said, holding my head high.

"Fine," he said, "an interpretive artist. But a New York showgirl through and through—that's how I see you. Very tough and experienced."

"Alright, that's how you see me. So what?"

"Given the scores of men who must be pursuing you night and day, I'd suspect you'd trust very few. But the more I'm with you, the more I see you trusting practically everyone."

"Bullshit."

"You trusted Fletcher, you trusted Bobby Marks, you even trusted Reverend Johnson."

"I think Reverend Johnson's a jerk, but don't tell me he murdered his own daughter."

"We don't know who murdered her, do we? Consequently, no one who knew her can be trusted."

The guy was right. He saw me as an easy touch. Funny, I didn't see myself that way. But at least he was looking at me—with that one green eye of his—looking at me harder and deeper than any other man I'd ever met. Bull and Sandy—well, maybe I was just a soft touch to them.

"When it comes to men," he went on, "I have a feeling your real pleasure comes in pleasing them, not accusing them of hideous crimes."

When he said that, I felt myself getting warm. Whether he was right or wrong, the way he said it—the words themselves—got me hot. That idea of pleasing men. How did he know? What did he see in me? I was hot but I was also mad. He was irritating me. He thought he knew more than he knew. I wasn't about to sit there and let him tell me who I was. "You know, Mr. Cal Bryant," I said, "you sure as hell know a lot about someone who you've spent a total of one hour with."

"We were together last night for far more than an hour."

"You weren't even sober for an hour. I bet you don't even remember the rest of the time."

"That's where you're wrong. I remember every word you said, every little gesture you made. At about eleven P.M., you excused yourself and went to the bathroom and came back with fresh lipstick and powder. You went from a pink shade to a red one. Isn't that right?"

That *was* right, but I just said, "Maybe. What does that prove?"

"You were interested in pleasing me."

"Enough of that shit."

"I mean it as a compliment. You're a giver. Givers are very rare in this world."

"Gee, thanks."

"When you're performing, I'm certain you give your all. But as a sleuth . . ."

"What's that?"

"A would-be detective. As a sleuth, you're well motivated but a little ill suited. I think you need a partner."

"And just who would that be?"

"Me." There was that smile again.

"And I suppose you'd be a good sleuth because you don't trust anyone."

"Not even myself."

"Then how am I supposed to trust you?"

"I'll show you where I live. I'll show you my Boy Scout medals and my short story. Then you're sure to trust me. What do you say?"

I said yes. I liked Cal's house. It was comfortable and roomy with old furniture in the living room and a kitchen with a green tile floor. You could tell he was a bachelor 'cause the dishes weren't washed and the empty glasses reeked of booze. He seated me on the couch and handed me the book with his short story. "Read," he said.

I'm a slow reader and this was pretty slow going except when it heated up with some sexy scenes. The murder mystery part wasn't too clear because at the end you didn't know if the murderer was Linda or Tom, these two people having an affair.

"Well, who did the killing?" I asked when I was through.

"I don't know," said Cal.

"If you don't know, who does?"

"No one."

"I hate that."

"That's just the point."

"For me to hate it?"

"To deny satisfaction in the traditional whodunit manner."

"What does that mean?"

"I'm trying something new."

"I think Linda did it."

"Of course. You trust the man."

"The man's mixed up. You're mixed up. Everyone's mixed up except Linda because she knows what she wants out of a man."

Cal brought out a bottle of brandy. "But I'm Linda. An author is all his characters."

"I'm surprised they'd print it in a regular book like that, the way you say 'stiff' all the time."

The windows were open, the summer night was cool, and I felt the air getting my nipples stiff. Or maybe it was the story that did that. Anyway, I have to admit I was anxious to see Cal's next move.

"I think we should go dancing."

"Dancing?"

"Dancing under the moonlight. Ohio has some things you can't find in New York City, and Paradise Lake is one of them."

By now he was a sweet drunk and I wasn't feeling half-bad myself. "I ain't letting you drive," I said.

"Good," he agreed. "I like the way you drive. I'll give directions. I'll even fix myself a thermos of coffee to insure my strict attention. What time is it? Only eight. Perfect. The band plays till ten. You'll love the setting."

The setting was outdoors, about a half-hour's ride out of town, by the side of a lake glowing with moonlight. Naturally the orchestra, seated in a bandshell that looked like a half-moon, was playing "Moonlight Serenade" and naturally all I wanted was a man to sweep me up in his arms and dance me around this patio where soldiers and sailors were holding their honeys tight while the band sailed into "Old Devil Moon" and "Sentimental Journey" and "For Sentimental Reasons" and "How Blue the Night." The night was silver blue, blue lights hung around the patio, me and Cal dancing to "Swinging on a Star," the night star-crazy, all clear and bright—I'd never seen a sky like that, never seen so many stars— and Cal was a smooth dancer, a little tipsy, he and I were nipping from his flask filled with brandy, he never did bring the coffee, but I didn't care 'cause I was feeling like we were floating through the heavens far away from little towns or big cities or anyplace on earth when he pressed closer to me, let me feel how stiff he was— here I go, talking the way he writes—and I felt like Linda in his story and I let him dance me off the patio, I wanted to be alone with him, I let him walk me down to the lake, the moonlit lake, to a little winding path, I let him lead me into a clearing hidden by bushes where we sat on top of a hill and could see the silver water and hear the music off in the distance playing "Long Ago and Far Away," far away was the way I was feeling, and when he kissed me with his tongue I let him, I let him snap off my bra and see what he was in for, I let him lick my tits all over, let him lick me real good, let him get my nipples stiff because he was so stiff he was about to burst. I let him slip off my panties. I slipped off his eye-patch and saw that his left eye was closed tight, like a little baby, and I let him love me there on the hill overlooking the lake with the dreamy music in our ears, he loved me strong and even though I started thinking about Bobby Marks and all his bulging muscles, even though I thought about all those sailors and the soldiers who were dancing on the patio coming over here and watching me spread my legs and kick high into the summer sky, I kept coming back to Cal and Cal alone because Cal wasn't a boy, I didn't have to say a thing, he knew just what to do, before, during and after, he knew how to make me wait, touch me soft, touch me hard, a little at a time, now a lot, now gentle, now slow, now crazy fast and faster until the lake began spinning and stars tumbled out of the sky, falling over all my body, shimmering like magic, my skin wet and tingly fresh like sweet morning dew.

"WOULD YOU CARE FOR A SPOT OF TEA, MY DEAR?"

How come Tush didn't tell me her mom was a limey? Or was she?

The Johnson home seemed American enough, with a little spinet piano in the corner and all this old-fashioned furniture that looked like it had belonged to George Washington. There were hooked rugs and rocking chairs and a big white bible sitting on a table all by itself and heavy curtains that blocked out the light and a painting that Tush showed me at the Metropolitan Museum of Jesus eating supper with his pals, only the one hanging over the Johnsons' vomit-green couch was a lot smaller than the one in the museum and the colors were washed out. "I saw that painting every day of my life," I remember Tush telling me. "And every time I looked at it I felt like crawling under the table where Jesus was sitting and tickling his feet." Now I knew what Tush meant. Especially in this house which looked like it could use a couple of good laughs.

"Sure, I'll have some tea, Mrs. Johnson," I said, not sure whether her accent was real British or fake.

I remembered seeing her that first day I hit town. She was sitting up on the podium looking like a bird. She seemed to twitter. Her skin was like perfect porcelain and her face looked frozen, her blue dress plain and stiff. Now seated in front of me, her knees were pressed together tight. As she got up and headed for the kitchen, I heard her humming under her breath—not any special melody, just a nervous sort of bee buzz.

It was two in the afternoon and I'd only been up a couple of hours. Cal and I had gone from Paradise to his house where we didn't get through doing what we did until daybreak. My back was breaking, my legs aching, but I wasn't complaining. Cal got up and went to work, leaving me asleep. When he came back it was noon. He handed me a Valleyview *Courier* opened to his editorial about Secretary of Commerce Henry A. Wallace. I was too groggy to read. He kissed me on the cheek and said, "I've fixed us some sandwiches for lunch." I wasn't used to men fixing me food, but it wasn't hard adjusting. The orange juice was sweet and the egg salad loaded with mayonnaise. When he dropped me off at the hotel he said, "I'll meet you at Tillie's for dinner." Tillie was behind the counter.

"Reverend Johnson called you," she said as she was piling up packages as part of her post office duties.

Jesus, I thought to myself, *he already knows what I did last night. What is it with this guy?* Like a nut, I started feeling guilty—like he was my father or something.

But on the phone, all the preacher said was, "Please be at my house at two."

"I trust you'll take a slice of sponge cake," his wife was saying now. The reverend was nowhere in sight.

"Sure."

The sponge cake was dry, not enough butter or sugar, just like the house was dry—boring dark green wallpaper, musty smells, copies of *Christian Life* magazine on the end tables.

"I understand you knew our daughter." Mrs. Johnson's accent started sounding a little more American. She had these thin lips which didn't move much when she talked.

"I was crazy about Teresa," I said.

She didn't smile or even nod. "Teresa made friends quite easily," is all she said. Her tone gave me the idea that she didn't approve of her friends. "She was a perfect daughter. I couldn't have asked for anyone more considerate or loving," she said, wiping a tear from her eye. "I only wonder if she was too trusting, poor thing."

"Trusting"—hey, isn't that what Cal said about me? Even though I was acting the part of a perfect lady, seated there in the reverend's house, my mind was mostly on Cal. The way he made me lunch. The way he made love all last night. The way he concentrated on me. Most men concentrate on themselves, in and out of bed. Cal was interested in me, *really* interested. That made me a little nervous, but it also made me feel good. All I could think about was the way he felt inside me. Talking to Mrs. Johnson, who seemed more like an old maid than someone's wife, I should have been concentrating on Tush, but I gotta admit—I was thinking about getting back together with Cal, tonight, tomorrow night, and the night after that. But wasn't I supposed to be leaving town? Shouldn't I be thinking about getting back to New York?

"Would you like to see my daughter's bedroom?" asked Mrs. Johnson suddenly.

"Sure thing."

The bedroom felt creepy. It was all powder blue and Pepto-Bismol pink. Weird, because it was a little girl's room, not even a teenager's room, no pennants or pictures of football stars like Bobby Marks, but only little dolls and teddy bears, and lots and lots of stuffed kittens on her dresser, just like the kittens she had in New York.

"She always wanted a real kitten," said Teresa's mom as I picked up a stuffed kitten, "but Reverend Johnson is allergic. I felt bad about that. Did she have a cat in New York?"

Come to think of it, she did. Snuggles. What happened to Snuggles? I didn't see Snuggles on that Sunday morning when Captain Donegan called me over there. Maybe Snuggles was in the corner hiding, or maybe she ran out in the hallway. Hey, what became of Snuggles?

"Yeah," I told her mom, "she had Snuggles."

"Such a cute name. Our Teresa had a cute name for everyone. She called me her Mommykins." Her lips formed a half-smile, like it hurt her to smile.

It hurt me to look at this bedroom, I thought as Mrs. Johnson sat on the bed beside me and started showing snapshots of Teresa as a little girl. She looked a little like me. Why was I feeling so bad? I know I was feeling bad for Teresa, but I was also feeling bad for myself. I never had a bedroom like this. So neat and pretty with stuffed animals to hug when you're scared at night and your parents aren't around. I wondered if I would have turned out different had this been my bedroom. But how did Tush turn out? Not that different from me. She trusted men. She trusted everyone.

"I trust you'll remember Teresa in your prayers," Mrs. Johnson said.

"Sure I will."

"What church do you attend in New York?"

Jesus, here we go again. "Jewish. A Jewish synagogue."

"Oh, I see." Cold as ice. "Well, if you people pray for your deceased, then it wouldn't hurt to mention Teresa in your prayers, would it?"

"I don't know," I said in a voice just as cold as Mrs. Johnson's. "I ain't God."

I wish I *was* God, I thought to myself while walking back to the hotel. It wasn't far, but I decided to take a long stroll and get a little lost. The streets were clean and all the old houses were scrubbed, white picket fences and trees and flowers and neatly cut lawns. If I was God, I'd make the world less complicated. Maybe I'd make it so sex wasn't such a big deal. I'd turn down the heat on sex. All that heat—that's what makes us crazy. I was trying to concentrate on the mystery of Tush and here I was concentrating on Cal, thinking of last night with Cal, and what happened my last night at Plotsky's, thinking of Bobby Marks and Tush, the way she couldn't resist Bobby and the boys on the football team, couldn't resist Billie Holiday and maybe a bunch of different guys in New York and maybe even Bull—I still didn't know what to believe about her and Bull—but I couldn't blame her, and I couldn't blame myself, because I know how it feels when the heat comes over you and the whole shitty world—and your problems and your parents—just disappear and you're pleasing someone and someone's pleasing you, all the teasing and squeezing and just plain fun of getting naked with someone new. I think that's fun. I want to have fun. When your parents are screaming at you all day—like mine were, like I knew Teresa's had to be—you figure out ways to slip away and have fun. That's all there is to it. Some girls got the guts to have fun, and some don't. I do. Tush did. So what . . . Tush didn't turn out to be the innocent little girl from the smalltown like I thought she was. More power to her. Except she was killed by some fucked-up lunatic. And even though I still didn't know who or why, it had to do with sex. That I know. If you ask me, everything has to do with sex—too much sex, too little sex, the wrong kind, the right kind—the world runs on sex. Sex starts us off, gets us born, gets us lovers, boyfriends, girlfriends, husbands, wives . . . makes us poor or maybe gets us rich . . . gets us families . . . gets us in trouble . . . and sometimes gets us killed.

"You're still not thinking of suspects," said Cal. "You're just philosophizing about sex. That's fascinating, you're fascinating, Rhonda, but what about the case? What about the motives? What about the people you've met in Valleyview?"

Cal's eye-patch gave him this double look, like his eyes were both open and closed; he was serious and funny, sober serious and a little drunk at the same time. We were back at his house where we'd just listened to Burns and Allen on the radio. Cal loved Gracie. Sure, Gracie was sweet, but why did the woman have to be so stupid and why did the jokes always have to be on her? Cal explained about straight men and foils and how Gracie was the real star. Of course I knew all about that from burlesque but I didn't say nothing since Cal thought I was a Broadway showgirl, not a stripper.

"I'm a stripper," I blurted out. "I know all about top bananas and second bananas and straight men. I worked with them." There; now he knew. I felt better. Why should I pretend to be something I wasn't? What was wrong with stripping? I wasn't any good at living lies. If I'd told my mother and father, I could sure as hell tell Cal Bryant. Besides, I trusted this guy. Wasn't he the one who said I trusted all the guys?

I waited for him to react while he sipped his whiskey, lit a cigarette, smoothly inhaling, then slowly exhaling.

Finally he asked me a question. "Did Teresa work with you at the strip bar?"

"It wasn't a bar, it was Plotsky's, a regular theater, with business guys and executives and boys back from the war. Top-drawer clientele. And yeah, Tush stripped. I was teaching her."

"I see."

"You see what?"

"The complications."

"What do you mean complications?"

"The greater number of suspects—all her admirers. She must have had many."

"I had a few myself."

He smiled, and when he said, "Count me among them," I knew he didn't think bad of me. He probably liked the idea of sleeping with a stripper. Most men do. I was waiting for him to ask me to strip. Maybe I was wanting him to ask me. Every guy loves a private show. Sandy did. And Bull went nuts when I went through my drawn-out peel-off-the-panties routine. But Cal didn't really say anything; he sat there, looking at me, shaking his head and smiling.

"So you like being a bad girl, is that it?"

Was that it? I didn't like the way he put it. Now I wasn't sure I liked his attitude. "No, that ain't it, Mr. Know It All," I told him. "You don't know me as well as you think you do."

He poured more booze in his glass and smiled even wider. "I don't know if I know you," he said, "but getting to know you is the best thing that's happened to me in years."

I liked the way that sounded. My eyes said, Go on, Cal. Tell me more. He read my eyes right and kept talking.

"You see, Rhonda, I'm stuck. Stuck in Ohio. My father was a farmer outside of town and my mom never left the state, not once. Her specialty was apple pie. Mom's apple pie won contests in counties all over Ohio. I went to Ohio State and afterwards made up my mind to go to New York City to become a writer. Real original, right? Well, that didn't work out. Two weeks in some flea-bag hotel, being turned out on my ear by those tough cynical newspaper editors—that was enough big city for me. So I decided to come home and write fiction. I didn't need New York; I didn't need those editors. All I needed was my imagination. I'd become Upton Sinclair or Sinclair Lewis. It hasn't worked out that way. Instead of writing novels I'm writing articles about Valleyview's homecoming war heroes."

"But how 'bout that short story you got published?"

"That was one story."

"You'll write more," I said, feeling bad for him.

"Look, I'm not telling you this sad story to get sympathy. I just wanted you to know that when I called you a bad girl I said it with affection, and admiration. I admire people who break rules . . . and boundaries. That's something I've never been able to do. When the war came, I thought that was a way out. Then the accident with my eye."

I'd been waiting to hear about this. I'd been wondering and wanting to ask ever since I met him.

"Happened when I first got back from that trip to New York. Car accident. I was driving my old man's De Soto. It was a miracle that I came out alive. My wife didn't."

Chilly silence.

"I'm . . . I'm sorry," I finally said.

"To be honest—I'm not sure the marriage would have lasted. She was a schoolteacher."

"Pretty?"

"Very pretty, very happy about my decision to come home and

work for the newspaper here. Very settled in Valleyview and anxious to stay put. It was all very safe and secure."

"But after the accident, you weren't tempted to go off again?"

"I thought about Chicago or Los Angeles. Even thought about
Europe. Thought about a lot of places. But I stayed. I guess that's
why I'm interested in your story—and Teresa's. She at least had
the guts to go."

"Hell, she had the guts to go up to Harlem."

"Tell me about that."

I told him the story of Abraham Jones and Teresa Johnson and
Billie Holiday. His one green eye looked at me hard as he drained
the glass of whiskey. Then I told him a little bit about Plotsky's
and the girls who worked there.

"It's a full plate," he said when I was through. "You have
suspects everywhere—downtown, uptown, suspects from New
Jersey to Ohio."

"But I'm no closer to who or why than I was when I started."

"At least you're developing the right cast of characters—that's
the first step."

"This ain't no story, Cal, it's real life."

"That's what makes it exciting."

"Come back to New York with me." I said it—just like that.
Usually I never talked that way to a man; I always wait for a man
to make his move. "You need to get out of here, that's what you
need to do." My heart was beating real fast. It was like my heart
was talking instead of my head.

"Now why in the world would you want me in New York?"

" 'Cause I'm probably falling for you." The words fell out of
my mouth. I wanted to pull them back. I never talked like that.
That wasn't my style. I'd only known this guy for a couple of days
and here I was acting the fool. Love? Me? Me saying I was falling
in love? Just because he was sweet and smart and interested in
everything about me? Just because he was different? Just because
he loved me so good? Just because why? Well, just because. I didn't
know then. I still don't know now. There was just something about

Cal Bryant that made me want to be with him and stay with him. I didn't want to leave him behind in Ohio. He made me feel comfortable and safe and wanted, like the way he came over to me after I said what I said and put his arms around me and kissed me and had me warm all over, warm on my mouth, warm on my neck, warm on my breasts and on my back, his skin was so warm and I said, let's not go to the bedroom, let's do it right here on the couch, let's pile up the pillows and do it. Which is just what happened. It was beautiful.

We had dinner at Tillie's and she could see what was happening. She saw the look in Cal's eye, she saw I had the glow.

"It's a lot easier to be a writer in New York," I told him, " 'cause there are more stories, more characters. New York is a writer's paradise."

"What am I going to do for money?"

"I got a little saved and I'll be working soon. Does that make you uneasy?"

"Having you strip? No. Not at all."

See, he had the right attitude. "I got a place in Brooklyn you'll really like," I told him. "Brooklyn ain't as loud as the city. More like this."

"Brooklyn's like Valleyview?"

"Not exactly, but we got trees and flowers and a big park. We'll go for walks in the park. And we'll figure out what happened to Teresa. We'll figure it out together, and that'll be your book. You'll do a book about Teresa. Ain't that an idea?"

I hit home. He was all smiles. "You see," I said, "you know where she came from, and I know where she went, and once we solve the mystery you'll have a slam-bang ending. Okay?"

For a long time, he didn't say anything. Then he reached over and took my hand and said, "Did you like that bar outside of town?"

"Where you passed out on me?"

He smiled. "Let's take a ride through the country."

I was feeling terrific. Every minute I was with Cal, I was feeling better and better. Unlike Sandy, he was calm; unlike Bull, he didn't have any sex problems. Okay, he drank too much and he'd been hiding out in Ohio too long, but I could give him everything he needed. Rhonda Silverstar knew how to be a woman. Especially for the right man.

The country smelled like heaven. It had rained earlier in the evening when me and Cal were making love, so the woods were dewy and perfumed and tingling like me, the sky was clear with stars, a half-moon shining bright. I heard crickets and saw fireflies and held Cal's hand while he drove real slow through the countryside. It was one of those times when the world didn't have no wars, people didn't have no problems, I was all peaceful inside with my man.

"I love this place," he said when we got to the Robin Hood and his merry men bar.

"I love it, too."

We started drinking brandy and that got me feeling even warmer about the world.

"So what do you say?" I asked him. "What do you say about going to New York with me?"

"I say it's a hell of an idea. I never thought of myself as a kept man."

"You won't be kept. You'll be working on the book."

"You'd want me to meet all the girls from Plotsky's, this Abraham, Billie Holiday? And what about Bull?"

"Bull's the past," I said, not even mentioning Sandy. "You're the present. Besides, we got a job to do, and you do it good. You're suspicious. I bet you're even suspicious of me right now."

"Well . . ."

"Come clean. You're worried about me. You're worried about my old boyfriends. You're trying to figure out my angle, aren't you?"

Cal smiled. "I'm not used to all this flattery. Not many exotic dancers have invited me to move in."

"I'm different."

"I noticed. *Vive la différence.*" We clinked glasses and threw back the brandy. We were flying. We were excited. I was excited because I'd found someone who made me feel right; and he was excited because—well, he was falling in love too; I knew he was— he was seeing me with loving eyes, and seeing me as his way out of his smalltown blues.

Things started to blur—I wasn't used to this much booze—but I was still feeling fine. I was listening to Cal talk about the first time he went to a New York deli and how he loved hot pastrami so much he wound up eating it three times a day. He lived on hot pastrami, he thought hot pastrami was the answer to the world's problems, and I promised him I'd take him to the hottest hot pastrami joints on the face of the earth, I'd plaster him with hot pastrami and feed him big fat matzoh balls and he wanted to know all about my family and, well, with all this brandy I was telling him everything, how my brother Leo was the star egghead of the family and how Mom and Pops were at each other's throat, how Mom liked to go off to the opera by herself and maybe she had a boyfriend, and maybe Pops also had something on the side, but mainly he wanted to open a corset shop and how they wanted me and my savings in the middle of their rotten marriage but I had my own life, I ran out when I was a kid and I wasn't running back.

"They sound fascinating," Cal said.

"That's 'cause you come from Ohio. If you came from Brooklyn they wouldn't seem so fascinating."

Everything about me was fascinating to him, and maybe that's why I was loving him. He saw me as different and exotic and couldn't stop asking questions and getting deeper into what it was like running off with the circus and that time I went out to California—how did a kid like me have the guts to do that?—and one more drink and we'd head back to my place, and I was ready, I was ready to have him love me for the rest of my life.

I remember staggering out of the bar. I remember I couldn't even think about driving. I remember I was laughing and holding onto Cal. I remember the stars were still out—I looked up at the moon—

and I remember the car started with no trouble and we were easing down the road and my head was on Cal's shoulder and his arm was around me and we were cuddling and cruising and on a highway to heaven, we weren't driving any more, we were flying, we had taken off from the ground and the car was flying and when it landed everything went dark and Cal was gone. I remember crying, "Cal! Cal!"

But Cal was gone.

I'LL BE
SEEING
YOU

It was a nurse, not a doctor, who told me. "Cal Bryant is dead. Fractured skull. Massive concussion." Just like that. No emotion, no pity, no nothing. "Cal Bryant is dead."

I was in the Valleyview Community Hospital. Tillie Rosslyn was seated next to my bed. "Honeychile," she said in that low husky voice of hers, "you were lucky. The door blew open and you flew out and landed on soft ground. The doctor couldn't find a thing broken. He said you can leave here tomorrow. You're just in shock."

Too shocked to cry. Too shocked to realize this wasn't a dream, me in bed, Tillie next to me, Cal dead. Cal dead. Cal is dead. I kept repeating it over in my mind to see whether I believed it. I didn't. I was drunk, he was drunk, and soon I'd wake up and the nightmare would be over, and I'd put my arm around him and he'd lean over and kiss me and we'd talk some more about going to New York. It was all set. He was going back home with me and he was moving in, he was going to write a book about Tush—and maybe he'd put something about me in there too, maybe the book could also be the story of me and Cal, the book that finally got him to leave the little newspaper and little town that he always wanted to leave, the book that led us to Tush's murderer, the book of love, the book about his life and my life and Tush's life, the book that would give us a better new life. I kept babbling about the book and Tillie thought I was delirious, she called over the nurse to calm me down, but I wouldn't be calmed, I wouldn't believe what happened. Tell me Cal's in the next room recovering just fine, tell me he's home waiting for me, he's back at the newspaper, he's packing to go to New York with me, he's fine, he's healthy as a horse, he's a little hungover, but he's alright, it'll all be alright, just tell me, Tillie, tell me Cal's here and it'll be alright.

The whole town was there. I waited around for three days so I could be there too. I couldn't leave without saying goodbye, no matter how much it might hurt. And it hurt plenty.

No one sat next to me in the church except Tillie. Everyone stared at me—Principal Birchdale, Miss Fletcher, Mrs. Johnson—like I was the Wicked Witch of the West. Like I was poison. Like I had done it. Like I had come to town and killed this man by falling in love with him. But they didn't even know that we had fallen in love. That was the hard part. No one knew it. There was no one to talk to except Tillie. Tillie saw it. She watched us falling in love right in front of her own eyes, she knew it was for real.

The closed casket made it harder. I knew it had to be closed 'cause they couldn't fix him up. But I wanted to see him anyway, wanted to touch him. Part of me still didn't believe he was really dead because I never saw him dead. Last time I saw him he was driving the car and he looked beautiful, he was smiling, his arm was around me. I could still feel his warm hand on my shoulder. They *told* me about the horrible injuries; they *told* me he was DOA. But telling and seeing are two different things. Maybe it would have been easier if I had seen him, no matter how horrible he looked, so I could believe he was really gone, so I could accept the truth. Seeing all those bitter scornful faces around me, I could easily get crazy and start imagining that these assholes took Cal away from me, stole him from the scene of the accident and hid him so he wouldn't leave Valleyview. Maybe it was all Reverend Johnson's idea; asshole Reverend Johnson who was starting to speak, maybe he arranged the whole thing. Maybe they'd doped

Cal up, maybe he was at the Johnsons' house right this very minute. Maybe I was going out of my mind.

Screw you, Reverend Johnson. That's what I kept saying inside my head as I tried to block out his words. His words were aimed at me 'cause he was talking about repentance and salvation but I didn't hear him saying shit about how Cal was talented and how Cal was beautiful and I remembered how Cal called Reverend Johnson a prick. I wanted to stand up and say, *The guy you're talking about said you were a prick. The guy couldn't stand you and you probably couldn't stand him so why the fuck all this two-faced bullshit?* But I didn't say it. I sat there with my head up high looking right at Reverend Johnson because I had as much right there as anyone. I wasn't going to be stared down, I was't going to be scared away, I wasn't going to be pushed out of that church. I was going to the cemetery along with the rest of them—Tillie drove me out there—and I could hear them whispering about me, but I stood there when they lowered the casket, I watched Cal go in the ground and I said a prayer, "God, take care of this good man," I said, and my face was wet. I even asked Tillie to show me Tush's grave which was in the same cemetery, the only cemetery in town. If I was going to say goodbye to Cal, I also wanted to say something to Tush. "I'm sorry, Tush," I said, standing there, determined not to fall apart, and I didn't . . . until that night.

Up in my room at Tillie's hotel, I was shaking and crying until I thought they'd have to take me back to the hospital, not a regular hospital but the loony bin 'cause my mind wasn't right, my mind so cloudy and confused and angry—angry at myself for letting Cal drive, angry at God for letting Cal die—angry at the whole fuckin' world, angry that life has to be so rotten that people you just meet and fall in love with, good people who you've been waiting your whole life to meet, people like Cal have to get killed and leave you alone and crying so hard that my insides ached and the tears kept coming. I just couldn't accept it, I just didn't know what to do, where to go, who to call. In the morning, after being up all night, my nerves shot to hell, I called my mother. Rhonda Silverstar needed her mommy. Can you believe *that*?

"Boy, do I have things to tell you," she said. "Where are you?"

"Ohio."

"You're still on your vacation? Aren't you about ready to come home, Rhonda?"

"Well, Ma, I . . ."

"I'm moving out of your place," she said. "Tomorrow I'm moving into my own apartment in the city. I'm filing for divorce."

Jesus, this wasn't what I wanted to hear.

"I finally got up the nerve. I'll be free as a bird, darling, and the best news is that I even got a job. You should see me. I'm running around like a kid. And you know the part that's killing your father? I'm selling corsets at *Klein's*. On Union Square. Not just selling, but buying. They made me an assistant buyer. All this experience I've had for years, all the help I gave your father, and what did I get back? Nothing. You think he's interested in how I feel or what I want out of life? Forget it. You think he's interested in romance? Don't even think about it. Don't even mention sex. Sex to him is one-two-three. He doesn't understand, your father will never understand how to take his time with a woman. Rush, rush, rush. It's over before it starts. You want to know the truth, Rhonda? The truth is that the man never learned how to lay me . . ."

"Ma! . . ." I tried to stop her.

"I know you're happy for me. You won't have to worry about giving me any money. I'm on my own. Well, almost. I got an apartment on Fifty-sixth Street between Eighth and Ninth. The Parc Vendôme. Beautiful building. They even got a swimming pool in there. Leo will be living with me. It was my idea. It's a good idea, don't you think? His lease is up on his place uptown and he says midtown is more convenient for him. We won't get in each other's way. It'll be good for both of us. As far as your father is concerned, he's back in Bensonhurst, still talking about opening his store but where's the money coming from? This cousin, that cousin, he's tried everyone. The man is hopeless. Now I'll be able to give *you* money if you need it, darling. When are you coming home? Already two men from the store have asked me out. One is very tall and dashing and from the side he looks like Clark

Gable. He's in notions. The other buys hats. A Canadian no less. Nice teeth. Do you think it's too early to start dating, Rhonda? I called the lawyer, Simon Berg—you remember Simon—to start drawing up papers, and you know what Simon told me? He said, 'Let's go out, Gert, I just left my Dottie and I think we should go out. You've always been a desirable woman, Gert, and I think we should go out.' Can you believe it? I told my friend Bea and Bea wasn't surprised. She said he always liked me. What did I know? I wasn't looking, I was being a good wife, I was thinking your father would really make something of himself. So now I'm ready to date. Simon Berg loves music. He said he used to play the fiddle. Him, he'll take me to Carnegie Hall. Your father, he'll take me to the Carnegie Deli. I don't think it's too soon to start dating. For thirty years I've been in prison, so why should I stay in prison a day longer? Your father calls all the time. You should hear him pleading on the phone, begging. It's pathetic. What do I have to say? When you get back, he'll call you. He'll want you to convince me to take him back. He'll use you like he's always used you. But Leo's not having anything to do with him. And if I were you I'd avoid him too, darling. As soon as you get back, we'll have dinner and talk. When will you be back? Leo says he needs to talk to you. Where can he call you? Will you call him?"

"Not now," I mumbled, my head hurting from everything Mom had said, everything happening to me. "Right now isn't a good time."

"What's wrong? You sound like something's wrong. What should be wrong on your vacation?"

"I'll call you when I get back," I said, wanting this call to end.

Wanting the world to end, I spent the rest of the day in bed, wanting the bed to open up and swallow me up so I could forget about Valleyview and Cal and everything else in the world. I slept, I got up and cried some more, I got dressed and went downstairs and nibbled on a piece of chopped steak. Afterwards Tillie came over with a hot piece of apple pie with ice cream piled on top. "Eat this, sugarplum," she said, "and when you're through I'll drive you out to the cemetery. Maybe you want to tell him goodbye again."

Tillie was a doll, if you can call someone her size a doll. She seemed to understand without asking. She drove me out there without talking. The moon was bright and the air was still. Fireflies. I thought of me and Cal dancing by Paradise Lake to that Glenn Miller music. If it was only meant to be for a few days and nights, they were awful sweet. But why couldn't there be more nights? Why . . . I told my mind to shut up. I said, "Cal, I just met you and I fell in love with you and I think you fell for me and this is what it's come to, me talking in the dark to the moon and the night air, but if you hear me, if you're up there or down there or anywhere around here, believe me, baby, I loved you. I think you were the first man I ever really did love."

"You're never going to feel good about this," Tillie told me on the way home, "but maybe now you feel a little better." She patted my arm.

"I do," I said, turning around to watch the cemetery disappear in the darkness.

"Where you headed to now?" asked Tillie, her silly-looking blond pageboy wig reflecting the light of the moon.

"I'm not sure."

"Didn't you say you were on your way to California? I know you're going to do right fine out there, honeychile. You'll do just swell."

"ARE YOU TRAVELING ALONE?"

Men love to ask that question to women on trains. If you answer honestly and say yes, you can just about see their natures rise. Me, if I don't like the tone of his voice or the look in his eyes, I just apply a little powder to my face and ignore him. On this trip out West, I did lots of ignoring.

During and after the war, lots of women traveled alone—lots of women were alone *period*—so I didn't feel all that strange. On the trip between Valleyview and Chicago, I didn't say a word to anyone, except the porters who served food and fixed my bed. I spent most of the time in my little roomette looking at the country passing me by, putting more miles between me and Cal's grave, getting farther away from Mom and her new apartment, Pops's predicament, Leo's problems and the Tush mystery. At this point I'd given up. I felt numb. I just wanted to be alone. A train ride was what I needed, a place where no one could bother me. What was I going to do in California? I had time to decide. Lots of time.

I changed in Chicago. The L.A.-bound train was beautiful, sleek and silver gray with a glass observation car. Everywhere you looked you saw chrome and mirrors, the lights all soft and romantic, the seats plush and roomy. I felt like I could stay on this train forever. I felt irresponsible heading west instead of heading back home, and I liked that feeling. What did I have to go home for? Mom and Pops? Leo? I wanted to go back to Cal. I wanted to bring Cal back to life. Cal was going to help me; he was the first one to care enough. Now no one cared. I was out of work but I still had decent savings. I could get Mom to wire me some of my money once I got to California. I'd buy clothes and I'd hang around until I got bored. Who knows—maybe I wouldn't get bored; maybe I'd look for work out there. Just like I did last time.

Last time was nine years ago, I remembered as I looked out the window of my little compartment. The porter had made up the bed but I couldn't sleep. I was too busy remembering. The night was dark and starless, making me think of the night I had arrived in San Pedro. I'd left the circus in Florida where I realized that even though I had pretty decent control over my body I wasn't made to be no acrobat or trapeze artist. I'd been an acrobat's assistant, working for a woman named Cleo, a worn-out old dame who was always so drunk I never understood how she stayed on that high wire. I'd also fallen for Jacques, the strongman who had muscles like boulders. Jacques was from France. He was thirty, I was seventeen, and to me he was God in heaven. I used to love to watch him lift those weights. He'd go into the crowd and lift two good-sized men, one with each arm. He liked being watched. He loved to undress in front of me and Jacques was the one, the first one, who taught me the art of peeling off clothes. Funny that I learned it from a man, but I did, and Jacques was all man: his waist was slender and his shoulders wide, he could make his pecs shake and his back muscles shimmy. He had these dramatic poses, the same poses that made him Mr. Europe before the war. Now he wanted to be Mr. America and he had me helping him with his English, he had me rubbing his back and oiling down his chest, he had me stripping for him, just the way he stripped for me, and I thought—*hell, this is new, this is exciting, this is wonderful.* I fully intended to be stripping for him—in private, mind you—for the rest of my life until I discovered him and Cleo behind the tiger's cage one dark night fucking like animals, right there on the ground.

That was the thing about the circus—sometimes the performers acted like the animals. Jacques got me feeling like an animal, and I wanted to rip into him, I wanted to kill him when I saw him screwing Cleo, but the two of them just looked at me like nothing was wrong. That's when I really knew the circus wasn't for me.

I had headed to California because California was the farthest place I could think of, far from two-timing Jacques and the Brooklyn home and family that was driving me nuts. I hitchhiked. Tonight I was taking the train—I was even treating myself to first-class—and I smiled thinking about that first trip. In those days, before the war, you didn't see many gals out there on their own. Any gal who'd thumb her way across the country had to be crazy. I was crazy. I didn't think anyone could stop me or hurt me and no one did. Oh, a couple of guys goosed me or grabbed me in the cabins of their trucks, but I'd laugh them off and move away, letting 'em know in a friendly way that they weren't getting any. I wouldn't get hysterical or angry. I'd show them I could handle them, and that got their respect. I think that's when I realized I could handle most men.

Then I saw this phone number in the Los Angeles want ads for a nightclub in San Pedro looking for dancers. I could dance. San Pedro was a port, just south of L.A., and I found a cheap hotel with a view of the water. It was wintertime, but it was warm, and I felt happy to be away from the circus and the smell of elephant shit—the San Pedro harbor smelled good to me—happy to be starting a new adventure, just like I needed a new adventure now. I had some savings, just like I have some savings now, only then I wasn't sure about my talent and wound up worrying too much. I worried I wasn't a real dancer, like the kind you see on Broadway, but it turned out this guy wasn't looking for real dancers; he wanted strippers. "Can you do it?" he asked. All I had to do was pretend I was stripping for Jacques. He had showed me how to work my hips and peel off my nylons; he was the guy who'd tell me to take forever in taking off my bra. "Peekaboo," he'd say in his thick French accent. "Be a little peekaboo. Peekaboo drives the boys crazeee." And suddenly there I was, on this little stage in this little joint, taking it off for all these screaming sailors, driving the boys crazeee. I pretended I was performing for a roomful of

Jacqueses. I liked that. I liked how I got excited by getting the guys excited. After a week or two the owner called me a natural and gave me an extra five bucks. The high wire, the acrobats—they were okay; but this was me. This was where I belonged.

I got up to Hollywood a couple of times, but Hollywood turned out to be a jive. See, I tried out for different clubs on the Strip but at every one they told me I'd do better with the sailors and merchant marines down in San Pedro—in other words, stay where you are. One guy just flat-out said I didn't have the class. "Well, fuck you, buddy," I said, trying to pretend I didn't care, trying not to show just how much he'd hurt me.

So I went back to my sailors and merchant marines. After a few months I had fans and a following. That felt pretty good. What did I need with those Sunset Strip movie stars and glamor pusses anyway? The guys who worked in San Pedro weren't phony, they weren't snobs. I gave 'em a good show and their tips got me back to New York, where with all this experience under my garter belt I eventually wound up at Plotsky's. Strange, then, to be going back to California.

The clickety-clack of the track below me and the memories in my mind, thinking of how much I missed Cal, how pissed I was to have such a good thing, a good man, snubbed out so soon . . . all these thoughts were keeping me up, making me antsy. I looked out the window into black night. Where were we? Nebraska? Kansas? Who knew? I decided to get dressed and go to the dining car. Maybe I could get a drink. Anything was better than this tossing and turning.

The night-shift porter got me a brandy—maybe it would make me sleepy—as I sat alone at a table, picking at a few cashew nuts, leafing through some magazine with pictures of the new 1946 car models. They looked just like the ones for 1945.

"Would you mind a little company?"

I looked up into a sailor's eyes. They were very light gray. This boy didn't look any older than nineteen or twenty. I would have told him no, except his big broad shoulders made me think of

Bobby Marks. He also had a twitch in his right eye which gave him a sort of vulnerable look. His dark wavy hair spilled over his forehead like Frank Sinatra's.

"You can sit down," I said.

He ordered a beer and said he was having trouble sleeping.

"That makes two of us. You going to California?"

"Denver," he said.

"Never been there."

"Not much to it."

"Is Denver home?"

"Yup." His eyes were a little watery. He had these large strong hands. I could see that his arms and legs, like his shoulders, were real developed. There wasn't an ounce of fat on this boy. I thought of Jacques. "But sometimes home," he added, "isn't what it's cracked up to be."

"I understand. You been overseas?"

"Italy."

"Pretty rough, huh."

"I seen things over there I never want to see again. But the worst thing wasn't nothing I saw. It was a letter I got."

He reached in his pocket and pulled out this piece of paper. Like they say, this kid wore his heart on his sleeve. He was so sincere it hurt. "Wanna read it?" he asked.

I did and didn't. But I did. It was written in flowery script, a "Dear John" letter except this guy's name was Paul. His girl's name was Lou Beth. She loved him, she'd always loved him, she said, but it turns out she loved his best friend Bill more. She loved Bill so much they were going off to Seattle to get hitched. Real sorry, Paul, she said, but that's how it is.

"I know it hurts," is all I could say, "but you ain't the only one who hurts. See, I had this guy . . ." I started, but I couldn't go on. I didn't want to tell him the Cal story, I didn't want to think about Cal.

"You can tell me," he said, taking my hand. His skin was warm. Suddenly I knew what I was going to do. I knew it was crazy, but it didn't matter. We were on a train in the middle of nowhere, strangers who had just met, hurting and needing a little companionship, a little love. While the world was asleep I was going to take this boy back to my roomette and strip for him and teach him to strip for me, I was going to teach him how to forget—at least for an hour or two or three—and I was going to forget myself. I was going to remember what it was like to be with someone just 'cause you want to be, just 'cause you're deep down lonely and you like his face and his broad shoulders and you're feeling sorry for him and he's feeling sorry for you and everyone's feeling sorry for themselves. Two strangers on a train in the middle of the night with broken hearts deserve some company, some pleasure, and I'll be damned if I wasn't going to give it and get it.

He was a little hesitant until I said it flat out: "We know what we need, Paul. Let's just do it."

I liked the idea that he'd been away for two years. Maybe he had some girl in Italy or maybe he hadn't. Either way, he'd appreciate me, and God knows I'd appreciate him. I could taste him and I could see him in front of me. Naked. I just wanted to rub his muscles and let him massage my back and move his lips over my nipples, I wanted all these things, and all these things happened as the train went across the country, its whistle piercing the night while Paul pierced me so deep I was crying, I was beating his back with my fists 'cause he was so alive, so good, this boy, this sailor was like a fucking machine, which was just what I wanted, just to lose myself and my pain, turn the pain to pleasure and give him pleasure, suck on him as long as he liked and let him suck on me, let him turn me over and do it doggie style, let me go on top and ride his rail, then let him get back on top, let him hump me hard. This kid was built, his stomach was tight and his equipment was right, thick and long and all-night strong, just keep it up, keep it in, move it higher, slide it, ride it, Paul, on the side and underneath, easy in and easy out, soaking wet and wild, he wasn't stopping, he wasn't losing it, he was beautiful, he'd been wounded like me and ready for a real live woman who wanted him just as much as he wanted her. Welcome home, baby, come on home, come on, Paul, just keep coming and coming and coming till you can't come no more . . .

In the morning, when the conductor called out "Denver!" Paul had to scramble, grabbing his clothes and his bags.

"Will I see you again, Rhonda?"

"In your dreams, honey," I said, kissing his lips.

He started to argue but there wasn't time. The last look I got of my sailor boy was him waving at me from the platform, smiling a big thank-you smile that warmed me almost all the way to California.

"AIRPLANE CRASHES INTO EMPIRE STATE BUILDING; 13 DEAD"

The newspapers at Union Station in L.A. were screaming with the headline. A bomber got lost in the fog and smacked into the seventy-ninth floor. I first thought about my family. Could they have been in the building? But that was ridiculous. What business would they have on the seventy-ninth floor of the Empire State Building? No matter, I was scared. You know how it is when you're far from home; you read about storms or earthquakes or plane crashes and the first thing you think about is your family. I had to call my family to make sure everything was alright. I didn't have Mom's new number, so I called Pops in the old apartment in Bensonhurst.

"California?" he said. "What in God's name are you doing in California?"

"I just called to make sure no one was in the Empire State Building."

"Your mother, who knows where she is? Did she tell you? Do you have any idea what this woman is putting me through?"

"I know, I know."

"You couldn't know. No one knows. She's taken our savings account—"

"Pops, please, I just called to make sure everyone's okay."

"No one's okay. Not me, not your mother, not your brother. Your brother needs to get away from your mother and there he is, living with her. Maybe he's even procuring for her. What do I know? I'm running around here like a chicken without a head. My store should be opening next week but the wholesalers are demanding another five thousand before they'll ship merchandise. Is anyone helping me? Your mother's working at Klein's. Have you heard? That's my reward for thirty years of devotion."

"Well, it sounds like you're making progress with the store. I'm glad to hear that."

"It wasn't easy, believe you me. You shouldn't know from the aggravation. But what about this other money? Where's it going to come from? Can you . . ."

"You'll find it, Pops. You'll come through."

"Thank you, Rhonda. That's the first encouraging word I've heard from a member of my family. But I need more than words, I need cash. And what's this business about California? I thought you were in Ohio or someplace. What's going on with you, Rhonda?"

"I'm not sure. I just needed to get away."

"You picked some time. Are you going to see Morris?"

"Morris?"

"My brother. Your Uncle Mo. He's out there someplace. God knows where."

"Jeez, I forgot about that. Uncle Mo. Yeah, maybe I'll look him up."

"If you do, tell him he's a bum. Tell him his brother said so."

Morris Silverstern—I looked up the name in the directory, standing right there in a phone booth in Union Station. It was a strange place to start my stay in L.A. In spite of all my feelings about the crazy Silversterns, here I was calling another Silverstern. Maybe I needed a family connection. And besides, I was curious about Uncle Mo, the man who disappeared a decade ago during the Depression. I remembered how he'd take me backstage and introduce me to Rags Ragland and Georgia Sothern. He knew all the showgirls and the bookies. Uncle Mo was the king of the delis, the guy who sat at the comic's table with Phil Silvers and Bert Lahr and Joe E. Brown. Once I even met Eddie Cantor ordering custom-made shirts in Mo's Men Store on Broadway. Last time I saw my Uncle Morris—it had to be eleven, twelve years ago—I couldn't have been older than fifteen. It was just before I'd run away with the circus. Now I suddenly wanted to see him. Without knowing it, maybe he was the deep-down reason I had come to California. Right now anything to keep my mind off Cal was good. The sailor on the train had done that. Maybe seeing a long-lost uncle might do it some more.

"Rhonda? Little Rhonda?"

"Not so little, Uncle Mo."

"Where are you?"

"Union Station."

"In Los Angeles? You're here in Los Angeles? Are you with your folks?"

"No, I'm alone."

"I'll come down and get you."

"You will?"

"Of course I will. What, I'm going to let my niece wander around this big city by herself? Give me a half-hour. Wait for me out front."

I was excited. After all, for years Mo was talked about like he was dead. I was about to see a dead man. He had run out when the Depression had shut down his business. My father was so furious with him all contact was cut off. I remembered trying to call Mo when I was in San Pedro nine years ago, but there was no number or clue to where he was living. And now, just like that, he was about to pop back in my life.

Walking through the train station, I thought the place looked like a big Spanish church. Outside the sun was shining through tall skinny palm trees. Compared to New York City, it seemed so quiet. I was looking for Uncle Mo to pull up in an old jalopy, so it took a while to realize that was him behind the wheel of this fancy English roadster—a Rolls-Royce or a Bentley, one of those things—with the top down. It was doubly hard recognizing him because he had on these big sunglasses, this wide-brimmed straw hat, a white suit and a banana yellow sport shirt open at the neck.

"Rhonda!" he yelled, waving at me. "Look at you!"

Before the train had pulled in, I had changed into a loose silk dress with flowers and oranges all over it, reminding me of California. It wasn't too revealing, but with a figure like mine you can't help revealing something.

As I got in the car, he pinched my cheek before kissing it. He smelled like cigar smoke and cologne. He face was too tan; there were sun splotches all over his forehead and lines around his eyes. I'd remembered Mo as a suave guy; now he was somewhere around fifty-five and trying hard to look younger. He'd gotten pudgy around the middle. When he smiled, though, his face turned sweet; you wouldn't call him handsome, but he had this charm, this something that said, "I like you and you gotta like me." Unlike Pops, who was too pissed off to be a really good salesman, Mo could sell jockstraps to *castrati*—that's what Mom always said. Fact is, Mom and Mo always seemed a better match than Mom and Pops. But Mo was one of those hard-core bachelors, so the first thing I asked him was whether some dame had finally caught him.

"You kidding? Never, kiddo, not Mo. How 'bout you? Look at you, you've turned into a ravishing beauty. You gotta have a fella. Lots of them."

He was looking at me like a man but talking to me like I was still a teenaged girl.

"I've been working at Plotsky's." I didn't want to put on no acts; I wanted to level with my uncle right away; I wanted to let him know I was all-the-way grown up. "I changed my name to Rhonda Silverstar."

"You been working burlesque?" He looked me over again. He didn't seemed displeased. In fact, he chuckled to himself. "Well, well, what do your folks have to say about that, Rhonda?"

"What can they say? I make good money. I been on my own a long time now, Uncle Mo. I'm doing good."

"And what are you doing out here?"

"I needed a breather. Me and old man Plotsky, we didn't see eye to eye."

"I remember Plotsky. Not a bad guy. But what happened, did the bum make a move on you?" asked Uncle Mo, ready to get angry.

"Nothing like that. He just didn't like my act. Anyway, I'm here to relax. I just wanted to get away."

We were driving up Wilshire Boulevard, driving past these beautiful department stores—Bullock's, I. Magnin—with the sun shining down and me feeling alright about being here. With his fancy car and crazy shades, my uncle was a character and now he was seeing that his niece had turned out to be something of a character herself.

"What about you, Uncle Mo? You look like you're doing good."

"I'm surviving, baby," he said. "What else can you do in this world? What about your father? I wrote him a letter—that must have been five, six years ago—but I never heard back. He's still mad with me. He'll be mad until the day he dies."

"Him and Mom have split up."

"Oy. He got involved with someone else?"

"I think it's the other way around."

"Poor Bernie. He was always such a *schlemiel*."

"You're talking about my father," I said defensively.

"A sweet *schlemiel*, but a *schlemiel*."

"I don't think he's so sweet."

"Sweet underneath it all."

"He was always mad at me, that's all I remember," I said.

"Me too. Didn't I try to take him into my business? Didn't I try to help him?"

"But you went broke."

"This was before I went broke, and after. Anyway, I'm not broke now."

We turned off Sunset Boulevard and pulled up to a nice-looking house with lots of pretty flowers in the front yard. The house looked like an oversized bungalow. It wasn't big, but painted fresh white. Inside, the place smelled of pot roast.

"Rhonda," he said, taking me through the living room, with its fancy upholstered furniture and seascape paintings, into the kitchen, "meet Tina." Standing over the stove, an apron covering her billowy green dress, was Tina Lovestrong. I recognized her right away. This a woman they called "The Bomb" when she was stripping in the thirties. She was hot shit back then. In fact, I began remembering that it was Uncle Mo who had introduced me to her one night backstage when I was just a kid. It had to be Tina because of the beauty mark on her left cheek and her trademark blond hair caught in a big fluffy bun above her neck. She looked old, sixty, maybe sixty-five, but pretty well preserved. The skin on her face was still tight. She had gotten fat—she had a big stomach and spread-out hips—and her nose had a little break about two-thirds of the way down. Her blue eyes were still bright, though, and I could tell that the dye job on her hair was high priced. Looking at her, I felt surprised, jealous and weird, like I was looking at myself as an old lady.

"Guess what," Mo told Tina. "My niece Rhonda here—she's gorgeous, ain't she?—she's been working at Plotsky's. Plotsky bills her as Rhonda Silverstar."

"I never trusted Plotsky," said Tina without missing a beat. She had a heavy flat-A Midwest accent. She looked in my eye—she didn't look over my body—which made me feel good. "In my book, that Plotsky was always a two-faced son of a bitch."

"Think so?" asked Mo.

"You're right, Miss Lovestrong."

"Call me Tina. So he gave you a hard time, huh?"

"I walked out."

"Good for you. Years ago, I wanted to form a union. But who ever heard of a strippers' union? I didn't even know Mo had family—and here you come out of nowhere. I'm happy to meet you, Rhonda, I really am. My family cut me off the minute they learned I was stripping. That was in Chicago, back in the twenties. Haven't heard from them since. But you know what I say? I say good riddance to bad garbage. How about your family, how'd they take it, sweetie?"

"Not all that great."

"There you go. You see," said Tina, shaking some salt into the pot roast and stirring it vigorously, "nothing changes. Oh, well, you here for vacation or you looking for work?"

"Not sure."

"Well, there's no reason to hurry up and decide. Your uncle and me, we got lots of room and we're happy to have you. We'll take you up to Miramba's on the Strip tonight. That's where the movie stars like to go dancing. Last week we saw Dorothy Lamour and Artie Shaw up there."

"Together?" I wanted to know.

"Who knows who's together? It doesn't matter 'cause this is Hollywood, it's fun out here, not like New York, where everyone takes everything so goddamn seriously. Ain't that right, Mo?"

"See how smart Tina is, Rhonda? I got me a sharp cookie here, don't I?" Mo put his finger in the pot roast pot and brought the dripping sauce to his lips. He tasted the stew as Tina lovingly tapped him on the top of the head with her spoon. They were a cute couple.

"Now, Rhonda," said Mo, taking me through the house, "this is your bedroom back here. Me and Tina, we're right across the hall from you. You even got your own bathroom."

"Driving over here you said you didn't have a girlfriend, Uncle Mo, but I see . . ."

"You asked me about a wife. Me and Tina, we're just friends. Real good friends. Now you unpack while I take a little nap."

The small bedroom looked out on the backyard. I never had a backyard before. There were trees out there with real oranges hanging from the branches.

"Let me air out this place for you," said Tina, walking in and pushing open the window. "Your uncle's already sleeping like a log. Every afternoon he sleeps. Maybe you wanna take a nap too, sweetie? You had a long train ride."

"I think I could sleep," I said. "But let me ask you something, Tina . . ."

"If you don't mind, Rhonda, I'd like you to call me *Aunt* Tina. See, I never had a niece before."

"Okay, Aunt Tina. I wanted to ask you about Uncle Mo. Does he still have a clothing store or what?"

"Oh, that. No, he's in a different line of work. He found some partners. Big men. They're in investments. I don't exactly know what investments, but the money's terrific. You see how he lives. Now if I could only get him to understand the value of marriage. Marriage is something he don't understand. He's scared of marriage. Maybe you could help me make him understand, Rhonda. I see how much he cares for you. From the minute you called from the station, he's been smiling."

"Well, Tina . . ."

"*Aunt* Tina . . ."

"Aunt Tina, I just gotta say I'm smiling too."

She kissed me on the cheek and left me alone. I closed the curtains, got undressed and stretched out on the bed. Across the hallway I could hear Mo snoring. Sleep sounded good. Sleep would be a relief. I thought about Cal in Ohio and Paul on the train. All I'd been through. I thought about my first trip out here and how much easier this was. How nice this was. How welcomed I felt. It was like these people really wanted me around. It was like Mo was the father I wanted and Tina the mother I never had, parents who understood. They didn't judge me or look down on me. They didn't need my money or my advice. Well, maybe Tina could use my help in getting Mo to marry her, but I understood that. It was sweet of her to ask. She trusted me. I trusted her. She was an old veteran of the burlesque wars who found a good life with a good man in sunny California. I really looked forward to getting to know her and talking to her more. I really looked forward to closing my eyes and letting sleep fall all over me . . .

. . . I woke with a scream . . . the knife . . . the wounds . . . the

blood everywhere . . . the knife plunging into her breasts, into her
. . . it was the same horror I was trying to forget . . .

"My God, what's wrong, sweetie?" Tina was there by my side.

"This dream," I said, short of breath, my heart hammering.

"Tell me about it."

"My friend Teresa. I dreamt about Tush. Jesus, I dreamt the
whole thing over again, and I was there, I was in the room, I saw
the knife going in, stabbing her where no one should ever be
stabbed, and I tried to stop the killer but I couldn't move my arms,
I couldn't even scream for help and the worst part was I couldn't
close my eyes, I had to stand there and watch 'cause my hands
were tied together and I was scared to death the killer would get
me next, and he was, he was moving over to me when I woke
up . . ."

"There, there," said Tina, "it's all over. It was just a dream."

"Except it really happened."

"What do you mean?"

I sat up in bed and told Tina the whole story, about the murder
and Captain Donegan and Sandy and Bull and Billie Holiday,
about Reverend Johnson and going to Valleyview and meeting Cal
and falling in love with Cal and what happened to Cal. I told her
everything except about meeting Paul on the train because that
was over and that didn't matter. I had thought Paul would help,
just like I thought Cal would help, but nothing was helping. Tush's
murder was just as fresh, just as awful, with me helpless to do a
goddamn thing.

"Poor baby," said Tina, mopping my brow with a wet towel,
"that's some horrible story you got there. And your friend . . .
that's no way to go. You know, sweetie, that's every stripper's
nightmare."

"It is?"

"I've had that nightmare hundreds of times, and so did most of
the girls I worked with over the years. We're afraid there's a maniac
out there. The idea is that we're supposed to be stimulatin' men,
and there ain't nothing wrong with that—you and me know there's
an art to it—but what happens when we stimulate the wrong guy?

In the back of our brains, no matter how gutsy we are—and girls like us are plenty gutsy—in the back of our brains we can't help thinking about that. With your friend Teresa, the nightmare came true. And of course the asshole cops don't give two shits, no one cares 'cause they don't got no respect for us anyways. We're the only ones who respect each other. That's why you been dying for your friend. I understand, Rhonda, I honest to God understand. I feel for you, and I see why you had to get the hell out of New York. And then everything that happened to you in Ohio . . . well, I don't see how you didn't go completely nuts. I'm so glad you're here with me and Mo. You need some people taking care of you instead of you trying to take care of everyone else."

"But I want to find out who killed her . . ."

"Sure you do, and you've been trying like hell. But now you need to stop, Rhonda. I want you to take a break and pretend like you're on vacation. Let me and Mo do for you. You just rest, sweetie . . . let me bring you some milk and cookies, I baked them myself . . ."

Slowly my shallow breathing stopped and I was starting to feel normal again. Tina came back with a tray she placed on my lap as I sat up in bed. The milk was cold and the chocolate chip cookies were sweet. I felt a little dumb. I wasn't a little girl; I was twenty-six years old and didn't need to be treated like a baby. Except I was liking it. I knew it was weird having this old burlesque queen wait on me hand and foot—it was almost like she was worrying after a poodle—but if it was making her happy and making me happy, why not? At least she knew just what I was going through.

That night, sitting in the back of Uncle Mo's car as we drove down to the Strip, I felt even more like a child with new parents. Morris and Tina were up front, whistling to Bing Crosby on the radio. They were dressed up in evening clothes. Tina had on diamond earrings and a necklace dripping with more diamonds. I kept wondering about Uncle Mo's business. I was wearing the only good dress I'd brought for the trip, a fancy black affair, and was looking forward to tomorrow when Tina . . . Aunt Tina . . . said she'd take me shopping in Beverly Hills. I'd never been to Beverly

Hills. I also had never been to Miramba's. Miramba's wasn't one of the clubs where I auditioned the last time I was in L.A. It wasn't in business back then. Now it was the hottest thing on the Strip.

The waiters wore tuxes and there were antique mirrors and marble columns and vases stuffed with yellow roses on every table. Morris ordered champagne and Caesar salads and filet mignons with mushroom caps and chocolate soufflés and afterwards there was a floor show and when the Harry James big band came out and played "Two O'Clock Jump" Uncle Mo asked me to dance and whirled me around the floor, laughing all the while, waving to his cronies, and when Harry James played "Ciribiribin" Mo danced with Tina who despite her size was still very graceful. By her moves I could see what a great stripper she used to be.

"Morris," said an older man who came over to our table, "who's your young friend?"

"My niece Rhonda. She's a dancer. A professional. You could give her work, Jake, but keep in mind she gets top dollar. Jake Epstein, Rhonda Silverstern . . . no, Silverstar . . . Rhonda Silverstar, that's her professional name."

"My pleasure," said Jake. He had to be in his sixties, but he had all his hair, gray and wavy, and was very trim and tall and I could see that even his eyebrows were plucked and his nails were buffed and polished. He smelled good.

"Jake's a producer," said Mo.

"What was that?" asked Jake.

"I said you're a *producer*," repeated Mo in a louder voice, whispering to me that Jake was hard of hearing.

"A *New York* producer," Jake corrected. "I'm just in Hollywood looking for talent. Would you mind, Miss Silverstar, if I gave you my card? I wish you'd call me tomorrow at my hotel." He handed me a card.

"Any interviews, Jake," said Mo loudly, winking, "and I come along. Got it?"

"You'd be more than welcome, my friend," Jake was quick to say, taking my hand and kissing it.

"Pretty slick," I said to Tina when Jake was gone.

"I think he's legit," Tina told me. "He's put on a couple of Broadway shows. Jake's legit, ain't he, Mo?"

"No one's legit in this world," said Mo. "He just ain't been caught yet."

Tina and I laughed. Seeing the way everyone in the joint knew Uncle Mo, the way the waiters were making such a fuss over him, it looked like he'd really come up in the world. He'd become a big shot in Hollywood, my uncle, and on top of that he was protective and proud of me and when some sleazy guy asked me to dance Morris gave him such a look the guy disappeared P.D.Q.

"You know, Mo," said Tina, "all this classy stuff is nice, but maybe Rhonda would like to hear some jazz. Most of the girls like jazz these days. What do you say, Rhonda?"

I thought of Sandy and Abraham and how Tush loved jazz. "Sure," I said.

"Swell. Let's hit Billy Berg's. He's got the best jazz club in town. No telling who we'll see there."

We saw Clark Gable, honest to God, *Clark Gable*. I tried not to stare, but who wouldn't stare at Clark Gable? The club was down on Vine Street and the singer was called Harry "the Hipster" Gibson, a wiry guy who played hot boogie woogie piano and sang songs like "Who Put the Benzedrine in Mrs. Murphy's Ovaltine?", "4F Ferdinand the Frantic Freak," and "Get Your Juices at the Deuces." He was funny and crazy and when Gable left Orson Welles walked in and so did Robert Mitchum who I'd seen last year in "Thirty Seconds Over Tokyo"—he was gorgeous—and my head was spinning from the music and the stars when Tina, I mean Aunt Tina, turned to me and asked me whether I'd ever smoked reefer because Uncle Mo hated it, he didn't understand it, but she had learned to like it from some of her jazz friends, and why didn't we go to the ladies' room because she had a stick of pot. Why not?

When we got back to the table the jazz sounded better than ever and there were Orson and Robert across the room and here I was in Hollywood having the time of my life, I wasn't even feeling guilty, for the first time in days I wasn't thinking about Cal or Tush, wasn't thinking about nothing except what a funny lady this Aunt Tina was with her reefer and sticking her elbow in my ribs when Robert Mitchum walked by—she raised her eyebrows as if to say, "Get a load of this hunk of man!"—but she was holding Mo's hand the whole time, and I didn't think she was two-timing him, I really didn't, and I started to believe that yes, he should marry her and yes, they should adopt me so I could become their little girl and live happily ever after just like in a fairy tale.

Back in the car, riding home, Mo smelled the pot on our breath and smiled. If he'd been my old man he'd have had a heart attack, probably have had me arrested. "You're corrupting my little niece," is all Mo told Tina, but he was smiling when he said it.

"Rhonda can't be corrupted," said my new aunt. "She's too sweet." Tina kissed me on the cheek.

That night I slept like a baby. I didn't have no bad dreams, no scary nightmares. I felt so secure in the little bedroom with the orange trees in the backyard. When I woke up, Uncle Mo was still snoring. Aunt Tina made me eggs and toast and reminded me to call Jake Epstein at his hotel. He wanted to have dinner with me.

"What do you think?" I asked Tina.

"I think he's looking to get laid."

"Sounds like it."

"On the other hand, he does hire dancers for his shows, and you can dance. You and me, sweetie, we both know that stripping is harder than dancing. Dancing's part of stripping—the easy part."

I'd been saying the same thing for years.

"The problem is . . . who wants to sleep with Jake Epstein? Certainly not you."

"Certainly not."

"Now maybe—just maybe—he's one of those guys who wants to have a beautiful companion for dinner. How many guys like that have you known?"

I just smiled.

"If you're lucky, that's all he wants. A chance to impress the gents when he walks into the club with you on his arm. Did he mention anything about dancing?"

"He said he'd audition me in his room."

Tina laughed out loud. "At least he's letting you know where you stand. What'd you tell him?"

"I said I'd call him back."

"That's my gal. Keep him waiting, keep him praying. You'll think about it while we're shopping. Meanwhile, let's hit the stores. But first, let's hit up Uncle Mo. He did good business last week."

Mo was in a bathrobe, eating a grapefruit which he topped off with his morning cigar, a cup of strong java and the racing form. "While you girls go shopping I'll make my calls and then go to the track."

"How much you risking today, Mo?" asked Tina.

"Couple of thou."

"Well, we gals deserve equal rights with the ponies. Put two on them and two on us—and we'll come back with something gorgeous on our backs. What do you say?"

Mo reached into his robe, grabbed a roll of hundreds and started peeling them off. I was trying not to act too impressed—I'd been around lots of cash before—but this was my uncle. And while Tina went off to get dressed, I couldn't help thinking of Pops. Maybe he wasn't the greatest guy in the world, and maybe he never understood me, maybe he was a loser and maybe Mom was right to leave him, but there he was in Brooklyn all alone—me out here, Leo and Mom in Manhattan—looking for another five thousand to get the merchandise in his store that he'd been dying to reopen. And here was his brother with all this money.

"Look, Uncle Mo," I said, "I don't want you to think I'm being greedy."

He reached for his roll again. "What do you need, Rhonda? Just let me know. It's not a problem."

"It's not me. It's my father."

"Oy. Bernie. Do we have to talk about Bernie?"

I told him the story about Pops and his store and the cash he needed. I told Mo I didn't need money—I had some savings of my own—but I didn't have enough to see Pops through and maybe, as his brother, he could help him out.

"You know something, Rhonda, you're a doll. You really are. You're begging for your old man and you're breaking my heart. I don't want to have to tell you about the aggravation he's given me. The jealousy. The backbiting. The money he's borrowed and never paid back. Things he said to our father. Things he told our mother about me. Things that never can be forgotten. *Never.* He didn't like the people I did business with and when I went broke he didn't like me moving out here. When I called, he didn't want to talk. When I wrote, I heard nothing back. Once, when I first got here, I asked for money. Once, mind you. I was desperate. But Bernie, he didn't send a dime. Fine, I forgot it. I forgave him. But now his daughter comes to me, an adorable child who has grown into a beautiful woman, and she asks me to help his new business get started. So what am I supposed to say to her? I don't want her to think I'm a louse. I don't want her to go around calling me cheap. She sees I have money. She sees California has been good to me, and no matter what Bernie might think I have *not* become a bum. You know what I'm going to tell her? I'm going to tell her yes because I never had a daughter so lovely, because I never had children of my own, I can't refuse her. That's right, Rhonda. Tomorrow I'll call my bookkeeper and I'll tell him, send your father a check. Send him the goddamn money. But I'm going to write him, I'm going to say, 'It's not because of you, Bernie, it's because of the beautiful daughter you produced'—that's what I'm going to say."

I threw my arms around Uncle Mo and kissed him on the cheek. "You're a wonderful man," I said.

That whole day was wonderful. Especially shopping with Tina. When I used to go shopping with my mother, especially lately, she was the main customer, not me. Ever since I'd started making good money, it turned out I'd be buying more for her than for myself. Why did I do that? Maybe it was because, unlike Pops, Mom never said nothing bad about me working at Plotsky's. Maybe buying her clothes was her payoff for leaving me alone, for not making me feel bad. Who knows? All I know is that I hated shopping with Gert Silverstern. When I'd get home I'd be mixed up—feeling good for being generous, feeling bad for being stupid. But with Tina, with Aunt Tina, there was none of that. I came first.

There was a Saks Fifth Avenue in Beverly Hills where Tina took me to the cosmetic counter and loaded me up with Merle Oberon eye makeup—mascara, eyebrow pencil and eye shadow—applying it right there on the spot where we piled up on perfumes and powders before taking off for the bathing suits. "You got the kind of figure I'd die for, even in my prime," said Tina. "Even in my prime my hips were too big." The one-piece Esther Williams models by Cole of California fit perfectly. "Take one in every color," insisted my new aunt, handing the saleswoman cash for four bathing suits. Then there were Lily Daché hats with feathers and hats with nets and a gorgeous pink suit by Adrian not to mention a couple of low-cut blouses and high-heeled Ferragamo shoes in brown and gray suede. "But what are you getting for yourself?" I asked Tina. "Pleasure," she answered. "I'm getting pleasure out of watching you. Just enjoy."

Over lunch in the ladies' tearoom we talked turkey. "You got two, maybe three years left in burlesque," said Tina. "Some of us tried to push it past thirty. You can do it, but you pay a price. It's a young girl's game. The sooner you're out, the better. I waited too long. Between us chickens, I was sagging pretty bad. Oh, I had ways of hiding the fat and puffing myself up and out, but I was hurting. I waited too long to try and go legit. If you're going to make a move, make it now."

"You're saying I should see Jake Epstein."

"I'm saying be smart."

I called his hotel and arranged to meet him there that night.

"Good," said Tina when I got back to the table. "Now, what are you going to wear?"

"I think I got enough stuff."

"We haven't been to lingerie. The lingerie at Saks is to die for."

Why lingerie? I started wondering whether Tina was in on something with Jake . . . whether she was setting me up.

"I really don't need no lingerie," I said.

"A girl never has enough lingerie."

The silk dressing gown was fabulously sexy and cost twenty bucks. Before we left the store we added a few handbags to our haul and needed two guys to carry our boxes to the cab.

When we got home, Mo was counting his cash; his roll had doubled. Right there at the kitchen table he was flipping through tens of hundred-dollar bills. The man must have had $20,000 in cold cash.

"Good day at the track?" asked Tina.

"The track, the business, everything's going right. Do I get a fashion show?"

"Show him, Rhonda. Show him what you got."

After a half-hour of modeling, I decided to take a rest. I was happy but tired, my head spinning from feeling like a ten-year-old girl. From the bedroom, I could hear them talking.

"She's seeing Epstein tonight," Tina told Mo.

"We'll all have dinner together," Mo said.

"No, let her go alone. It's business."

My suspicions came back, but I slept anyway. No dreams, just deep-dead sleep. An hour later I woke up, bathed, put on the new eyeliner, the new pink suit, the new shoes. Tina handed me the new bag. "Gorgeous," she said. "Simply gorgeous."

Mo kissed me goodbye and walked me to the door. Jake Epstein sent a limo and a driver. On the way over, I kept thinking—*what am I getting into?*

When I saw him in his hotel suite, I was startled. He'd dyed his gray hair jet black. It didn't make him look younger, just strange. Wearing a double-breasted blue flannel robe, he was pacing in front of a half-dozen paintings leaning against the wall. Very crazy-looking paintings.

"Do you like art, Rhonda?" he asked.

"Sure."

"What was that?"

I forgot about his hearing problem and had to shout to be heard. "*I love art!*"

"Now today," he said, "today everything is different. Look at this picture of a woman. She's got three noses and four chins. They call this modern. Do you like it? I don't. Personally, I think it's nuts, but everyone says buy this stuff today and tomorrow it'll double in value. Go modern. You think I should go modern?"

"I wouldn't know."

"What?"

"*I don't know!*"

"Who does? I know dancing, though. And I know figures." He turned his attention to me. "And you, dear girl, you got a knockout of a figure."

I reached in my purse for a cigarette and saw the silk dressing gown had been stuffed in there. Tina must have put it there.

"I talked to Tina today," he said. "I didn't know she had retired."

"She retired from burlesque ages ago."

"I don't mean burlesque. That was a long time ago. I knew her back then too. Beautiful dame. I mean, she's not in business anymore. Mo made her quit."

"Quit what?"

"I presume that's how you know her . . . from her old business."

"I'm her niece. Her *niece!*"

"She called all the girls her nieces. No one was ever more devoted to her girls than Tina."

My heart sank. I'd halfway seen it coming earlier in the day but didn't want to believe it. Oh, well. Who was I to judge? But here I was, sent by Tina.

"Look, Mr. Epstein . . ."

"I'm not a small-time operator, I'll tell you that, Rhonda. In the fall, I'm mounting a musical, *America on Parade*. It might not be Rodgers and Hammerstein, maybe it won't be *Carousel*, but the costumes are out of this world and I'm sparing no expense. We're opening at the Royale Theater on Forty-fifth Street. A Broadway theater. My lead singer is better than Dick Haymes and I'm picking all the chorus girls myself. Already I have five girls. You want to have dinner up here or downstairs?"

"I want to tell you something, Mr. Epstein."

"A little louder, honey."

"*Okay*," I shouted. "*There's been a mistake. Tina, well, Tina is a nice lady . . .*"

"Wonderful person. Known her for years. Always gotten me the best girls."

"*Well, there's been a mistake. You see, Mo Silverstern is my uncle, he really is my father's brother, and I was just visiting him out here and I'm not . . . I don't want to—*"

"Who's asking? Did I ask? I never force myself. I don't believe in forcing. You're a Jewish girl, aren't you, Rhonda?"

"Yes."

"Never in my life would I impose myself on a Jewish girl. I can respect whatever you need for me to respect. No one's forcing nothing. I ask only one thing. Take off your clothes. That way I can tell if you're right for my musical revue. It won't kill you. You can do me the favor. You can change in the bathroom, you can take them off in front of me, you can do it any way you want."

The old man was being decent about this. I appreciated his attitude and figured, since this was some kind of audition, I might as well put my best foot forward. I'd do a little strip for him. I went to the bathroom and came out wearing the flimsy dressing gown with a pair of black panties underneath. I didn't want to go overboard or give Epstein a heart attack, but I did want to show him that I knew my stuff. When I was through, he was all smiles, saying just what I wanted to hear.

"You're a pro."

"Thank you."

He came over to me and stroked my cheek. I could see he was excited. "If it's a matter of money . . ." he said.

"I don't need no money, Mr. Epstein," I shouted.

"We don't have to do everything, we could play around, maybe just a little suck . . ."

Why not make the old guy happy by sucking him off? Because, well, because I just didn't want to. I didn't want to feel cheap, I didn't want to see his schlong, I didn't want to fake it like I was coming. I just wasn't interested.

"Okay," he said, backing down. "I said you're a professional, and I meant it. Rehearsals start next month and I expect you to be there. Now if you'll excuse me, I have another appointment."

By the time I went to the bathroom, changed, fixed my face, told him goodbye and headed down the hallway for the elevator, another woman was on her way up. Epstein worked fast. She was even younger than me. I could tell by her hungry face that she wouldn't disappoint him.

It didn't bother me that Jake had withdrawn his dinner invitation. At least he had the driver take me back. But I wasn't ready to go back. I didn't want to face Tina tonight. It hurt me to think about her as a madam. I didn't want her to know that I knew what was happening. Not that she'd care—or not that I even cared that much. Or did I? She'd gone from stripping to running call girls. For the past two days I thought she was so classy, I thought she'd gone from stripping to just living a good life. Another false impression. Like Tush?

Riding in the limo, my eyes half-closed, a theater caught my eye—the Los Angeles Philharmonic Auditorium. People were pouring in. I glanced up at the marquee. TONIGHT ONLY! DUKE ELLINGTON. SPECIAL GUEST STAR MISS BILLIE HOLIDAY

"Stop!" I told the driver. "Let me out here."

I bought one of the last tickets, way up in the balcony. The place was packed. I had gotten there just in time. Hey, I was excited. The lights went down and the emcee introduced Billie who came out in a white sleeveless gown with white gloves going all up her arms and the white gardenia in her hair. The emcee gave her the Esquire Award as the best jazz singer of 1945 and introduced celebrities in the audience—Danny Kaye, Lionel Barrymore and Johnny Mercer—who came up to congratulate her and kiss her on the cheek. She sang "Body and Soul" and "Strange Fruit," "He's Funny that Way" and "Travelin' Light" in a way that I thought she was singing right to me, her little-girl-wise-woman voice small but deep with so much feeling her fans went wild. I knew she knew all about the Plotskys and Epsteins of the world. I knew she knew all there was to know about women and our troubles with men. When she sang "God bless the child that's got her own," I knew her message was my message and I decided to go backstage and say hello and let her know that I thought she was a goddamn great artist, tough as nails and sweet as sugar at the same time. I loved the way the woman sang.

"You're Teresa's friend," she said in that smooth slurry voice of hers. She was in her dressing room smoking a cigarette and sipping a glass of something. "What are you doing out here, baby?"

"Just wanted to tell you that you're the greatest."

"Appreciate it. I guess you heard about Bull."

"No. What about Bull?"

"Abraham Jones hipped me just before I left the city. Said they picked him up on rape. Raped a white girl in Queens. Cut her too. Guess they'll make the connection to Tush. Hope the motherfucker fries."

Bull . . . rape . . . just like Billie told me last time . . . Bull had been leaning on Tush . . . I should have known it . . . Billie was so honest . . . but Bull was so gentle, such a tender teddy bear of a guy . . . how could I have been so wrong about Bull?

"Sorry to break the news to you, baby," said Billie. "But sometimes we see what we wanna see, not what's really there."

I needed to get out of there. Needed to sleep and forget everything because my mind couldn't handle this. First, I'd been wrong about Teresa. Then Tina. Now Bull. All this time I thought I was so sharp about the world, but I was duller than dishwater. I was stupid. Billie was right; I'd been blind to everyone and everything. I hailed a cab and gave him Mo's address. "Step on it," I said.

Driving down Sunset, a kid was hawking papers, calling out the news—"Atom Bomb Dropped on Japan! 20,000 Tons of TNT!" I felt a jolt, like the whole world was coming apart, like *I* was coming apart.

"Look, lady," said the cabbie as he tried turning onto Uncle Mo's street. "We can't get in here."

"Why? What's wrong?"

"The cops got the street blocked off. Something happened. It looks like the bomb squad."

I got out. I looked down the street. Now my heart really started thumping. Atom bombs. Bombs. Fire. A house was on fire. I started running, running towards the house . . . it couldn't be Uncle Mo's house . . . but the closer I got the more I was sure . . . I wasn't crazy, wasn't making it up . . . I saw the house . . . the house burning . . . burning! . . . not all of it but the back . . . the back of the house in flames . . . fire shooting into the sky . . . cops everywhere . . . firemen running around . . . ambulances . . . sirens . . . I grabbed the cops and the firemen . . . "what happened? where are they?" . . . "it was a bomb . . . back in the bedroom" . . . what kind of bomb? . . . was it the Japanese? What the fuck was happening? A newspaper reporter was shaking his head. "Gangland execution . . . Mo Silverstern and some dame . . . sticks of dynamite thrown through his bedroom window . . . both on their way to the morgue . . ."

OUT OF NOWHERE

Nothing. Blank. I opened my eyes hoping my eyes wouldn't work. I didn't want to see the lamp next to the bed. I didn't want to look around the hotel room and remember where I was. I didn't want to hear the ringing phone or the cars outside or the the baby crying down the hall. The baby could have been me. I wanted to be a baby 'cause babies don't have to think or remember or figure things out. I couldn't sleep anymore. My dreams were so jumbled I was glad I'd forgotten them, but wide-awake real-life staring me in the face was crazier and scarier than any dream. It was August and I could feel the heat of the sun pushing against the shade. I could feel my brain pushing against my skull. I was feeling fire, still seeing the fire from two nights ago—but I was also feeling frozen. Staring across the room from me were the clothes Tina had bought me. I knew she'd want me to have them. Mo too. They were in a closet in the living room and didn't get burned. I took all the stuff to the hotel. It was almost like if I had the clothes I could also have my uncle and my "aunt"; I could bring them back to life. I could put the fire out. I wouldn't have to think about talking to my mother and my father who had read the papers in New York about how Morris Silverstern and his lady were rubbed out in a mob hit, Morris Silverstern, the rags said, "who reputedly had ties to Nathan Waller, the most notorious underworld boss on the West Coast."

"I told you he was a bum!" my father was screaming at me when I told him I was alright. "He was covered with dirt when he had his store on Broadway. That's why he ran to California. So

153

what does he do out there? He finds more dirt. You didn't believe me. Now you do. My God, Rhonda, you could have been killed!"

"You never said anything about mobsters."

"You never listened. You hear what you want to hear, Rhonda. But this brother of mine has been playing around with hoodlums ever since we were kids. Our mother warned him. Our father beat him. But nothing sank in. He'd play one loan shark against another. He'd cheat the numbers men, carry their money—he started off as a runner—but he'd always take for himself. The older he got, the more he took, the bigger the gangsters. He got caught a couple of times but weaseled his way out. Now there's no more weaseling. Mo thought he was so smart."

"He was all set to send you money," I told Pops.

"He told you that? He's been telling me that for the past forty years."

"I'm wiring you money!" was all Mom said. "I want you out of California. I want you to leave tomorrow."

Feeling like a fool, like I didn't know anything or anyone, feeling like God was playing tricks on me, feeling that nothing mattered anymore, that anyone I touched or anyone who touched me turned out dead—Tush, Cal, Tina, Mo. Who's ever heard of losing four people during one summer? I was jinxed. There was something very wrong with me, something so rotten that I couldn't keep anyone who loved me. Tush was like a sister, Tina and Mo like Mom and Dad, Cal like the perfect boyfriend, a boyfriend who really loved me and I loved him. I loved them all, except I didn't know them. I thought Tush was so innocent when she wasn't; I thought Cal was so terrific when Cal was really a terrific drunk; I called Bull a teddy bear, and now the teddy bear was going around raping and killing; Tina ran hookers and Mo was running with mobsters, and I thought they were the most wonderful couple on the face of the earth. All these people dying, people right next to me, people wanting to help me. So why was I alive? Why did Cal's head get smashed in while nothing happened to me? Why did I stop at the Philharmonic Auditorium instead of going straight to the house where I would have been blown up with Tina and Mo?

Seeing Billie Holiday's name stopped me. Seeing Billie saved me. Why did God spare me? Maybe God didn't have shit to do with it. Maybe it was just the throw of the dice. Cal got drunk. Mo crossed the wrong guy. Tina was sleeping next to Mo. But what about Tush? I still didn't understand. My head ached. Inside I was empty. I didn't want to admit it, but I think what I wanted was my mommy and daddy, my *real* mommy and daddy.

I thought about them as I took the train the next day—back to Chicago, and from Chicago to New York. Coming out here the train ride had turned into a sex ride. Paul. My soldier boy. He helped me, but that was a one-time shot. Sex was the last thing on my mind as I looked at the desert turn into mountains turn into farmland turn into night into morning into afternoon and a rainy Chicago train station. I nibbled on crackers and ate half a shrimp, but mainly I just stared out the window, not focusing on nothing, like I was shellshocked. You're with a person one minute—laughing and joking and buying clothes—and before the day is over that person's dead. Mo did some bad things, but to get blown up in your bed . . . is that any better, or worse, than going through the windshield like Cal? Worst was Tush. Tina and Mo, at least they didn't know what hit 'em. Neither did Cal. But Tush . . . the knife going into her, she didn't die right away. Bull. Bull raping a woman. Killing Tush? I couldn't imagine it, but if I'd been wrong about everyone else, why couldn't I be that wrong about Bull?

I put the question out of my mind because in Chicago the papers were full of stories about Uncle Morris. They said he was caught in a gang war between Nathan Waller and Sid Furio, the two big mobsters on the West Coast. Insiders were claiming that Mo, Waller's man, was getting big cash to feed information to Furio. The smart money said Waller ordered the hit. So my uncle was a two-timing hoodlum, the same uncle who treated me like a princess. My own father always treated me bad, he was a schnook, but an honest schnook. At least what you saw was what you got. Like it or not, Mom and Pops and Leo were all I had. And I needed them now. I needed people to hold on to . . .

The trip went on forever. The train stalled somewhere in Illinois.

I kept dozing. It started up again and there was a chattering old lady next to me, talking about her grandchildren, and then she got off and a young salesman schlepping his samples got on, a guy with a red face puffing on a pipe, the sweet tobacco making me sleepy, making me dreamy, and when I woke up the salesman was gone and the train was speeding through a station. I looked up and saw the sign that said "Valleyview, Ohio" but there was no one on the platform and I thought about Principal Birchdale and Mrs. Fletcher and Reverend and Mrs. Johnson, I thought of how Bobby Marks looked that afternoon at the gas station and what it was like dancing with Cal under the moonlight and I was glad to be speeding through Valleyview and not stopping, it was just another town like a million towns in Ohio and Pennsylvania and I didn't want to think about the cemetery and the grave where Cal was buried. Did it really matter, I mean, I'd only know him a week, and how can you really fall in love with a man in just a week? Keep asking, Rhonda. Ask and you'll get no answers . . .

When we pulled into Penn Station it was Sunday and I couldn't wait to get off that train. When I looked out the window I saw the three of them standing there—Mom, Pops and Leo. I couldn't remember another time when they were all smiling at the same time. They actually looked happy to see me.

"Sure we're happy," said Mom, hugging me hard. "You're *alive*."

Pops and Leo covered me with kisses. I was back from the war, I was among the lucky living.

"I feel bad that none of us were at my brother's funeral," said Pops. "But considering the circumstances, you did right to come right home."

"Leo and I came home," said Mom, taking my arm as we walked through the station to the street. "We're all back in Bensonhurst. Leo's been very good for me. He made me realize some things, darling, that I hadn't seen before. He's been talking to your father and talking to me and, well, you should be very proud of your little brother because he's convinced me to go home and give it another try."

"The store opened this week and doing business like you wouldn't believe," added Pops. "Your mother's helping out. She's terrific in the store."

"And there's a place for you, Rhonda," said Mom. "I know you can sell."

"I can't believe this," I said.

"Come on, sis," said Leo, putting his arm around me. "Everything's going to be just fine."

"Leo's dating the Brotman girl," Mom announced. "You remember Joanie Brotman from down the street."

I gave Leo a look. He looked the other way.

"Your bedroom's waiting for you," said Pops.

"We moved all your clothes from Empire Boulevard," Mom informed me. "We put your furniture in storage and closed down the apartment."

"What!" But before I could really get mad I noticed the *Journal-American* Pops was carrying and the headline:

BALL PLAYER SUSPENDED
NEWARK BEAR RAPE RAP

I stopped walking and read. The article confirmed everything Billie had said. The picture of Bull, taken from game action, made him look like a damned monster. He was grimacing, showing his teeth. It was awful.

"What's wrong?" Leo wanted to know.

I couldn't go into it. They didn't know from Bull; they didn't know from any of the men I dated. And the men didn't know my real name, so there was no way for them to get in touch with my family. God knows what Bull and Sandy thought happened to me. I didn't want to think about them, not now; now we were piling into the family car and heading home. As impossible and crazy as it might seem, this was what I wanted.

Driving across Manhattan, the city looked beautiful, the skyscrapers and the theaters, Times Square and Forty-second Street, movie houses and cabs and buses and red-white-and-blue posters welcoming the boys back from the war, the calm energy of the place on a Sunday afternoon. Going over the bridge to Brooklyn, with Dad and Mom in front and me and Leo in back, it was like when I was a little girl and we'd drive to Jersey to buy fruits and vegetables. I was in the middle of an old dream about an old life as a young kid. But it was also like being in a play—acting, pretending that things weren't what they were but what they used to be. Like the old times, Mom started giving directions to Pops—"Don't take Coney Island Avenue, take Ocean Parkway"—and, like old times, Pops got mad. "Who's driving?" he wanted to know, "you or me?" "With you driving, Bernie," said Mom, "we'll wind up in Canarsie." "Listen to her," Pops told us. "Has she changed? Has anything changed?"

No, which is probably why me and Leo were sitting back there like two happy idiots. At this point anything seemed better than being out there alone in the big cold world. We liked being snuggled in the back of Pops's old Packard, remembering a time when our parents took care of us, when we didn't have to think or decide anything for ourselves.

"Go to the store," said Mom. "Rhonda wants to see the store."

Now Mom was even talking for me; but that was alright. Sure, let's go by and see the store.

The store was on Fort Hamilton Parkway, a regular nice Jewish neighborhood in Borough Park with mothers pushing baby carriages and kids playing in the street. GERT AND BERNIE'S FOUNDATION GARMENTS read the sign. The place was small, squeezed between a candy store and a radiator-repair shop. Pops opened the door and showed me around. He had loaded up with merchandise—all colors, shapes and sizes of bras, garter belts, stockings, slips, in and out of boxes, boxes everywhere you looked. "Without a decent inventory," said Pops, "you don't have a chance. This time I got a decent inventory."

Leo seemed uncomfortable among all this stuff. Mom looked happy. "This time," she told me, "your father and I are equal partners. Did you see the sign?"

"I saw," I said.

"I got top billing."

"Tomorrow morning," said Pops, "we're all here by seven-thirty. The truck arrives at nine with more merchandise that has to be inventoried—unpacked, priced, tagged. You'll help, Rhonda."

I still didn't argue, still amazed that the family was all together, standing around this girdle shop. Who'd ever heard of girdles bringing a family together?

That night Mom made a potato kugel, Pops's favorite. There was flanken and chicken and coffeecake like we were celebrating some kind of holiday. Leo was talking about this new job he got teaching at Brooklyn College, so he'd be living at home, at least for a while, and they assumed I'd be there too. Home. With the living room furniture covered with faded doilies and the photographs of the grandparents from the old country and the heavy smells from the kitchen and my bedroom where I went crazy as a kid, crazy to get out. Go figure.

I was sleeping. Sleeping lots. The first couple of days I was just recuperating. I tried going into the store but couldn't stay there longer than a few minutes. Mom and Pops were already yelling at each other, even with customers around. By my third day back home I was wiping away the dust from my eyes and starting to realize I couldn't keep up this act. Leo and I talked about it.

"You're actually going to stay around here?" I asked.

"What's wrong with that?"

"What happened to your boyfriend?"

"I decided . . ." He hesitated, looking at the floor. "I decided it wasn't right for me. Then Mom mentioned Joanie Brotman. I didn't know she always liked me."

"Mom set you up with Joanie and then you set her up with Pops? Is that what happened?"

"I decided to be reasonable. Those times when I was talking about California . . . well, look what happened when you went to California. It was madness. Abnormal. I'm opting for normalcy."

"*Opting?*"

"We do have a choice, Rhonda. You don't have to go around stripping in front of strange men and I don't have to indulge my perversions—"

"Wait a *minute*. Stripping's a perversion?"

"I was talking about myself."

"So what you like and what I like are both awful?"

"It's not a question of what we like. It's a compulsion, an obsession."

"So you're saying we're sick?"

"Maybe that's what I'm saying . . . yes."

I started to argue, then walked away. On the breakfast table the newspaper had stories about General MacArthur taking over Japan and Joseph Stalin and Truman and plans to do away with all the trolley cars in the Bronx. I didn't concentrate on any of it. I just thought about what my brother had said. We were sick. Our thrills were sick thrills. We were *perverts*. That's what he thought, and he was a pretty smart guy, Ph.D. and all. So what was he doing? He was starting all over again, coming back home, back to his boyhood bedroom and dating this girl down the street so this time it would all turn out okay. *Normal*. He wanted to be normal. And what about me? Did I want to start all over again and this time around become a nice Jewish girl who listened to mommy and daddy and helped out in the store where maybe I'd meet a woman with a son who's a dentist, fall in love and live happy sappy ever after?

The question was staring me in the face. I thought about it that day and that night and the next day and the next night, all the time eating dinner with the family and acting like nothing was wrong, like all this family stuff was protecting me from the terrible things that had hurt me out in the world. But the question didn't go away, the question stayed the same:

Should Rhonda Silverstar go back to being Rhonda Silverstern? Should Rhonda "grow up," as Pops put it, and finally learn to behave?

Are you kidding me?

STRAIGHTEN
UP AND
FLY RIGHT

The panties are always the last to go. The panties are the key to the whole thing. They love the tits, sure, the tits can drive them crazy, but, believe me, it always comes down to the panties. I'll spend days, weeks, maybe months looking for the right panties, see, 'cause the panties are more important than the G-string. Some of the gals don't even wear panties; they go right to the G-string, but not me. The boys want to see panties. Once I take off that last garment—the robe, the dress, whatever the hell—the boys focus on the panties like a bee on honey. And I tell you something else funny, that first night I went back to stripping, even though it was just a little joint in Coney Island run by an old friend of mine, I kept thinking how happy I was *not* being in Gert and Bernie's Foundation Garments. I hated that place, hated all the fuckin' corsets and bras and straps and all the other torture shit that holds in your body and makes you feel like a mummy. "Take it off, baby . . ." Goddamn right! Fling it off! Rip it off! Get free! Get going, start showing what you got without a bunch of bullshit about hiding or being ashamed. You can say what you want, but I ain't really ashamed of nothing. I'm out there, even if it's a dive in Coney. I'm *expressing* myself.

I couldn't take any more of Mom or Pops. That's what I was saying inside my head while I was moving to the music out there in Coney, the jukebox playing "Ac-cent-tchu-ate the Positive." Well, I was ac-cent-tchu-ating it alright, I was pushing myself into

the positive, into the action because back in Bensonhurst I was
going nuts living with people I just didn't much like. I hate to
admit it, but the truth is the truth. You could say I loved them—
maybe you always love your family no matter what—but you
couldn't say I *liked* them. I tried, believe me, this time I tried like
crazy. I tried to behave and act real sweet and go along with the
program. But the program, it stunk like it stunk when I was a kid.
Pops was so irritable and short-tempered and Mom was interested
in nothing but money and fancy clothes and besides, I kept asking
myself: What was she doing back with Pops when I knew she
didn't like him any more than I did? She'd wanted to explore the
world and date other men, so what happened? She got scared—
that's what happened—she lost her nerve and came running home
to help her Bernie sell girdles. Hey, I did it too. But selling corsets
side-by-side with her and Pops like nothing was wrong, I felt like
a liar, a hypocrite. Maybe Uncle Mo was a mobster and Tina ran
hookers, but at least they took chances. I missed them. And Leo,
Leo was living in a dream world. All this make-believe shit. Trying
to be normal. Maybe it worked for Leo, but not for me. The more
I hung around the house the more I felt dead inside. I was ready
to *explode*.

And you know I explode when I strip.

The place was filled with soldiers and sailors and guys who
worked at the Brooklyn Navy Yard. Afterwards I hung around
and had some drinks, joked with the boys and realized I had my
pick among maybe twenty or thirty guys. I left alone. I got the
attention I needed. That was all I needed. See, I didn't even trust
myself anymore. Didn't trust my instincts about who was good or
bad, sweet or sour, right or wrong. That night I went back and
slept in Bensonhurst, but the next morning I was out early. I didn't
say anything to Mom or Pops; I didn't want no long discussions.
I just left them and Leo a little note that said, "Getting a place of
my own. Will call. Rhonda." I found what I was looking for over
in Brooklyn Heights. It wasn't fancy, just a little one-bedroom
apartment on the top floor of a beat-up old building, but it looked

across the river to the city. It wasn't anything like the penthouse I'd planned to move into before this business with Tush, but I was a different person now. I didn't care about penthouses. I cared about some peace and quiet, a place where I could just sit and think.

I thought for a few days before I knew what I had to do. I had to stop playing games in my head, stop thinking about ever hiding out again from the world. That couldn't even be a consideration. On October 1, I was going to be twenty-seven years old, and you know the thing that bothered me the most? Tush. I still couldn't get Tush off my mind. Sure, I was still mixed up from getting canned by Plotsky, from running around from Ohio to California and back, crashing with Cal and nearly getting blown up with my uncle and his madam. I know all those things mixed me up, scared me, made me crazy. I had to be crazy to think living with my folks would make me *less* crazy. But the craziness wouldn't go away— at least this is how I was thinking—until I found out—once and for all—what had really happened to Teresa Johnson. That was a pledge I made to myself when I left for Valleyview. When Cal couldn't help me, I quit. Well, that wasn't right. I had to know. Before I got on with my life, I had to have that settled. Staring out the window, gazing across at the twinkling lights on the bridges and buildings as a steaming mist rose over the East River on this hot August night, I started thinking straight. I guess I hadn't been able to think about the real probability that Bull killed her. I'd put it out of my mind. Well, it was time to put it back in my mind. Time to get back into it, to go back over that bridge and see what the hell was really going on. I thought again about Sandy, but Sandy wasn't the main point. The main point was Bull. I had to see Bull. I had to look him in the eye and see for myself how I could have been so wrong about a guy I thought was so sweet.

BULL

The first thing that went through my head when I saw Bull sitting in jail was that this guy ain't no killer.

The jail was on Staten Island, and going over on the ferry I looked out on the rainy morning feeling real down. I got there right at the start of visiting hour and Bull was waiting for me, sitting there behind the bars. They had told him I was coming.

"Jeez," he said, "I ain't never been so worried about anyone. I figured you for dead."

He reached out for my hand. There were tears in his eyes.

"Where you been, Rhonda?"

"Away. But I'm fine. What's with you, Bull? What's the story? What's this about you raping this dame?"

"I didn't do it, Rhonda, you gotta believe that I didn't do it."

I wanted to believe him.

"Why should I believe you?"

"Because I wasn't anywhere near where she was attacked. It happened in Queens, and I was home alone in Hoboken."

"But the lady named you. I read it in the paper. She identified you. And so did someone else."

"I wasn't anywhere near there."

"If you got an alibi you better tell the cops."

"I can't . . . I couldn't turn him in . . ."

"*Who?*"

"My brother."

"What brother?"

"Pete, my twin."

"Come on . . . Suddenly you got a twin brother?"

"He's been shadowing me for years. I don't like to talk about it . . ."

"You expect me to believe this?"

"Rhonda, you know me. Would I hurt a fly?"

"Tell me about this Pete."

"Mean. We ain't nothing alike. For years we had nothing to do with each other. Then, soon as I start playing for the Bears, he shows up, telling people he's me."

"Did he take out Tush?"

"Tush?"

"You remember, the girl that got murdered, the one who stripped with me—Teresa Johnson. Did he ever date her?"

"Could have. I know he once followed me to Plotsky's."

"And he told Tush that he was you?"

"Could be. Does it all the time. Did it when we were kids. I hate it."

"And how in hell do you expect me to believe all this?"

"Meet him. See for yourself."

"Where is he?"

"Home. Buffalo."

"Well, if all this is true, Bull, why don't you just tell the cops about Pete and get yourself sprung?"

"How can I do that to my brother?"

"How can *he* do this to *you*?"

"You talk to him, Rhonda. You'll see. But be careful, honey."

Some way to see Niagara Falls.

There I was, looking at all that water spilling over into the river below. I gotta admit—it was pretty amazing, the roar, the spray coming up in my nose, the sun beating down on my face. I liked it a lot and for a while I didn't feel sad about being there without a man or a husband. But since this is honeymoon haven, and since the place was crawling with newlyweds—soldiers and their sweethearts—it did cross my mind that Rhonda Silverstar, in her green and orange flower print dress and her big-brimmed straw hat, Rhonda with her makeup on so neat and her lipstick just the right color and the new brown shoes and the nice nylons, Miss Rhonda was all alone. And being alone in Niagara Falls, no matter how beautiful the place might be on a breezy morning in August, ain't no fun.

But who knew I'd wind up here? See, when I got to Buffalo to look up Bull's brother Pete, the landlord said Pete had moved to Niagara Falls, fifteen or twenty miles up the road. He didn't have his address but told me the name of the bar where he worked. So I caught a cab, and the cabbie kept asking why a nice-looking gal like me was traveling alone to Niagara Falls. That didn't help. "Where's your beau?" he wanted to know. Thinking of Cal, I wanted to say he was dead, but why bum out the cabbie? I kept quiet, although inside I was picturing myself in Niagara Falls with Cal, talking to Cal, listening to Cal, sleeping with Cal, watching Cal wake up in the morning and maybe write a little short story or take a leisurely bath, taking a walk in the park along the falls with Cal, buying Cal a hat that he'd slouch over his patched eye and look like a movie star or a detective, having Cal help me figure out what this goddamn mystery was all about. I sighed just thinking about Cal. How long was I going to carry the torch for Cal?

Cal wasn't in Niagara Falls. I was. And I was ready to snap out of it, ready to see what was what. I got to the bar early. The joint—called Lovers Lounge—was next to a seedy hotel and didn't open till two. More time to think. Wandering around the falls, watching the torrents of water spilling over and over, I had plenty of time to kill. If Pete had killed Tush, I should have been plenty scared—what the hell was I doing looking for a murderer?—except I wasn't. I was worried, sure, and I planned on being extra careful, but at this point I wasn't shaking in my boots. Not after all the wrecks and bombings I'd seen. If Pete was the one, I wanted to look him in the face. I had to see this monster for myself.

At two I was back at the Lovers Lounge looking for Pete.

"Haven't seen him for a couple of days," the owner told me. "If you talk to him before me, tell him he's fired."

"Got his address?"

"Maybe in the back. Hold on. But I'm telling you, this guy ain't worth the trouble."

Aside from the falls, Niagara ain't pretty, and the part where Pete lived was your typical slum. The cab dropped me in front of a rundown six-story apartment house. Inside it smelled like a hundred old ladies cooking cabbage. No name on the mailbox, but my slip of paper said apartment 6A, so I schlepped up the steps which is when, huffing and puffing, I started hearing weird noises. By the time I got to the fourth floor, the noises were getting louder. I went ever faster and the noises got louder and when I finally got there I banged on the door and I heard all these screams, like someone was getting hurt, so I started yelling—"Open the door or I'm calling the cops"—and then the screams got muffled and I got scared—the door still wasn't opening—and I started hollering for help and a guy from downstairs came running up and then this other guy came out of an apartment from across the hall and the two of them kicked in the door and there on the couch with her dress pulled up was this girl—couldn't have been more than sixteen—and on top of her, his big fat ass high in the air, was Bull. Except it wasn't Bull, it had to be his twin brother Pete since Bull was in the slammer, and, pulling up his pants, Pete ran for the window and started climbing out on the fire escape but this son of a bitch wasn't going anywhere, not if I could help it, and I reached for the first thing I saw, this heavy ashtray, and heaved it at him with all my might. His back was turned so he wasn't ready when the ashtray hit him smack on the side of the head. He went down. And that gave the guys time to jump him and put out his lights.

Next thing I knew I was in the Buffalo papers, and it even made the New York *Daily News*. I was sure I'd got my man.

MY MAN
IS
SLIPPERY

I figured it was all over. Back in Brooklyn, I called Captain Mickey Donegan.

"You're really something, Rhonda," he said. "You got guts. You go up to Buffalo all alone and go after some bum who's been raping women, maybe killing them."

"Not maybe. He's the one. I know he took out Tush. He pretended to be his brother, he called himself Bull but it was Pete who killed Tush. The guy's violent, Mickey, he's out of his mind."

"He confessed to raping that broad in Queens. He said he did it."

"Of course he did it."

"He also confessed to using his brother's name. He said his brother always got the attention—he was the good boy—all the girls liked him, and poor Pete didn't get no play."

"I want to see poor Pete fry."

"We released Bull. Can you believe that guy? He's so good-hearted he takes the rap for his own brother? He told me to tell you that he owes you."

"The lug doesn't owe me nothing."

"I owe you too, Rhonda. Why don't we get together and go over all this in person? I could run over to your place right now."

"Back to business . . ."

"The Bears are putting Bull back in the starting lineup. He'll be playing tonight. I'll take you."

"I'm busy."

"But we've got more to discuss."

"Discuss what? The case is closed."

"Except for one thing . . ."

"What?"

"Your friend Teresa Johnson and this Pete Wallinsky."

"He was dating her. He told her he was Bull."

"That's right. He's confessed as much."

"So what's the problem?"

"He says he didn't kill her."

"Bullshit."

"That's what I said. And I kept saying it until I started calling around. The bum's got an alibi."

"I don't believe him."

"I didn't either, but it looks like on the night of Saturday, June ninth, our boy Pete was four hundred miles away tending bar in Buffalo. The owner's records show it, and at least a dozen people remember him being there. Turns out that same night he got into a fistfight with one of his customers."

"Shit. So where does that leave us?"

"Back to square one."

I barely hung up with Donegan when the phone rang. I figured it was Mom or Pops calling again to say I was crazy for chasing after criminals.

"Is this Rhonda Silverstar?"

"Speaking."

"Jake Epstein here. Remember me?"

"Sure. You're the guy looking for blowjobs."

"Please, Rhonda, I told you I was legit. And I am. First, I want to say I was sorry to hear about your uncle. Very sorry."

"Thanks."

"But I'm calling about business. It turns out we have a friend in common."

"Who's that?"

"Sandy Singer."

"You know Sandy?"

"He's working with me. He's playing piano in my new musical. We were talking the other day and your name came up. He said he's been trying to reach you."

"How'd you get my number?" I was unlisted.

"I'm a producer, remember? Legit producers have everyone's number. Anyways, this Sandy Singer tells me I was right about you. He says you're a dynamite dancer. He says you can dance legit. So if you're interested, the auditions are at the Royale on Forty-fifth Street Thursday at three. What else can I say?"

"Nothing, Jake. I'll see how I'm feeling on Thursday."

By Thursday I was feeling lousy. First of all, Mickey Donegan was driving me nuts. I'd gone over to the station to talk more about Tush and Pete Wallinsky. I had to see all those statements for myself, the sworn statements from the guys who were at the bar with Pete the night of the murder. Damn if the statements didn't look legit—there were too many of them for the alibi to be cooked—so I had to believe Pete was in Buffalo that night, not New York City. That meant the case would have to be reopened, and this time, I thought, Mickey would have to take it seriously. But think again, Rhonda. Think about men; think about cops; think about what they think about strippers. Nothing had changed. Mickey wanted to fuck me; he didn't care nothing about this fuckin' case even after I went to the trouble to travel to Buffalo. He didn't feel sorry for me, he didn't feel sorry for Tush. He wanted what Jake Epstein wanted—his own private show with his own private stripper. All he could do was sing that same old song about how all the police resources were used up and how they didn't have time to go over no old cases. "Mickey," I finally told him, removing his arm from around my shoulders, "you're going to have to suck your own dick."

I don't usually talk like that, but I was fed up. I stormed out of the police station and headed for Horn and Hardart's. When I was a kid, eating at the automat used to put me in a good mood. I needed to be put in a good mood before I started chewing glass. The place was crowded, and I got a half-dollar worth of nickels which would give me all the lunch I needed. I liked putting the nickels in the slot and watching the food pop out of the little glass compartments, the macaroni and cheese, the hot chocolate, the apple pie. I remember how Pops used to take me and Leo here when we were kids and show us how to make free soup from tomato ketchup, hot water and pepper. Pops was always cheap.

Was I feeling cheap? To be honest about it, I didn't know what the hell I was feeling. That's what I was trying to figure out when I dipped into the macaroni and cheese. If I was smart about this thing I'd do what Mickey Donegan was doing. I'd forget it. I mean, what the hell—Tush had been running around with one of my boyfriends. I mean, she thought Pete was Bull, and it didn't bother her none. That should make me mad. Here she was, my little sister, my pal, and she didn't think nothing about two-timing. But how mad could I get when Bull really didn't know about Sandy and Sandy didn't know about Bull, and Tush, well, she knew how I was playing them both. So if I could do it, why couldn't she? I guess I didn't set a very good example. I remember telling her that they each had their good points but it wasn't that I was madly in love with either one. Maybe she took that as license to steal. But she really wasn't stealing, she was playing, just like I was playing. And maybe one of the reasons I couldn't get her off my mind was that she was like me in so many ways. It was like someone had broken in and stabbed *me* to death. I took it personally, and *that's* what made me mad, made me want to find out what asshole, what pervert, what fucked-up excuse for a human being would do that to *me*. Mickey was right—back to square one.

I polished off my apple pie and started sipping coffee, thinking about Bull and Sandy. How long had I been working my two-man option plan? A year, maybe eighteen months. Bull was still an option. He was out of jail and back in centerfield. But in this morning's paper, next to an ad of Barbara Stanwyck selling Chesterfields, the box score showed he was hitless yesterday, the last game of the season. That meant his schlong was down and out. And I was in no mood for a repair job. On the other hand, Sandy never had those kinds of problems. Sandy was usually up, he was a cheerful guy, especially when he played the piano. In his own way he was a writer like Cal, a composer. 'Course Cal was smarter and deeper, Cal had a mystery about him, but Sandy wasn't no drunk. He was a hypochondriac and he was nervous about mobsters—imagine what he'd think about Uncle Mo—but me and Sandy, we always got along without a lot of hassles. I suddenly realized how I took the guy for granted.

Sandy, I started thinking as I went for another cup of java, Sandy could be very nice. He believed in me. He respected me. He always pushed my talent. Look what happened when he met Jake Epstein . . . the first thing he does is tell him I'm a great dancer. He's pushing me to go legit, just like he always did. Well, why not? What else was I doing? I was sitting there killing time—that's what I was doing. Besides, my savings were running low and I had to try to get this business with Tush out of my mind. I had my own business to tend to. This very afternoon auditions were going on over at the Royale Theater and I'd be an idiot not to try out.

Sure, I was uneasy. I was out of shape. Aside from the stint in Coney, I hadn't been working. And as far as legit dancing goes, well, I'd just have to go with my gut. But why should that be a problem? Hell, I could dance. I could always dance. Even as a little girl I could waltz, jitterbug, whatever you wanted. If Sandy was playing piano, he'd give me just the music I needed, the right rhythm to get me moving. I could be graceful, I could be sweet, I could be just as legit as the next gal. So what was wrong with me? Why was I sitting around in the automat feeling sorry for myself when I had a producer waiting to watch me strut my stuff and a piano player who loved me more than his own mother?

When I drained my third cup of coffee—maybe it was even my

fourth—I was ready to rip and run, ready to fly over to the theater and show them just what I could do. Sandy was a doll, that's what he was. Sandy had always been there for me, and now Sandy was just what I needed—someone I could count on.

The minute I arrived at the theater, he threw his arms around me.

"Baby!" he shouted, just like I knew he would. "You look terrific. Boy, have I missed you! What the hell were you doing in California?"

"Oh, I'll tell you all about it later."

We were on stage at the Royale Theater, and never was I happier to see anyone. Sandy's bowling-ball bald head never looked cuter. The man was all smiles. Jake was sitting in the first row, yelling, "Come on already, let me see her dance."

I'd changed into a leotard and felt terrific. Because of all my traveling and worrying I'd lost weight. My thighs were thinner and my ass tighter. I felt light on my feet and ready to romp.

"How 'bout 'Fascinating Rhythm'?" asked Sandy.

"Perfect."

Sandy put the rhythm just right and I did a little soft shoe, a little light shuffle before breaking into some straight-out kicking and dipping. I made up the moves as I went along—just like I did my strip—but I'm telling you, it had a real form to it. My body was telling a story with a beginning, middle and end. Sandy knew just where to push me—we were so happy to see each other—and at some point I felt like I was leaving my body and floating out there in space.

"Fine!" Jake yelled when I was through. "Very good. I like what I see. We'll give her a featured spot with your Nancy, Sandy."

"Who's your Nancy?" I asked.

Sandy looked the other way. Something was wrong.

"And by the way," Jake was still shouting from the first row, "did you tell Nancy she's going to have to change her name. Nancy Nips is too burlesque. This ain't burlesque. This is legit."

"*Nancy Nips!*" I exploded. That bitch from Plotsky's—the one who opened for me, the slut who was always stealing my stuff, what the hell did Nancy Nips have to do with this show? "This ain't the Nancy Nips from Plotsky's?" I said to Sandy.

He was still looking the other way. "Well . . . to tell you the truth . . . she's really a good dancer, Rhonda—"

"She's *shit*," I said. "She's got an ugly puss and she's fat in the ass. All she's got are nipples the size of truck tires. All you see are her huge sloppy boobs, Sandy, you're a boob man, you can't see past her goddamn boobs . . ."

"Well . . ." He started to say something else but stopped.

"Well *what*?" I wanted to know.

"You were gone, Rhonda. You just disappeared—no calls, no nothing. What was I supposed to think? And besides, Nancy's really a nice girl."

"How can you say that? How the hell do you know?"

He took a deep breath, stood up from the piano bench, and finally found the courage to look me in the eye, at least for a few seconds. "Me and Nancy, Rhonda . . . well . . . last weekend we got married."

GOOD
MORNING,
HEARTACHE

Billie was singing. No one sings like Billie Holiday. "Good morning, heartache, you old gloomy sight," she moaned. The melody like the music was written across her heart. "I've got those Monday blues straight through Sunday blues."

I was sitting at Kelly's Stables up on Fifty-second Street, nursing a highball, watching Lady say everything I wanted to say. "Lover Man, Where Can You Be?" "Don't Explain," "No More," "The Blues Are Brewin'," "No Good Man." I felt like she was singing the story of my life, singing with this little swinging lilt that seemed so sad but salty enough to make me order another drink and smile. "Listen, Jack, your sweet Jill will be out with some Bill. Baby," sang Billie, "I don't cry over you."

"You look like you been crying, baby," said Billie, sitting at my table after her first set. When she talked she slurred her words like she was still singing. She had this slow, hypnotic rhythm, this way of peeking at the pain behind the mask. I guess my feelings were all over my face.

"I fucked up, Lady. I've been trying to get to the bottom of Teresa's mess and all I've done is made a bigger mess of my own life. I'm down."

"Now, now, sugar, it can't be that bad."

"It's worse."

"You got your heart broken, that it?"

"That's it."

"You trusted some dog."

"A lot of dogs."

"It's something, ain't it? Way we feel sorry for them, way we let 'em in and then how they turn us out."

"But it's not only them, Lady. It's me. I've been spreading myself so thin, it feels like there's nothing left of me."

"Trying to understand them, we wind up misunderstanding ourselves. I been misunderstandin' so long it's gotten to be a habit. Got so many habits. But what about that Bull cat?"

"It was bull*shit*. Wasn't him. He didn't turn out to be who we thought he was."

"No one is."

"He had a twin brother and . . . anyway, it's a long story with no ending. The killer's still out there."

"You scared, baby?"

"A little. But mostly disgusted at being stupid."

"You ain't stupid, this killer is smart. Plenty smart. But you know something, looking at you I do believe you gonna get your man. You got that attitude. Baby, you got guts."

"Thanks, Billie."

"And by the way, a good friend of yours asked about you just the other day."

"Who's that?"

"Abraham Jones."

"The sax player?"

"Call him. He's good people."

I wanted to go to Harlem. Maybe it's because I wanted to get out of my world, the white world, and lose myself in another world where everyone was dark and different and a lot more sincere than the schmucks running in and out of my life. As far as I was concerned, Sandy Singer was a schmuck. He didn't see women, he saw tits, and as soon as my tits were out of sight he grabbed the first big pair that came along. Let him have Nancy Nips. Let him have his Broadway show. Maybe Nancy was servicing Sandy and Jake at the same time. How else could she get the job? She was a snake. A no-good conniving bitch, and I didn't want to be around her or Sandy or Jake Epstein. I didn't want nothing do with his hotsy-totsy "legit" show. There wasn't anything legit about any of those assholes. I didn't need to be legit, I just wanted to lose myself and get away from the people who were driving me crazy—like my family . . .

The big news with my family was that Leo was marrying Joanie Brotman, the nice Jewish girl from down the street. Leo was lying, sentencing himself to hell. I cringed when I thought about his life. He made Mom and Pops happy, but what about him? How long would it take before he'd be out there looking for what Joanie Brotman could never give him? No, I didn't want to go the wedding and I didn't want to go back to Brooklyn to see what a big success the girdle shop had become. I didn't even want them to loan me money, although I needed some 'cause my savings were about out. I didn't want anything to do with them. I wanted to lose myself up here in Harlem.

Abraham Jones gave me the address of the chili house where he was jamming on Seventh Avenue between 139th and 140th Street. First he suggested I come to Newark and meet him at Plotsky's, where he was still playing with the house band. I said no. "Well, if you really wanna hear what I'm about," he said, "come up to the chili house."

The music was sort of nutty but that was okay. I felt the same nuttiness running through my mind. The music was fast, frantic with bits of melody thrown in, but mainly lots of crazy rhythm, with the horn players all over their instruments: Abraham on tenor sax, a skinny guy on trumpet plus two-fisted piano, drums and bass behind them, lot of notes, lots of ideas, songs called "Meandering" and "Moose the Mooche" and "Max Making Wax." It was exhausting, like running around the block four or five times instead of sitting there in a 100mful of colored people nodding their heads and snapping their fingers. "You understand what we're doing?" Abraham asked me afterwards. He was all sweaty from playing so hard, but his voice was soft and he spoke in breathy whispers like the way he played sax. His white linen shirt clung to his sweaty chest and the short sleeves showed off the muscles in his arms. He had the kind of muscles where the veins pop out and you wouldn't mind touching them, just to feel their hardness.

"I think I understand," I answered. "You guys are trying something new."

"How does it sound to you?"

"Like you ain't bullshitting."

"You're getting to be a jazz fan, Rhonda."

"I've always been a fan of yours, Abraham. But to tell you the truth," I said, "I think I like it a lot better when you play slow."

"That can be arranged."

Next set he played "Body and Soul," announcing beforehand that "this is for a very special friend of mine." A dim spot hit his face and blacked out the rest of the band so that all you saw was Abraham, his thick scholarly looking glasses, his pretty face, his puffy cheeks, the big sax in his mouth, beads of sweat across his forehead and the slow, slow sound of gorgeous melody climbing out of the bell of his horn like a poem, like the body of a woman, like lazy white clouds on a perfect sky blue afternoon, like stars sprinkled over the midnight city. I'm telling you, Abraham was blowing so pretty I felt all warm inside, his "Body and Soul" was deep, like he was showing me his soul and looking into mine, and when he was through he wanted to know if I wanted to go to the Braddock Grill at the Braddock Hotel on Eighth Avenue and 126th Street and I said yes, sure, I'd love to.

If you're a white chick with a black cat in Harlem, you might get some looks, but not the kind of nasty looks you'd get downtown. Maybe one of the older colored guys might stare, maybe a jealous colored gal might scowl, but the young musicians, well, they're artists and they don't give a shit and I felt fine, I felt accepted and Abraham couldn't have been more of a gentleman.

"I'm glad you came up to hear me, Rhonda," he said. "This is the stuff I really wanted you to hear. This is my heart music."

"You play from the heart, even down at Plotsky's," I told him.

"Only when you were there. These days the ticker's pretty cold."

"Business off?" I asked, wanting the answer to be "yes."

"Business stinks. The house is half-empty."

"Let's not talk about Plotsky's."

"Alright, let's not. I know you've been having a hard time. Still no luck with the Teresa thing?"

"Trying to forget it."

"And your friend Sandy . . ."

"Ain't my friend anymore."

"I'm glad to hear *you* say it, 'cause he's not mine either."

"Why? What happened?"

"That song we wrote together . . ."

"I remember, 'She Sure Can Swing' . . ."

"Right; well someone actually recorded it. Problem is, Sandy's name is on the label as a songwriter, the *only* songwriter."

"The putz screwed you."

"I figured he would, but I wrote with him anyway, just for the experience."

"How'd you know he'd screw you?"

"Well, he screwed you, didn't he?"

"Yeah, with Nancy Nips."

"That happened after you left. I'm talking about Teresa."

"Tush? He was screwing Tush?"

"I tried to hip you back in the summer but I could see you weren't ready to listen."

"Sandy fucked her? Jesus, Sandy fucked her too. This is a joke. Who *didn't* fuck her?"

"Me. Not that I didn't try . . ."

"I know, but Sandy, *fuckin' Sandy*! Maybe he killed her!" I started screaming so loud people were staring at me like I was nuts. "Sandy's the snake, Sandy would do anybody in—"

Abraham put his arm around me, trying to calm me down, but

while I was yelling I was also remembering that the night Tush was killed, Sandy had slept with me in Brooklyn. Shit. Sandy might be the biggest prick of 1945, but Sandy wasn't the killer.

"Look, Rhonda," said Abraham, "you gotta find a way to get this stuff out of your mind before you lose it. Let's order you something to eat and you'll tell me all about it."

"You know, Abraham, I'm all talked out. I don't know what the hell to say."

"Then eat."

Eating did me good. Especially the sweet-potato pie. And the peach cobbler. I wanted something sweet, something or someone. Abraham was sweet, and serious too. He was serious about his music and his books. He started telling me about all the books he was reading—history books, books on art in France and Italy, books on religions I hadn't even heard of. When he stopped talking I started hearing voices inside my head, old voices and new voices, voices screaming that I was stupid to care about Sandy, stupid to care about Tush, stupid to care about Uncle Mo and Aunt Tina who wasn't even my aunt but just someone who hired hookers but, damnit, she seemed so nice—she seemed, he seemed, they seemed, the whole fuckin' world seemed to be hiding behind masks. So what was Abraham's mask? He seemed so calm, cool and collected . . . *seemed* . . . seemed so bright, seemed so concerned, but why the hell should I trust him anymore than I trusted Sandy? Okay, Bull was playing it straight with me but Bull was dumb as an ox and Abraham was so smart, talking about how making music is like dreaming—the freer you are the better—and me remembering that the music he made on his sax always made me strip the best. He'd follow my moves and sometimes he led me on, and once in a while I'd look back there and watch him lift that golden horn straight at me, and he'd wink, and I'd wink, and the guy was really part of my act 'cause when he wasn't there I felt it, I lost the spirit and the spirit is what good stripping is all about.

"You miss stripping?" he asked me.

"Now why would you ask something like that?"

"Because I know you liked it. You took it seriously. You took it all the way out . . ."

"You're talking about the night I went nuts . . ."

"You weren't nuts that night," said Abraham, "you were expressing yourself. You had this rage inside you."

He understood, Abraham really understood. But I also understood that I was probably building myself up for another fall. I was about to fall for another guy who was so kind, so understanding, so interested in me that, well, why not give him what he wanted? Only this time I couldn't. I was beginning to see that I had no judgment when it came to men. Besides, Abraham was colored. I'd never been with a colored before. I ain't saying I'm prejudiced— I don't think I am—but I didn't need the trouble. Even if this guy was whiter than snow, I wouldn't, I couldn't take another chance on making another mistake.

Then what was I doing leaving the Braddock Grill with him, walking the streets of Harlem with him? What was I doing going up to his apartment? It was two in the morning and a fall nip was in the city air. I heard music—jazz music, blues music—coming out of little cellar nightclubs nestled in old buildings. Down the block a couple was kissing under the streetlight. From an apartment way up high I heard a baby cry. On someone's phonograph Billie Holiday was singing "Guilty." I had to smile. You could recognize her voice anywhere. Abraham smiled too. I took his arm. I was crazy.

If Mama could see me, if Pops could see me . . . why was I thinking about Mama and Pops? Why wasn't I thinking straight? What was I doing heading up the stairs, schlepping up five floors? Was I out of my *mind*? Was I drunk? I was cold sober and the truth is that I was doing just what I wanted to do. Like with my soldier boy on the train. Abraham was my sax man. He knew how to play me.

Oh, God, he knew.

BRAVE
NEW
WORLD

That was the name of the book he was reading when I woke up the next morning. *Brave New World*, by a guy named Aldous Huxley.

"What's it about?" I wanted to know.

"Utopia."

"What do you mean?"

"Well, it's about a natural man in an unnatural world."

"That's you."

He put down the book and looked at me. "Nothing feels unnatural today," he said, kissing my lips.

I liked being in his bed. I liked the way he looked at me. I liked the pot we smoked, I liked all these books piled up around his apartment, I liked his records and his sheet music and the out of tune little upright piano where he sat and figured out chords and wrote these strange melodies. I liked the fact that he liked me the way I am, and that last night he loved me so long and good that I forgot about everything except being with him in his own world, unnatural or not. I guess I liked being crazy.

He picked up a flute and started blowing. The sound was gorgeous.

"Hey, I know that song," I said. "It's from that movie where Frank Sinatra and Gene Kelly are sailors. I saw it last year. What's it called?"

" 'I Fall in Love Too Easily.' "

I flushed. I felt myself getting irritated. "Now why would you say something like that about me?"

"I wasn't saying, baby, I was just playing."

He was right. I *do* fall in love too easily. I was falling in love again. Only this time it was doubly dangerous. This time I was with a colored.

"You don't have to worry," Abraham told me, reading my mind. "We don't have to carry this thing past Harlem. We don't have to take it downtown."

"I'll take it wherever the hell I want to take it," I said. "I ain't ashamed."

He smiled, bent down and kissed me again. I took him in my arms and showed him just how much I appreciated his beautiful flute.

It was more than making good music together. It was a different thrill, different, I knew, because he was colored and we were in Harlem and this was something that would shock everyone I knew. Coming here, I also knew I was following Tush, who'd been here before me. I was the one who'd been shocked when Abraham first told me about Tush fooling around in Harlem, and here I was shocking myself. I guess I liked the shock. I felt good about it, and I wasn't nervous, I wasn't scared 'cause Abraham made me feel safe, Abraham made me feel a lot of things I hadn't felt before. It was new—his sounds and his shapes and his smells, the way he cooked me hot cereal and started talking about how his father was a music teacher in Austin, Texas, and his mom was a nurse to old folks. They had a nice little house in the country where he went to church and played the piano. His father expected him to follow in his footsteps, but Abraham heard music differently than his dad and went his own way.

"When I first came to New York City," he said, "I thought I'd landed on the moon. That was five, six years ago. I'd just graduated from college—a colored college in Texas—and, with all my education I figured I'd get a job with a symphony orchestra playing clarinet. No legit orchestra would even look at me, not even the pit bands for the Broadway shows. Jim Crow is as thick here as anywhere. It's just not official. That's how I wound up at Plotsky's. But being in the city, I started hearing stuff I'd never heard before— Bird and Diz—all these geniuses running around Harlem, inventing new music. I can't get enough of it."

"You're a real artist," I told him.

"You too."

"Come on, Abraham, I'm a stripper."

"You're an interpretive dancer."

"That's bullshit."

"No, it's not, it's real. Look, I've watched you long and close. You push it to its limits. And the night you were fired? Man, that was wild. You were taking your feelings all the way out and no one or nothing could stop you. It took guts." He smiled. "It was the ultimate strip. Your own passion play."

"I was just pissed. Never mind passion play."

"But dig it—you turned your anger into art."

"I did?" I was beginning to be a believer.

"You did, like I take all the heat inside me and blow it out my horn. It's what all these good writers I'm reading try for—to release the shit, the confusion, to get it out and get free."

"You're just trying to make me feel better."

"You've always made *me* feel better. I thought gigging at a strip joint would make me feel bad, but when you were up there I felt your honesty. I could make honest music too."

Honesty. Maybe that's why I was feeling so strong about Abraham. The guy seemed so honest. Maybe that's why I spent the rest of the week with him up in Harlem. When we'd go out to eat, even the food tasted honest. The clubs he took me to, the blues sounded honest too. Abraham didn't know anything about baseball but he didn't mind when I wanted to listen to the World Series on the radio. It was the Tigers and the Cubs, and in the second game, when Hank Greenberg hit a home run, I knew Pops would be happy, Greenberg being Jewish. I hadn't called home in weeks.

"Greenberg's something, ain't he?" I said when Pops answered the phone.

"He's a terrific ballplayer. Where you been, Rhonda? You run out of town again?"

"No, I'm in New York."

"I thought you were in Brooklyn Heights."

"I've been fine. What about Mom and Leo?"

"Your mother's in the store. I can't keep her out. She's a regular salesman. Business isn't bad. It could always be better but I won't complain. The wedding's a week from this Sunday. The Brotman girl is lovely, but her father's a *schnorrer*, he's already trying to borrow money from me. If he thinks I'm going to pay for this wedding he better think again. But there's another problem—wait, I'll let you talk to Leo . . ."

"Rhonda?"

"Hi."

"Where are you?"

"At a phone booth." I didn't mention that the booth was on 125th Street. I could read the marquee on the Apollo Theater. BILLY ECKSTINE'S BIG BAND PLUS THE INK SPOTS.

"I need you at the wedding."

"Look, Leo, I really—"

"Really nothing. You're my only sister. You've got to be there. If you're not"—he lowered his voice—"it looks like . . . well, it looks like the whole thing's a lie. Or at least it feels that way."

I wanted to say it was a lie, but I didn't. I didn't say anything.

"And besides," Leo continued, "you gotta help me find a band. The one Mom hired just canceled. Look, you know musicians. You can find someone to put together a band, can't you?"

You should have seen Abraham in a *yarmulke*. The little skullcap looked funny sitting on top of his woolly head. And the idea of going to my brother's wedding with him and his salt-and-pepper bebop band playing *Hava Nagila* with all my relatives bouncing around the dance floor doing the *hora* . . . well, I gotta say I was amazed by all the whole thing—amazed that Leo was marrying this Brotman girl, amazed that Abraham really wanted to play there—he said he could use the money and he liked weddings, everyone was happy at weddings and how else would he ever meet my family?—amazed that the boys in the band were having a good time—the heavyset colored drummer, the white red-haired bass player, the tan piano player with the floppy beret. Seeing it through Abraham's eyes, I was having a good time. I was there, but I wasn't there. I could look at myself and laugh. Being a little tipsy didn't hurt either.

I dressed up for the occasion. I wore a snazzy red linen suit, and instead of a blouse, I tucked a sheer chiffon scarf in the bodice. Plenty of cleavage was showing. I had on these navy blue alligator sling-back pumps with a matching envelope clutch, Bakelite fruit earrings and lots of jangly gold bracelets. Up in Harlem, I'd been letting my hair stay kinky, loose and free—that's its natural state— but the day before the wedding I'd gone to Wanda, who has a beauty shop down the street from Abraham's, and this gal fixed me up in a soft beautiful bun that circled all the way around the back of my head—it was a work of art, I swear—and Aunt Goldie told me I looked like a movie star and Uncle Nushky pinched my waist and said I should be ashamed that I don't need a girdle 'cause I'll put my parents out of business if I don't put on some weight.

All this was happening on the second floor of a restaurant on Thirteenth Avenue in Brooklyn where tables had been set up and there was a bar, a cake the size of Staten Island, the newlyweds' names scripted in chopped liver, and Abraham and his guys up on a bandstand where they switched between Jewish music and Benny Goodman swing. The old folks liked the old-world music and my cousins liked the jitterbug. Abraham mixed it up real good. The later the party went on, the giddier I got because of the wine in my head and the secret in my heart—that the bandleader, who now was playing clarinet and sounding like Artie Shaw, the colored guy I came in with and I'd go home with . . . he was my boyfriend. No one would even notice or say nothing about us because they just thought I was part of show biz and he was show biz and look how nice he was being, swinging "Don't Be That Way" and "Begin the Beguine" so that my little cousins were dancing with me, and Leo was dancing with Mama, Mama wearing way too much jewelry and acting like the Queen of England, but so what? Tonight Mama didn't bother me, and Pops, handing out quarters to the little kids, Pops didn't bother me, and Leo looked handsome and his Joanie looked very small and shy with her shoulders slumped something awful, but what the hell . . . the tiny knishes were delicious and the liquor was flowing and Abraham was having a ball, he wasn't looking down, he was looking up, he was holding his clarinet high in the air—who knew he could play the licorice stick like a regular Jew?—he was seeing my people kibitzing and hugging and kissing and telling funny stories and not caring if the man making the music was purple, pink or green.

On that night, everything seemed okay. Different worlds were getting on. In real life, of course, things weren't that way. I wasn't the nice little daughter I was supposed to be, but I could act that way and not feel bad. I could act that way because I knew I'd be running back up with Abraham to Harlem, where I felt wanted and he made me feel good. When the party was over, I beheld the strange sight of my father paying Abraham good money and patting him on the back for a job well done.

"They're beautiful people," Abraham had told me that same night after we'd made love.

"You were nice to them, Abraham. You played your heart out."

"I enjoyed myself. They were well-meaning folk."

"You don't know the half of it." I started to set him straight, to tell him the real deal about Leo, about how Mom and Pops make me nuts—but why? Why ruin a nice evening?

"Your old man reminds me of Plotsky," said Abraham.

"Me too."

"By the way, I told Plotsky you were back in the city."

"Why?"

"I figured you could use the work. I also figured you're ready to come back. Did I figure wrong?"

"Maybe not," I said, kissing him on a spot behind his ear that drove him crazy.

We made love a second time, and then I had this dream. I was in Oz with those people in the Judy Garland movie where first it's in black-and-white and then color, except the little people were all my relatives and they weren't white, they were black, dark black, Mom and Pops and Leo had turned colored and Joanie Brotman and her mother and father were flying white-faced monkeys pointing at us and screaming, "You're niggers! The Silversterns are niggers . . ."

I woke up in a cold sweat, at first not realizing where I was, or who I was with.

"You okay?"

Abraham startled me. I was in bed with a colored man, up in the colored neighborhood. Was I going crazy?

"Nightmare?" he asked me.

I felt like running out of there. Maybe I'd gone too far. He put his arms around me and didn't say another word, like he understood my nightmare.

"I'm playing Plotsky's tomorrow night," he said a little while later. "Why don't you come over there with me? It might make you feel better."

Abraham had his reasons.

"LOOK
WHO'S
BACK!"

That's what the poster said out front—with a new picture of me in star-shaped pasties plastered all over the place. It was November, the weather had turned chilly and the crowds—a lot of my old fans—were coming back to Plotsky's. I was back in my old slot in Newark, a headliner again. That felt good. Plotsky apologizing felt even better; he practically begged me to come back. And Abraham was the one who got us together.

"Okay, I was wrong," said the old man. "You had one crazy night. We're all entitled to one crazy night. So you're sorry, so I'm sorry, so we're all sorry."

He looked sorry. He had bags under his eyes, he'd put on weight, and word was that his wife Dolores, the former showgirl, had left him. Nancy Nips, trying to make it on Broadway with those schmucks Sandy and Jake Epstein, was also gone. All the new strippers Plotsky had hired were lame. He even gave me a little raise. I wasn't unhappy.

I wasn't ashamed of being with Abraham, but we both decided that only the hip people needed to know—musicians and friends up in Harlem. Abraham needed the work with Plotsky, and now that I was back in the old man's good graces, why complicate things? The couple of times that Abraham took me back to Brooklyn Heights, we got dirty looks like you wouldn't believe, and once a gang of white assholes looked like they were ready to attack us. We decided to play it low-key; things were a lot easier in Harlem.

I didn't think I'd ever forgive Plotsky, but there I was, stripping for him again like nothing had happened. Abraham had a lot to do with that. Abraham was always reading these philosophy books—some of them written by Chinamen, I think—telling him to be compassionate and understanding about all God's creatures. Abraham was a little bit of a preacher, but not the kind who talks about sin and burning in hell. He said Jesus was a good guy, but he really liked Buddha. Every time I'd complain about my family, Abraham would make me see the bright side, the right side, so even Plotsky didn't seem so bad. After the show, Abraham would leave the theater before me and wait at the Tubes station, where we'd ride into the city together. Then he and his be-bop buddies would jam at the uptown chili house on Seventh Avenue till dawn. What a blast! I was even getting to understand what they were saying. On Sundays, Abraham would take me to museums and have me look at abstract art where I was also starting to see what the scrawlings and scribblings were all about. "Feelings," said the sax player, "can't always be logical—or contained." That's what he said. I tried to get with it.

Things were changing between me and Abraham. At first, it was just weird and different and, I guess, daring on my part—going with a colored guy. But now, well . . . now I'd really fallen for the guy. Abraham Jones was one beautiful human being.

Abraham had gotten me back on my feet, out on stage and in the spotlight. I was back to giving the boys what they wanted. Some of my old fans were waiting for another night like the night I went wild, and for the first week or so when I didn't go all the way they were disappointed. I even got a few boos. But before long they were cheering 'cause they saw my strip was still the classiest in Jersey—*and* the most exciting. Abraham helped. During my shows he used his horn, like I used my strip, for secret signals. Without anyone knowing, we were performing and playing to each other. It was a private show put on for public consumption. I heard the boys yelling, "Take it off . . . take it *all* off!" but I was really listening to Abraham's sax, the sax making me wait, making me wiggle. Because the sax was a secret—because Abraham and I were a secret—my whole act got even sexier. Plotsky said, "Long as you don't go crazy, you're still the biggest star I ever had."

I liked being a star again, and naturally I liked the money. I even liked telling Mom and Pops that I was back at Plotsky's because any illusions they may have had of my going good, settling down or selling girdles . . . well, they could forget that stuff. I was back on my own. In fact, everything would have been okay were it not for one lousy thing, the same goddamn thing that had me crazy since last summer.

Tush.

When old man Plotsky told me to hire some backup dancers, I had to audition a whole crew of girls and don't you know each one, in some way, reminded me of Tush. One especially. Her name was Betsy, and she came from Troy, a little town in Ohio. Betsy had the same cheerleader look as Tush, so I hired her but didn't have the heart to get friendly with her. Every time I looked at Betsy I thought of Tush. Every time I went to work I thought of Tush. God knows I wanted to be rid of the memory. I tried to forget, believe me, but at night when I closed my eyes, whether I was alone in Brooklyn Heights or in Abraham's bed in Harlem, there was Tush again with the horrible stab wounds and her face drained of life, and I knew that this sick angry murdering cocksucker was out there running around loose with me still wondering . . . how? . . . who? . . . why?

Then the nightmares came back and I'd be the one getting stabbed instead of Tush and I'd wake up screaming in the middle of the freezing cold night.

"Baby," Abraham would say, taking me in his arms, "everything's gonna be alright."

I'd tell him my dreams and I'd be shaking until he took out his flute. He'd blow soft, play a little lullaby or a beautiful thing like "Star Dust" until the music whispering in my ear and soothing my fears put me back to sleep and the nightmares went away for maybe another night or two when another horrible dream, with some guy stabbing at me, with more butcher knives and more blood, would start all over again. It got to the point where only the music would make the nightmares go away. And that was okay with Abraham. He lived for music, he loved music more than he loved anything, including me, but I didn't mind because he'd take me to these sessions, jam sessions, and I never got bored because of the sounds. But there was another reason.

Because my nightmares were driving me crazy, because they seemed to be waiting for me the minute I fell asleep, I welcomed the all-night sessions. Sunday was a tough day for me; Plotsky's was closed and I had time to kill and even after the museums in the afternoons there was Sunday night—that was the worst— when Abraham was studying French (learning the language like he'd learned music, with his perfect ear, with no effort) while I was thinking that even after all this time it was still so vivid, this thing with Tush, so that when Abraham mentioned he felt like blowing his horn I said, "Great! Let's go!" and we grabbed our coats and we were out the door into the December night with fresh snow falling over Harlem and holiday lights in store windows and a cute little Christmas tree in the corner of a cellar club over on Lenox Avenue where Abraham unpacked his sax and joined Curley the bass player and Bud on piano and a white trumpet player called Hy who was pals with Max the drummer. There were twenty, maybe thirty people crowded around the bandstand, drinking whiskey and eggnog and listening to the beautiful strange music that talked to me in the way my dreams had been talking to me— bits of feelings, of memories, sometimes fast, sometimes furious, all these things out in the open and no easy-to-follow melody like you hear in the movies, no easy-to-follow story like you read in fairy tales.

The jazz went on till two in the morning and I was sad when it stopped. I wanted the jazz to go on forever. Afterwards we went to an all-night restaurant and I saw how the cats looked up to Abraham as someone who read and studied. They had these heavy discussions about the new music that left me feeling dumb but mostly I felt accepted 'cause the musicians knew what I did and Abraham never showed any shame—he liked me for what I was—and there were lots of laughs and Hy the trumpet man liked Dick Tracy comics and he could do all the voices like The Shadow from the radio. He cracked us up, and the baby-back ribs were scrumptious and the crust on the cherry pie melted in my mouth, the Christmas feeling so strong this year because the war was over; peace had finally come to the U.S. of A. and I kept praying for peace to come to my mind. On the way back to Abraham's place I rested my head on his shoulder, his arm wrapped around me, the snow falling in slow motion, the city hush-baby quiet. After all the wonderful music and all the good times, I knew tonight I'd get a good night's sleep.

But first we made sweet slow love, and I remember my dream started off real nice with me and Abraham in front of a fireplace up in Alaska with no one except for elves bringing us hot chocolate and maybe there was a merry Santa Claus or a smiling Mrs. Claus cooking up fried chicken in the kitchen—this was a deep-down Christmas dream—with jingle bells ringing be-bop riffs, when all of a sudden there's this *BANG! BANG! BANG!* and Abraham jumps up and the door breaks down and my eyes are opening and I'm realizing . . . wait a *minute*, this ain't no dream, it's real as real can be, it's the cops crashing in, a half-dozen cops with Captain Mickey Donegan leading them in, grabbing Abraham, choking him, nearly breaking his arms while snapping cuffs around his wrists, throwing him on the floor and me grabbing my robe and screaming, "Get the fuck *out* of here!" and Donegan talking about a search warrant and arresting Abraham for the murder of Teresa Johnson. Next thing I knew, Stickman the photographer had slipped in out of nowhere and was popping flashbulbs in my face. If you saw the picture in the papers the next morning you'd think I'd seen a ghost. There I was on page one, one arm around Abraham's head, another arm trying to beat back the cops, the headline saying STRIPPER'S BEAU HELD ON MURDER RAP!

My nightmare had just begun.

FRAME
FOR THE
BLUES

I slapped Sandy Singer hard enough to knock him down. I heard the shower running in the bathroom and figured that must be Nancy Nips. So I went in and whipped open the shower curtain so hard it flew off the rod. Sure enough, the bitch was standing there shivering, looking like she'd gained ten pounds since I'd last seen her. By then Sandy was up off the floor trying to restrain me, but I was pulling Nips out of the shower by her wet hair and she was screaming and somehow slipped away, grabbing her clothes and running out the door.

"Have you gone crazy?" Sandy asked me.

"You're an asshole," I told him, calming myself down a bit. "You're worse than an asshole. You're a sick fucked-up piece of shit, that's what you are."

"I did it for your own good."

"So you admit you did it? I knew you were the one who told Donegan about me and Abraham."

"Look, Donegan never closed the case. You thought he did but he didn't. He put you off because you were being a pain in the ass. He kept questioning me, he kept wanting to know stuff."

"Oh, sure . . . and did you tell him that you fucked Tush, you two-faced creep? Did you?"

"A lot of people had Tush, I tried to tell you that."

"You didn't try too hard."

"I wasn't going to say anything to Donegan about Abraham till someone from Plotsky's told Nancy you'd shacked up with him. Then I got scared."

"Of what? Scared someone was finally laying me right? Scared he'd come after you for cheating him out of that song he wrote?"

"Ninety-nine percent of that song was written by me—"

"Bull."

"Maybe he added a couple of notes to the melody, but the chorus, the lyrics, the ideas were all mine. Anyway, that's not the point . . .".

"The point is that the guy's a lovely gentle man—"

"Don't make me laugh, Rhonda. The nigger's violent. He carries a razor. I've seen it. He cut up that girl because she wouldn't fuck him any more."

"Abraham never fucked her to begin with. And don't call him a nigger."

"Well, what would you call him?"

"I already told you."

"He's a goddamn killer. Instead of slapping me you should be thanking me for saving your stupid life. Did Donegan tell you about the letters from Tush he found in the apartment? Love letters. From Teresa Johnson."

"Tush talked to him about music. She sang with him. Hell, you were the first one to tell me that. Now how does that make him the murderer? And why, all of a sudden, should you be running to the cops?"

"Because I see you're losing your mind, that's why. This thing with Tush got you so crazy you can't see danger when danger is smacking you in the face," he said, touching his own face, still sore from where I'd smacked him. "All year you've been nutty as a fruitcake and now you've gone all over the edge, living with a nigger—"

"You know something, Sandy, I feel sorry for you, I really do. You're pathetic. You can't make it as a songwriter so you steal someone else's ideas. You try to put together a musical, but the musical flops. You marry a second-string peabrain stripper, then your marriage turns to shit. You're not happy to see me happy so you get the cops after Abraham—"

"Donegan was ready to get him. He was madder than me, madder than hell—"

"Yeah, Donegan's been trying to get into my drawers for years. The minute he learns I'm with a colored guy—"

"Donegan knows niggers. He works with them every day. He sees what they do to each other, what they do to white women . . ."

"You're *sick*," I said, ready to slap him again but too disgusted to waste my time. "You're *all* fuckin' sick."

Sick.

"Mom's sick," said Pops. "The picture in the paper made her sick. The way you were holding the *schwarza*. You looked like a *schwarza* . . . the way your hair looked."

"What are you talking about? That's my natural hair. I have kinky hair."

"You have *wavy* hair, not kinky. Kinky is colored. The picture in the newspaper practically put your mother in the hospital. She wants nothing to do with you. If I tell her you're calling she won't even pick up the phone."

"I'm not calling to talk to her . . ."

"How could you do something like this?"

"Look, Pops, I don't expect you to understand . . ."

"You not only disgrace yourself, you disgrace your whole family. Even your brother Leo, a liberal like Leo, even Leo has to answer to his in-laws . . . he can't explain it . . ."

"Explain *what* for Christ's sake! Explain that some innocent guy is being charged for something he didn't do?"

"But you were in his apartment, in his . . . I can't even say it. I can't think about it. My own daughter . . ."

"Is that a crime?"

"You're goddamn right it's a crime, a crime against God, a crime against the Jewish people, a crime against your parents who tried to raise you right, but look what happened . . . first the circus, then this striptease business. I knew one thing would lead to another. It always does. Then when you went to California to see my brother, I should have known then. Did he have a colored woman out there? Is that where you got the idea of sleeping with the colored? Don't tell me. I don't want to know."

"Would you just give me the name of a lawyer?" I asked.

"A lawyer? *A lawyer*! You think a lawyer—you think a respectable Jewish lawyer, a man like Arthur Wasserman, is going to have anything to do with you and that colored bum . . . ?"

I hung up in my father's ear. I was in my little place in Brooklyn Heights and I was in a hurry. I had to get Abraham sprung. He was being held without bail and the only hope was a smart lawyer. I didn't have time to put up with my family; I didn't have time to worry about being fired from Plotsky's again; I didn't care about any of that. I just wanted Abraham free because I knew Abraham didn't do it. I also knew the charges were trumped-up bullshit. Abraham had told me when I went to see him last summer that the night of the murder he was jamming with the cats at the chili house. He had an ironclad alibi and he had witnesses. What he didn't have, though, was a lawyer.

"Of course I know your father," said Arthur Wasserman, "and your mother as well, but I'm not a criminal lawyer. You'll need a criminal lawyer for this matter."

"Can you give me a name?"

His names finally led to a guy in a nasty office off Union Square. He was sort of walleyed and looked like a walrus. He had this way of coughing and talking at the same time so I could barely understand him. What I did understand, though, was that he wanted five hundred smackers before taking the case. Either that or a tumble in the hay with me. I said no on both counts. There had to be a better way.

Other names, other lawyers, other meetings. It all came down to this: no respectable attorney would defend a colored guy accused of killing a white stripper, especially when another white stripper was caught in his bed. These lawyers were gutless, the whole world was gutless. Pops was right when he said even Leo was spooked 'cause when I talked to Leo about finding a lawyer all he said, "You've gone too far this time, Rhonda . . . this time you've really gone crazy." Sandy, Leo, Mom, Pops, Plotsky . . . not a single one believed me or gave a shit when I told them Abraham was being framed. The best I could do was a public defender.

Jimmy Elkins was a *schlepper*. His glasses kept sliding down his nose. He looked like a frazzled bookkeeper. For sure, this guy was no sharpshooter. He took the case because he had to, and when he looked into it all he could do was worry. He read the letters from Tush to Abraham and said that a jury would assume something hot and heavy had been going on even though she was only thanking him for helping her with her music. Thank God the letters didn't mention Billie, and I wasn't about to mention her either, since Billie was having enough trouble with the law and, besides, Billie couldn't help Abraham with an alibi. The musicians could, though, the guys who were with him at the chili house on the night of the murder.

I told Jimmy Elkins he had to chase the cats down, and I offered to help. But of the four names Abraham gave us, one guy was dead, another in the slammer for narcotics possession, the third in the nut house and the fourth nowhere to be found. What about the people in the chili house who heard him play? They wouldn't be reliable, said Jimmy Elkins; the place was notorious for reefer and the prosecutor would destroy their testimony. Meanwhile, things got worse. Among Tush's possessions, which had been locked up by the cops, they pulled out a pair of men's boxer shorts the same size and brand that Abraham wears. "So do a million other men," I told Elkins. "But a million other men," he told me back, "didn't work with her, didn't take her up to Harlem, *and* weren't seen with her in places in Jersey and New York." Besides, Elkins said, everyone was lined up to appear before the grand jury—Sandy Singer, Nancy Nips, Plotsky, plus ten other Plotsky stagehands and musicians—all white guys, naturally—to testify that Abraham and Tush had been sleeping together. Maybe, maybe not, but *don't* tell me Abraham killed her. I wouldn't believe that. The lunatic, or whoever it was, was still out there. Now I had to set things straight, even though no one was helping except a second-rate lawyer who didn't know his ass from third base.

UNHAPPY
NEW YEAR

Don't ask me why, but I went to Times Square to ring in 1946. It might seem like a dumb thing to do, but I figured anything was better than hanging around Brooklyn Heights and feeling sorry for myself.

Things had gotten worse. Much.

A reporter at the *Mirror*, for example, had dug up that my uncle was rubbed out in L.A. and that I was there when it happened. I don't know how he knew. I remembered how Sandy was fascinated by mobsters, so maybe Sandy told the reporter. The same reporter had tried to talk to me, but I hung up in his ear. His article was bullshit, a hack trying to smear me and my family with gangster connections. I wouldn't have cared nothing about it except Pops said the publicity was killing his business and I was killing my mother and my brother for having turned out so rotten.

I gotta admit that there were times when I thought maybe my father was right; starting with the circus, maybe I had been on the wrong track. I didn't want to think about that, didn't want to think about having no job, no family to talk to, only this colored guy sitting in jail who broke my heart when he played the sax so pretty and made love to me so sweet and gentle I knew he couldn't kill, not the way I'd seen Tush killed. But then I started thinking about being wrong. Being wrong all the time. And this line I'd been feeding myself—that I knew men better than I knew any-thing—that was bullshit 'cause look at Sandy, who'd turned mean and spiteful. Look at all the mistakes I'd made, and sleeping with Abraham had to be the biggest. You go with colored, you ask for trouble. You trust colored, you get trouble. Pops had been telling me that all my life. Colored and white don't mix. When Plotsky fired me the second time, he said, "If God meant for us to mix, God would have made one color." I'd decided to mix 'cause I'm different and no one can tell Rhonda Silverstar what to do. But when I looked in the mirror and ran my hand through my hair I saw it was kinky, not kinky like the coloreds but kinky like a lot of Jews have kinky hair and what was a Jewish girl doing up in Harlem living the life of a colored? What the hell did I know, except my feelings? And look where they'd got me.

"You live in a dream world," my mother would say to me when I was a kid. That was it. I was dreaming I could go with a colored guy and everything would be peachy. He'd play his jazz and I'd do my strip and we'd live happily ever after. Like with Cal. I really thought Cal would come to New York and start writing novels and live happily ever after with me. Except Cal would have had a nervous breakdown in New York, the place scared him to death, but you couldn't tell me that because I was in love with Cal—or I thought I was—but at least Cal was white. Bull Wallinsky was white. Bull . . . at times like these I thought about the centerfielder for the Newark Bears. Maybe if I called him he'd come running back, but Bull wanted a mother, not a girlfriend, Bull was so weak he made me feel weaker than I was already feeling. I didn't want to feel that way. I didn't like doubting Abraham . . . except *maybe* what everyone was saying was true . . . coloreds are violent, you think you know them but you don't, they talk one way and act another, Dr. Jekyll and Mr. Hyde. Abraham could have a split personality, I only saw one side. The other side might be this crazy dark man driven to murder white women. I mean, there was no way to *prove* he was up at the chili house that night, no way to prove he didn't go up the wall and kill Tush. He said he was dying to lay her, he admitted she wouldn't let him, so maybe he went bonkers. Men do that. Sex makes men nuts. But sex is right where Abraham showed he was the most caring guy I'd ever met. Abraham played sex like he played his music, played it from his heart, not like most guys who rush to get it over and act so selfish they don't even know if you got any pleasure out of the deal or not.

Well, for now just forget it all. Go to the biggest party of all, Times Square with all the people screaming their heads off, happy just to be alive. Which, I told myself, I should be too.

The movie marquees were plastered with stars—Ray Milland, Joan Crawford, *A Tree Grows in Brooklyn, The Lost Weekend.* I was glad to be lost in the huge crowd, couples hugging, the Camel man puffing out his perfect smoke rings, "Happy New Year, New York!" rotating 'round the New York *Times* building, the cold night air warm with good feeling among strangers, me looking for as much good feeling as I could find, looking to *forget* and just start all over again, new year, new attitude, and the big newsstand hawking tomorrow's papers about a year of peace ahead. So why couldn't I find peace? Why couldn't I just buy a romance magazine and go home and read myself to sleep? Why was I glancing at the out-of-town papers? Why did my eye stop at a newspaper from Dayton, Ohio, and a headline about a man who was murdered? I wasn't even paying attention—it was just one of those quick glances—I was about to move on and head back home when my eye stayed on the newspaper long enough to read the word "Valleyview." The man was murdered in Valleyview. It said he was stabbed in the heart and stabbed in his "genitals," stabbed until they were "grotesquely mutilated."

It also said his name was Bobby Marks.

Ohio was the last place I wanted to go, but the train had left the station and I was on it. I had no choice. I had no job, nothing to do in New York anymore except listen to lawyer Jimmy Elkins tell me how he didn't think Abraham had a chance, his ass was grass. "But the evidence is shit," I protested. "The evidence is good enough," he said. "Once the jury learns he sleeps with white women—strippers at that—he won't have a chance." "That's crazy," I protested some more. "That's life," he let me know.

"There's gotta be a way," I insisted. "Short of proving someone else did it," said Elkins, "I don't think there *is* a way."

Proving someone else did it. The words turned inside my head. *Proving someone else did it.* "I will," I told Abraham when I visited him in jail. "I promise I will." He could only manage a little smile. He had me go to a French bookstore in Rockefeller Center where he wanted a certain play he said described his condition—*No Exit.* There he was in jail, playing music—they let him have his flute— and reading books in French. Deep down he had to be scared but he still acted sweet to me, not even angry. "Whatever happens happens," he said. "How can you talk like that?" "Because if I talk any other way I'll lose my mind." "I'm working to get you out." "I know you are, I always knew you were an amazing woman."

"Amazing"—that's how Abraham described the gal who helped land him in jail and maybe lose his life. *He* was the amazing one, and I knew if I didn't help him I could never live with myself. That's why when I saw the item about Bobby Marks—Tush's old hometown boyfriend, Mr. Body Beautiful—I realized something I guess I knew all along but didn't want to admit. Back in July I'd run out of Valleyview without getting the job done. The answer, just like I somehow knew all along, was in Valleyview. Now I figured the person who killed Bobby killed Tush. Girl, get your ass back to Valleyview.

The train ride wasn't exactly a joy ride. I had to be thinking about Cal Bryant; if he hadn't gone out with me that night, *he'd* still be alive. If I hadn't gone out with Abraham, *he* wouldn't be in jail charged with murder. Did I have the fatal touch? Bad feelings piled up inside my head as the train sped into Ohio. I fought back the feelings 'cause I had a job to do in a place where I didn't want to do it. All my life I'd managed to fight back bad feelings that came from my family and the rest of the world that didn't approve of this or that, and now I was fighting for my sanity, and Abraham's life. In *Life* magazine there were pictures of bombed-out buildings in London. That's how I felt. I picked up *Vogue* and saw that some dresses were going to be shorter in 1946. Good. I liked dresses that showed off my legs. The green dress I was wearing today was too long. It was old. In this past year I'd aged ten years, or felt I had. A young guy sitting across the row didn't even notice me. I didn't like that. I wanted to feel good about my legs, feel good about something, feel good *period*. The closer the train got to Valleyview, though, the worse I felt. Memories came back. I wrote down the names of the people I'd met—Principal Birchdale, Miss Fletcher, Reverend Johnson and his squirrelly wife. They were all jerks, every one of them, but killers? I couldn't imagine it, but that didn't mean much. I'd been wrong about everything and everyone so far.

A nasty storm was blowing through Valleyview when I arrived—the wind was howling something fierce—and my overcoat felt thin against the cold. But the Rosslyn House was warm as toast inside and, I'll tell you, I was glad to see Tillie, smiling 300-pound Tillie in her silly-looking blonde pageboy wig inventorying stamps at her lobby post-office desk. I remembered how she treated me in the hospital and at Cal's funeral when all those assholes in Valleyview—including Tush's old man—looked at me like poison. That's why coming back was hard—that and the memory of Cal. But Cal was also the one who said I trusted everyone and in the matter of murder you can't trust no one. That was the ticket—*trust no one.*

"Why, honeychile," said Tillie in that Tallulah Bankhead foggy-bottom voice of hers, "you're the last person in the world I'd expect to see on a day like this. What brings you back to our little burg?"

"Bobby Marks."

"They put that in the newspapers way out in California?"

"I'm coming from New York."

"Thought you were planning to settle down in California. What happened in California? You were going to be a movie star. I swear, I thought you'd be a movie star."

"It's a long story, Tillie. Have they found Bobby's murderer?"

"Merciful heavens, everyone 'round here is frightened to death. I don't think they even have a clue. Rhonda, I'm just so happy to see you, let me just fix you up in a pretty room and get you a hot bowl of soup."

Dinner was delicious, and even though it was tough being back in Tillie's restaurant without Cal I kept hearing Cal's voice telling me *"trust no one."* That night the storm was still blowing while I made plans for the next day—see the police; find out what they'd learned; talk to the people I'd met before. They wouldn't want to see me, but tough. Thinking about them, I couldn't sleep. I started seeing how each of them could be a secret sickie—Principal Birchdale as a psychopath with this thing about murdering his best-looking ex-students; Miss Fletcher, a so proper suppressed killer; the Reverend Johnson or even his wife, hating their sinful daughter so much for being a stripper they had to murder her, then murder the boy they thought had taken her virginity, stabbing out sex in the holy name of Jesus. As night wore on, and turned to dawn, my view of the suspects sharpened. In the morning I took a shower and without a wink of sleep, tired but fired up, I was ready to roll.

The police station was right there on the town square. Chief of Police Ralph Kinston wanted to know why I wanted to know. "Teresa Johnson was my friend," I said. "I think whoever murdered her might have murdered Bobby Marks too."

"Teresa Johnson was murdered in New York. That's way out of our jurisdiction."

Great, I had a genius on my hands. *Of course it's out of your jurisdiction, bozo,* I wanted to say, but I kept my cool. "The murders were alike."

"How's that?"

"Do I got to spell it out? I'm talking about their private parts."

No comment.

"You have any suspects on Bobby?" I asked.

"You knew him? Maybe you're a suspect, Miss . . . what did you say your name was?"

"Silverstar."

"Silverstar . . . Silverstar . . . you aren't the one who was with Cal Bryant when he died in that accident, are you?"

Oh, God, here we go. "I was with him."

"I heard about you."

"What'd you hear?"

He didn't answer. Silent Ralph. Finally, "What are you doing back in Valleyview?"

"I just got through telling you. I gotta get to the bottom of this thing. Back in New York they locked up an innocent man for killing Teresa, a guy who did not do it."

"What's his name? Where was he on December 30, the night Bobby Marks was killed?"

"He was with me!"

"You sure of that?"

"Hell, yes, I'm sure. As a matter of fact, I was sleeping with him . . ."

"You married to him?"

"What is this, the fuckin' Inquisition?"

"No need to be vulgar, young lady. I don't know how women talk in New York, but here in Valleyview, Ohio, a lady always—"

"Look, chief, do you have any suspects? Yes or no."

"I'm really not at liberty to say."

I looked in his eyes and saw a great big vacancy sign. He didn't have a clue.

Next stop, the Valleyview *Courier*. I was surprised I didn't get any grief from the man who'd replaced Cal. I was expecting grief from everyone.

"The police don't know anything," said Fred Sinclair, the new editor. "I've looked into it myself. Marks was locking up his father's gas station, about 6:30 P.M. He was alone. He was hit over the head from behind by a heavy object, knocked unconscious, then . . . well, you read the papers."

This was worse than New York, worse than Captain Mickey

Donegan—no one knew nothing, there was nothing to go on. I had to get going for myself.

I caught Principal Birchdale just as he was leaving the high school. He was not glad to see me. What else was new? I gave it to him straight. "There's gotta be a connection between the two murders, Mr. Birchdale. Catch up with one and you've caught up with the other . . ."

"You've come to our city, Miss Silverstar, at a very difficult moment. Bobby Marks was loved by a lot of people. Nobody disliked him. We were shocked beyond words. I was in the middle of a faculty conference when word came to us that same night."

"What time did the meeting start?"

"Approximately five-thirty."

"And when was it over?"

"Miss Silverstar . . ."

"Just tell me when the fuck it was over." I was losing it.

My ladylike language went right by him. "We had dinner at school and weren't through until nine or ten."

"And what about Miss Fletcher"—that nervous ex-nun was strange enough to do anything—"was Miss Fletcher there?"

"She was sitting right next to me."

That took care of Birchdale and Fletcher, unless, of course, they were in cahoots. Except why should that be? Why should anything be? Why should I go around talking to another ten teachers to make sure that Birchdale was telling the truth? Or should I just pack it in? No. I swallowed hard and had a broken-down old Studebaker cab—I think it was the only cab in town—drive me to Reverend Johnson's house.

His bird wife with the phony English accent answered the door. She was not smiling, she did not invite me in, she looked at me like I wasn't there.

"Don't you think you've done enough harm?"

"I'm just trying to help. May I please come in?"

She hesitated. I took a step and she finally moved out of my way. I was in the living room, and before I knew it she was running through the house like a scared mouse. Meanwhile, I went down the hall and looked into Tush's room. Everything was the same—the stuffed kittens all in place on her dresser. Then I heard voices. I knew Mrs. Johnson was getting her husband, and *I* got scared. What if he came out with a gun and started shooting? What if both him and his wife were in on it together . . . religious nuts who hated their own daughter . . . and now that they knew I knew, or thought I did, I'd have to be eliminated. Suddenly I saw myself on a suicide mission and actually started to leave, but no, Rhonda Silverstar was not about to chicken out.

"*You are not welcome in this house*," the reverend was saying as he came back down the hallway toward me, his hair messed up, his black suspenders hanging down.

"I didn't come over for chicken dinner," I said, scared and wiseass at the same time.

"We have nothing—absolutely nothing—to say to you, Miss Silverberg."

"Silverstar."

"Leave, please. *Now.*"

"I know you hate Jewish people—"

"At once, I said!"

"I'm staying and I'm saying my piece. You're mad at me because you think I got Teresa in trouble. Well, L didn't. I didn't have nothing to do with it. We were strippers at the same burlesque joint—"

Mrs. Johnson held her hands over her ears while the reverend shouted out, "Lies, lies . . . I will not sit here and listen to these damnable lies . . ."

"You're standing, and they ain't lies. I'm just saying what happened, and what happened is that—"

"You ruined her. You pulled her down, down . . . into your world of sin and degradation . . ."

"I'm thinking the same person who killed Bobby Marks killed your daughter . . ."

"You're incapable of thinking. You merely respond to the flesh, to the—"

I couldn't take it anymore. "You're an old windbag, Johnson, and you probably spend more time playing with your little dingaling than reading that Holy Bible of yours. No wonder your daughter became a stripper. Anything to get out of this fucked-up house . . ."

"Which is exactly where you're headed! Either that, or I phone the police."

I left, slamming the door, certain I'd spotted a murderous glint in the old man's eye. No question, the old geezer was capable of killing. But his own daughter? If he wouldn't give me any answers I'd get them on my own. I had the waiting cab take me over to his church, to see where *he'd* been last June when his daughter got it, and last week when Bobby got it. I gave his secretary this bullshit story about how I was there to sell Bingo games. She gave me a look, but when she turned away I spotted his desk calendar and slipped it in my purse on the way out. Gold!

The minute I got back to my room, though, the gold turned to fool's gold. There'd been church meetings on both murder nights, with the one last week going from 5:00 to 8:00 P.M. But maybe he wasn't at those meetings. I called back Sinclair, the newspaper editor, who gave me the names of a half-dozen church members. By seven that night at least five people had told me they remembered Johnson at both meetings.

Over dinner I was depressed, confused, crazy. Silverstar was no Sherlock. A cat had run into Tillie's dining room and she chased it out and I started talking about Tush's stuffed kittens, and Tillie was saying how cute they looked up there on Teresa's bed and all of a sudden I started thinking about Cal's short story.

"He told me it wasn't a traditional whodunit."

"It was sexy, wasn't it?" Tillie asked with a broad wink.

"Cal was sexy, but maybe this thing with Teresa and Bobby is like Cal's story. We don't know. Maybe we'll never know."

"Maybe. That's what the man from New York was saying last week."

"What man?"

"I thought you knew about him. Didn't Chief Kinston mention him?"

"No. Who is he?"

"Done-something. An Irish name."

"Donegan? Mickey Donegan?"

"That's it. New York accent, like yours, honeychile."

"What the hell was he doing here?"

"Oh, it was just before Bobby was killed. He said he'd come to learn about Teresa. Just like you."

"Donegan was here? Captain Donegan?"

Donegan. Why had Donegan come to Valleyview? Of course. Donegan was the crazy one. He'd always been crazy for women, crazy for me, probably crazy for Tush who didn't want nothing to do with him so he killed her and waited a long time till he could find the perfect frame-up. And now that he had, he was so obsessed with Tush he couldn't leave it alone, needed to see more of her, what was left of her in her hometown . . . But what about *Bobby*? Why should he care a damn about Bobby?

I had to learn more about Bobby.

What I learned was that he had still lived at home and that after his funeral his parents, in shock, had gone off to Indianapolis to stay with relatives. I didn't have no choice; I had to get into his house and see what was up. I went to the general store, bought a big black flashlight and waited till night. It was at least a mile walk to the Marks's, and it couldn't have been any warmer than ten degrees. Thank God the people of Ohio are trusting souls, though, 'cause the backdoor was locked with a little latch that came undone with a couple of bangs. I didn't even have to climb through a window. Following the yellow beam from the flashlight, it didn't take long to find Bobby's room, with books on baseball and football and a little rolltop desk that I flipped open and then rifled through, reading all the pieces of papers, finding nothing there and then going through the drawers where I discovered a dirty magazine with a huge-breasted woman on the cover who looked like

Nancy Nips, and then underneath a piece of paper with a letter that began with the words "Dear Captain Donegan of New York City. You don't know me, but my name is Bobby Marks, and I used to go steady with Teresa Johnson who was killed in New York City, and now I think I know more about how she was killed, so please, I don't have your number, but you can call me at my father's gas station or at our house here in Valleyview, Ohio, where I live . . ." And then it stopped.

It was the first draft of a letter—I could see that—'cause a lot of the words were crossed out so he probably started again and wrote out the whole thing more neatly and mailed it to New York. I remember that I was the one who'd mentioned Donegan's name to Bobby. But what had Bobby learned and what had he written? Maybe he learned something that let Donegan know that Bobby was onto the real murderer, and if the real murderer was Donegan, he had to run rub out Bobby in a hurry. That's why Donegan had come to Valleyview and that's why Donegan had done in Bobby . . .

Donegan. As police captain, Mickey Donegan was in the perfect position to do whatever the hell he wanted to do and then hide it. For years I'd been hearing Donegan was on the take. It was Donegan who went after Abraham 'cause the Irish hate the coloreds, and Donegan couldn't stand the idea of Abraham getting mixed up with Tush and with me. Donegan. *Don't trust no one*, my creed, and here I'd been trusting the worst crook of them all, the one guy with the power to fool everyone! Donegan! He was it.

The next day I had the long distance operator call his precinct in New York. It took hours to make the connection.

"Captain Donegan, please."

"Not in."

"May I ask where he is?"

"Been off-duty for the past two weeks. Out of town."

"Where?" *I had to know where.*

"Don't know. Private business. Should be back next week."

That was it! Nails-in-the-coffin. Donegan. I packed my bags in a flash, threw some money at Tillie for the room and hustled down to the station, just in time for the late afternoon train that headed east.

Sure, I was scared. I had no goddamn idea how Rhonda Silverstar, for God's sake, was going to prove that a police captain had killed Teresa Johnson and Bobby Marks. Think. All right, I'd get Stickman to find me one of those muckraking reporters and I'd put him on the trail and we'd get evidence. We'd better, or Donegan's fall guy, Abraham, wasn't going to be around very long.

The train seemed to be moving in slow motion. The afternoon was gray and the scenery was dull and all I could do was sit there and think about how Donegan had done it, how Donegan had conned the world . . .

At Bridgewater, Ohio, a lady and her little girl got on board and sat across the aisle from me. The little girl looked a lot like the lady, who I assumed was her mother. They were holding hands. Made me think how I'd never held hands with my mother. Made me think how I still couldn't count on my mother—or any of the members of my family—to help me now. The little girl was real cute, innocent looking. She was holding this little stuffed kitten on her lap, which made me think of the stuffed kittens that had surrounded Tush's body and the stuffed kittens on Tush's dresser in her room in Valleyview. Stuffed kittens, *stuffed kittens—*

I jumped up and pulled the chain above my head. The train screeched to a jolting halt. Passengers lunged forward, the little girl screamed, luggage fell from the racks. Thank God we were barely out of the station. I grabbed my suitcase and ran like hell back down the tracks to the waiting room. There was one cabbie.

"How far to Valleyview?" I asked him.

"About a hundred miles."

I flipped through my money. "Fifty bucks is all I got. Will you take me for fifty bucks?"

"Hell, yes."

"Well, hit it."

* * *

The cab had a flat tire and the cabbie took a wrong turn that cost us an hour. By then I was glad. I didn't want to get back to Valleyview until well after nightfall, after the restaurant at the Rosslyn House was closed and the hotel was shut down. I had the cabbie drop me off a block away. What if I was wrong? What if I was about to make another mistake? Shit, I'd made so many . . . but this *had* to be right. I could go to the Chief of Police of Valleyview but he'd laugh at me and tell me to go home. He'd want to see proof, and that's what I was coming for. Proof. And stuffed kittens were my proof.

Looking outside the hotel, I saw a fire escape that zigzagged up to the third and top floor of the hotel. That's where she lived. I'd never been up there—she'd never invited me into her apartment—but from the big shadow walking back and forth behind the yellow shade, I knew it was her. As a kid I'd scooted up and down fire escapes like a little monkey, and this one, even in the cold, was nothing. I left my suitcase at the bottom and carried only my shoulder bag. I got to the third floor, with the cold wind blowing under my dress, and stretched out flat on the little landing, and I saw there was a little space where the shade wouldn't pull all the way down. I could see in. I tried to hold my breath, but in the cold it was hard. It was really hard not to fuckin' faint right then and there, hard not to scream out to all of Valleyview, Ohio, and the rest of the world . . .

Tillie had a dick! And balls!

Without her wig, Tillie wasn't a her at all, Tillie was a he, a guy with a crew cut who was packing a suitcase, hurrying around the apartment with his gut spilling over, his robe opened at the waist, his prick hanging down, his hairy thighs . . . I was about to choke, and then from out of nowhere a cat jumps at my face and I let out a scream and the cat screeches and all of a sudden Tillie's at the window, he's pulling up the shade and there I am and there he is, and he turns and starts running through the apartment, and I'm getting up, trying to figure out what to do next, and now he's coming back towards the landing, towards *me*, only this time he's got a butcher knife and I'm thinking that this is it, but at the same time I'm yelling at him. "Fuck you, you piece of shit, you sick *fuck*," and thinking of how he had done in Tush and Bobby Marks and knowing I'm a lot quicker than him 'cause while he's trying to grab me I'm ducking and dodging and he's halfway out on the landing himself, he's climbing out there, and he thinks I ain't no fighter, but I am, 'cause when her, I mean his, hulk of a body gets through the window I'm ready for him—this guy's not much when one sees him coming. He's good at stabbing people in the back— so when he finally climbs through the window I'm ready for him, I'm holding that big black flashlight with both hands and *whack*, I slug him over the head with that heavy thing and he goes down, and then I whack him again, and then again to make very damn sure his lights are out.

You should have seen what we found in the apartment and in the chests hidden in the basement. It was me, Sinclair, the newspaper editor, and Police Chief Kinston, looking through all this stuff. By then, Tillie had been hauled off to the can. We spent all night at it. First of all, there was a scrapbook of Tush going back to when she was in junior high. Dozens of pictures of her. There were ticket stubs for a train trip to New York that coincided with the week Tush was killed. Tillie must have had his eye on Tush for a long time, wanting her in his sick way and hating her for being with other guys and never being able to take care of her in his fashion until she left town. That would have been too risky, what with his disguise. But in New York he could "come out," be himself and do her in.

There was underwear later identified as Bobby Marks's and there were also Bobby Marks's letters—five to be exact—to the cops in New York which Tillie, through her post-office connection, had intercepted. See, Donegan had never even been to Valleyview.

She—I mean *he*—had said that to throw me off track. Bobby's letters showed he didn't know it was Tillie, but he was sure it was someone in Valleyview. Like me, he was getting warm, too warm, which is why Tillie whacked him and then was packing and getting ready to leave town when I showed up. I'd find out the lie about Donegan, but by then Tillie figured to be long gone from Valleyview.

I ain't all that smart, you know, but on the train when I saw the little girl's stuffed kitten I also remembered Tillie saying how cute the stuffed kittens looked on Tush's bed. Well, Sherlock Silverstar remembered the stuffed kittens in Tush's room in Valleyview were on her dresser. So many of them. But most of all, how did she even *know* about stuffed kittens? The only stuffed kittens on her bed *were the ones in New York—on the bed where she'd been murdered.* How would Tillie know *that* if Tillie hadn't been in Tush's bedroom?

And how could any of us know that Tillie was really one Horace Rutherford, a man who'd raped and killed a teen-aged girl twenty-five years before in Wheeling, West Virginia, and more since, and decided the only way to really hide was to hide his sex, buy this hotel in Nowhere Ohio, put on a wig and pretend he was just a chatty fat old widow.

Turned out Horace had cut up five other young girls in the last twenty years. He'd taken little short side trips of no more than a day. That's what was in the chests in the basement—articles of clothing, old panties and bras and newspaper clippings about the murders that took place nearby in Ohio, Kentucky, Tennessee and Indiana. Souvenirs of his sick pleasures. There was also a trunkload of knives, hatchets and saws.

When morning came and we'd gone through everything, I felt disgusted, proud, tired, fed up, relieved . . . I don't know how I felt . . . except I had to cry, which is what I did on the train all the way back to New York City.

P.S.
I LOVE
YOU

"You didn't even look surprised," I told Abraham, remembering the day he was sprung from the can.

"Hey, baby, I knew you'd come through. I said you were an amazing woman, didn't I?"

"Bullshit. I mean, when the cops let you out, you didn't blink an eye. You just kind of yawned. No one should be that cool."

"I'd already read the papers. STRIPPER BAGS SEX KILLER IN DRAG! Page one all over town. Someone on the radio said you were getting the key to the city."

"So far no calls from the mayor. Strippers still don't get no respect. Birds are already shitting on my picture in the paper."

"Heard from your family?"

"Leo says he's leaving his wife. Mom says she's leaving Pops, again—she's doing all the business and he's counting all the money. She says she's starting her own girdle store down the street. How's that for free enterprise?"

"You tell them our plans?"

"I mentioned Paris."

"And?"

"They wish I was going even further."

"Paris," he repeated with a smile. We were in my place in Brooklyn Heights. He'd already packed up his gear. The *Queen Mary* was leaving in a few hours, and *we'd* be on it. Sure, we were going third class, but at least we were going—first London, then Paris.

Paris made the most sense. First of all, Abraham could talk the talk. He also had the name of this little hotel on the Left Bank where jazz musicians could live for practically nothing. Plus, Paris loved the new jazz. They'd appreciate Abraham's talent and give him gigs. We'd heard they didn't have the kind of fucked-up attitudes against mixed couples like over here.

Far as I was concerned, Paris meant the Folies-Bergère and the greatest strip shows in the world. With the war over, things were kicking back up over there where strippers were looked on as artists, like jazz musicians were artists. Besides, Abraham had been telling me about Josephine Baker and how the Parisians adored her—she was a dancer who was also a war hero—and if a colored girl could make it in Paris, why couldn't a kinky-haired Jewish girl?

For all our heavy plans, we were traveling light. We had our tickets, we had our little nest egg, but mostly we had our desire to get out while the getting was still good. While I folded my last few undies and stacked them in my suitcase, Abraham took out his horn and started playing "Stormy Weather." I stopped to look out the window and saw what he meant. The sky over the East River was gloomy gray and clouds were building up. Across the water, the buildings of Manhattan were covered in mist. I knew how Abraham felt. We were leaving home. There wouldn't be anyone at the boat to tell us goodbye. There'd be storms at sea, but it didn't matter. Abraham was playing deep, taking that sad song and making it sound so pretty.